SUNNYWOOD HOUSE

BOOK ONE

BLAKE POLDEN

ALSO BY BLAKE POLDEN

The Strangest Criminals

Cover design by CARTOGRAPHYBIRD

ISBN: 978-1-7641265-2-6 (paperback)

ISBN: 978-1-7641265-3-3 (ebook)

Published by Thistle & Rune Press

*For Caleb—these characters are as much yours as mine.
And for Nan & Pop, who prove that age needn't tame mischief.*

"Inside every old person is a young person wondering what happened."
- Terry Pratchett, Moving Pictures

EPISODE 1

Excerpt from the transcript of
The Sunnywood Signal.

Episode 1: *"A Hero's Downfall"*

Transcribed by Kelzu's Sentinel, first-generation automaton model no: KS-01.

Broadcast every Sunday on The Upper Susshingham Radio 102.3EM.

~

HUK

I tell you what, I'm a bit nervous. My palms are all sweaty.

KELZU

Well, don't be. Gods, man—you've fought a dragon blind. This shouldn't make you nervous.

HUK

I can't help it, can I? My throat feels dry. What if I need to cough?

KELZU

Then cough, you idiot.

KS-01

Sir, you do realise we are broadcasting right now?

KELZU

Oh, fuck it.

HUK

Can we start again, KS?

KS-01

No, Huk. It's live.

HUK

What do you mean it's live? Look, I'd feel a lot better if we could just start again. Kelzu, can we please?

KELZU *(sighing)*

Sure we can, mate.

HUK

KS, count us in.

KS-01

3... 2... 1... and action!

KELZU

Welcome, adventurers past and present, to Sunnywood House, home for retired legends of the realm.

[A brief pause]

HUK

What'd you kick me for?

KELZU

It's your line, Huk.

HUK

It's my line? What'd you mean—oh... did you already give them the content warning, then? You know, explain that there will be murder, battles, blood and gore, swearing, drug use maybe, sex if we're lucky. You know, all that gear?

KELZU

No, because I do that after the cinematic introduction, don't I? It's all in the script. Look, do you want my reading glasses?

HUK

No. I've got mine here somewhere. *(pause)* Right. Here we go. Kelzu says, Welcome, adventurers past and present, blah-blah-blah, then I say—

KELZU *(prompting)*

We've got tales to tell—

HUK

Yeah, I can see it now. Right.

[Huk clears his throat]

We've got tales to tell and secrets to spill. Have you ever wondered what it's like to fight an entire horde of zombies with nothing but an old broomstick?

KELZU

Messy, I'd imagine. Or perhaps you've found yourself thinking about picking up your own sword, spell bag or backpack, and hitting the road on your own adventure?

[Another brief pause]

KS-01

Master, why are you kicking me now?

KELZU

Because now it's your line, you lumbering idiot. Do none of you know how a script works?

KS-01

Oh—well, you've come to the right place. At every week's end, join us as we delve into the best—and worst—ways to deal with anything from a thunder giant atop a volcano in the old town of Port Wyvern, to a reclusive but deadly elf at the edge of the Merivian Moors.
HUK
All that and more, KS. We've got stories, tips, and tricks from a lifetime of adventures, brought to you by the ones who lived them.
KELZU & HUK
We present The Sunnywood Signal.

[Yet another brief pause]

KS-01
I should be playing the cinematic introduction now, shouldn't I?
KELZU
Gods, help me.

[CINEMATIC INTRODUCTION PLAYS]

POPPY IS NOT DEAD (YET)

'Do you want to die, or are you just spectacularly careless?'

A figure dropped onto the branch above Poppy, steady enough that the leaves didn't move.

Poppy laughed awkwardly. 'No. Of course I don't want to die.'

She wanted to live. Frankly, that was half her problem. That was why she was out here, sleeping beneath the stars every night instead of in a comfortable bed back home.

A life full of adventure.

A life of meaning.

Not tedious, brain-numbing work at the local sodding grocer.

An arrow struck the tree beside her head—close enough to shower her with bark.

'Fuck.' She hit the ground with a grunt. 'If I wanted to die, I wouldn't have ducked that now, would I?'

'But you didn't duck,' grunted a man behind her. 'That goblin was just a shit shot. There's a difference.'

He shoved her out of the way as more arrows whistled past. Then he hurled his axe. It vanished—then reappeared in his hand, dripping goblin blood and half a hand. He kicked the hand off the blade, and it rolled on the ground in front of Poppy.

She gagged violently.

He was one of those adventurers who looked like he'd been born angry and handed a weapon at birth. Poppy had privately nicknamed him Axe Guy.

'I'm not sure you're cut out for this, kid.'

'I am. I just need practice.' She didn't want to beg. But she absolutely would if it came to it. 'I won't fuck up again. I promise.'

Her fellow adventurers had told Poppy their names earlier—she was almost sure of it—but she'd been too busy trying not to die to retain anything. Hence the nicknames. It would make the begging hard, not knowing their names.

The sword-wielding elf somersaulted out of the tree above her. The blade in her hand glowed blue, frosting the air. She was just so effortlessly competent, and nimble and lithe, and she was constantly flipping through the air with her magic sodding sword. What hopes did she leave for the rest of us? She was, thought Poppy bitterly, the kind of adventurer she could only dream of becoming.

'But you said that last time,' said the elf, her face unreadable.

'The last four times more like,' added Axe Guy. 'And we've only been at this since breakfast. And you can't keep knocking back all the healing potions that close together. You've had more than your fair share, and apart from bankrupting us, you'll just end up with the runs. Diarrhoea is not conducive to adventure.'

Poppy brightened. 'Not all. I haven't had them all.' She laughed, awkwardly. 'We have one left.' She fished in her pocket and held up the bottle. The ruby-red liquid glowed in the pre-dawn light. 'Here, you can have it.'

She tried to pass it to Axe Guy, but tripped over a tree root. The potion went flying and shattered at his feet, steaming in the cold morning air.

'...Okay. Well, now we have none,' he said, miserably.

The elf grimaced. 'If I'm being honest, I don't think this is going to work, Doppy.'

'It's Poppy.'

'Yeah, that's what I said.'

'It's just first-day jitters,' she tried.

'Yeah, but... I don't think it is? Like, you're kind of really shit at this? And somehow you're getting worse by the hour. Are you even sure you even *want* to do this? There's so much else out there for you, you know? You could be a baker. Or an innkeeper.'

'I've tried all that,' said Poppy, quietly. And she had. There wasn't a regular job she hadn't given a crack at. It was just that none of them did her any good. Sure, they put coin in her purse and food on the table and all that boring, mundane bullshit. But they didn't feed her soul. They didn't make her feel alive.

'What about a grocer, then?'

Poppy winced. 'I was a grocer.'

'And I bet you were bloody good at it,' chimed in Axe Guy.

The elf sheathed her sword with a sigh. 'No, we'll deal with the goblins from here on out, Doppy.'

'It's Poppy.'

'Yes, whatever.'

Poppy forced a smile. 'But what about the loot?'

'What about the loot?' said Axe Guy.

'Are we still going to divide it equally?'

They looked at each other and laughed.

The laughter seemed to last for longer than was strictly necessary, and then they were going. They turned their backs on her and wandered off further into the woods.

'She had a sense of humour. I'll give her that,' said the elf.

'*Has*,' Poppy shouted after them. '*Has* a sense of humour. I'm not dead. I'm not past tense. I'm still here. I'm literally standing *right* here.' She dusted some dirt from her palms and sighed.

The bastards didn't even look back.

Poppy sat on a log and undid her boots. One was full of mud. The other full of blisters. Adventures, she was beginning to realise, were mostly mud, injuries, and insults. No one talked about the cold, the hunger, the waiting. Or being thrown against a wall. Twice.

Her stomach growled.

She rummaged through her bag. It was empty.

'What are you doing with your life, huh?' she muttered.

She poked a blister.

It burst.

Nothing made you question your life choices quite like an oozing foot.

Then came the goblins. Screeching and chanting and drumming weapons on shields.

'Ohhh, fuck it.'

She ran, daggers in hand—why had she brought daggers, anyway? She didn't like stabbing things. She could barely look at a raw chicken breast without gagging.

She tossed them aside. They were clearly the wrong weapons. She wasn't quick or nimble. Maybe she needed something more distant. A bow, perhaps? Or magic?

Yes. Magic. That was it. Maybe she was Upper Susshingham's next great wizard.

She leapt over low stone fences, boots squelching, hair wild and left foot bleeding. The goblins faded behind her. The sun rose ahead.

'Magic,' she whispered. She shook her head with a smile. Why hadn't she thought of that? Of course, that was where her talents lay. *That* was her future. And so, despite the torn, filthy clothes. The scratches, the freshly healed scars, and the hollow stomach. The cold and mud-covered foot. Poppy found herself—as was her way—to be optimistic about it all.

Her best adventure lay just ahead. Of that, she was sure.

She tripped over a low stone fence and landed in cow shit.

Well, at least it couldn't get any worse.

(But of course, this is the beginning of Poppy's story. And things—as they often do—get a lot worse before they get any better.)

GIVING UP (JUST
FOR A WHILE)

Poppy stood in front of yet another Adventurer's Job Board in yet another tavern in yet another town. The town in question was charming. The Totswolds were all perfect gardens and lovely little cottages, hugged by green hills and distant snow-capped mountains.

It looked, thought Poppy, like a place you went to die.

Not to live.

Just like the village she'd grown up in, really. Where the biggest scandal of the week was someone repainting their front door an offensive shade of blue.

Her stomach rumbled. She needed new boots, a wash, and some food. For that, she needed coin. For that, a job. (A truly vicious cycle.) Preferably something simple. De-Kappa a garden. Banish a Will-o'-Wisp from a clogged drainpipe. Something she could knock out in half a day and still have some time left over. Most importantly, something she could do on her own.

The tavern was bustling with its breakfast rush. Everyone seemed to pause mid-bite to stare at her. She'd tried smiling. That only made it worse.

She turned back to the board. Not much on offer. Just one job.

'A plague of undead rabbits,' said a voice behind her. 'Think they still eat cabbages out of habit?'

Poppy turned to see a boy: half her age and twice her height.

She shrugged. It was decent pay. Ten gold for what should only take a few hours to fix. 'What do you think is making them undead, though?'

The boy snatched the job off the board. 'Dunno. I'll be sure to let you know when I find out, though.'

'What the fuck? I was just about to take that,' said Poppy.

'But you didn't, and now I have. So where does that leave us?'

'No, really, that was mine.' She scratched her left eyebrow and resisted the urge to thump him.

'I'm not sure it was, though.'

'Well, perhaps we could do it together, then? And go halves?'

He looked her up and down. 'What are you good at? Besides smelling like shit and losing your shoes?'

Poppy coughed; it was a shocked, angry sort of noise. 'How dare you!'

'It's only an observation. I mean no offence. Just seems like undead anything might be a bit much for you. Maybe start with a bath, yeah?'

Poppy clenched her jaw.

'Anyway,' he said, nodding at a table, 'we're already splitting the loot three ways. That's my party over there.'

Poppy's stomach dropped. Fuck sake.

Axe Guy and the elf waved at her lazily. 'Hello, Doppy!' bellowed Axe Guy. 'Still alive, then?'

Her cheeks burned. She pushed past the boy and marched out.

There was, of course, another job board in town.

The Regular Job Board. For regular jobs. For regular people.

Poppy hadn't looked at one in months and swore she never would again. But here she was, staring at a wall of parchment begging for farmhands, babysitters, shopkeepers, and on and on and *dull-boring-nothing* on it went. Her insides shrivelled up and died just at the sight of them.

A new Troll Bank needed a receptionist.

Poppy would rather chew off her own arm than work in a bank.

A gardener was wanted for general weeding and upkeep.

She barely knew a dandelion from a daffodil.

The least awful of the lot was a mysterious advertisement for a nearby retirement home. No duties listed. Just a place called Sunnywood House that needed help urgently with food, board, and good pay. She could do it for a week. Wash. Eat. Rest. Save a little gold.

It didn't have to be forever.

She looked around at the cobblestone streets, flower pots, and pastel bunting. Then, like a thief, she snatched the flyer and bolted.

It felt like giving up, and she didn't want to be seen by anyone—even strangers in a boring old village like the Totswolds—to be giving up.

And yet, just for a while, she sort of was.

SUNNYWOOD HOUSE

By the time Poppy reached the gatehouse at Sunnywood House, she'd broken a sweat. Outside, a postman was waiting, clutching a stick like he meant business.

He looked flustered. His dark blue uniform was in tatters, as if he'd gotten into a fight with a particularly savage leaf-shredder. He kept swearing—fantastical, heavy-duty swears. The kind you reserved for when you really meant them.

When he spotted Poppy, he dropped the stick.

'You scared the shit out of me.'

'Sorry,' said Poppy. Curiosity, as it often did, got the better of her. 'What are you doing, though, if you don't mind me asking?'

'Delivering the mail,' he grunted, reattaching letters to the end of the stick. 'What's it look like I'm doing?'

Poppy felt it would be better not to point out that most postmen, in her experience, didn't try to shove mail into a letterbox with a stick.

'How's it going for you?'

'FINE, THANK YOU.'

He jabbed the letterbox. It shivered, snapped, and bit down. Letters went flying.

'Lovely. That's just lovely, that is.' There was fury in his eyes. 'Are you going into the house, then?'

Poppy nodded. 'As long as I survive walking past the letterbox.'

'Oh yes, very funny.' The postman picked up his bulging leather satchel. 'Do me a favour and tell Matron she owes me *another* uniform. And unless she gets this sorted, she'll be hit with a fine and a promise of non-deliverable stamps for as long as I live. I swear to the gods. All of them. Even the ones I don't know about—and by fuck will I learn them just to spite her. What? I will!'

'Yeah, I believe you. New uniform, no mail, and ominous threat: I've got it.' Poppy grinned.

'What are you grinning at?'

'Nothing.' She tried very hard not to smile. 'It's just—it's not every day you get attacked by a letterbox, is it?' She thought it was rather marvellous.

'It is quite *literally* every day, yes.' The postman started to walk off, then stopped. 'You're not from around here, are you?'

Poppy shook her head. 'Why?'

The postman didn't answer.

She watched him go. He even walked angrily. It was splendid.

She turned to look at the letterbox. It looked ordinary enough. No great big teeth or deranged eyes popping out on either side of the no-junk-mail sign.

'You're not going to attack me if I walk past, are you?'

The letterbox didn't move. It looked, as far as letterboxes went, quite innocent.

Still, Poppy got a running start, just in case.

She didn't want to get her hopes up—this was, after all, just going to be a temporary thing. A way to get some food, wash herself and her clothes, with the added bonus of earning a little gold in the meantime.

And maybe, just maybe, it wasn't going to be half as dull as she'd first anticipated. Perhaps, as far as retirement homes go, Sunnywood House wouldn't be too bad.

As she jogged up the tree-lined drive, past wildflowers and hedgerows, she told herself again that this was just a detour. A job. A wash. A bit of gold. Then back to *real* adventuring.

There was a water fountain by a tall hedge. It stood in the shadow of Sunnywood House. There were a few fish in there. A frog watched her warily.

But if she stuck to one side, Poppy figured she could get herself reasonably clean and not risk killing them with her filth.

The fountain's water was ice-cold, but she scrubbed what she could and tried not to look directly at her reflection. She was covered in scratches and bruises. Her red hair, which should have sat just above her shoulders, was such a knotted mess that it clung to her scalp.

But she was clean-ish, if not quite presentable, when she approached the house.

The towering building loomed over her, inexplicably more intimidating than any goblin horde. Her stomach fluttered.

'Just a job,' she muttered. 'It's only temporary.'

So why did it feel as if her whole life were about to change?

EPISODE 2

Excerpt from the transcript of
The Sunnywood Signal.

Episode 2: *"A Door is a Dangerous Thing"*
Transcribed by KS-01.
Broadcast on The Upper Susshingham Radio 102.3EM.

KELZU

It is a truth universally acknowledged that if a door is closed, you want to open it.

HUK *(laughing)*

So it didn't matter that we told you not to?

KELZU

When would that ever have mattered?

KS-01

Master, I think—

KELZU *(cutting KS-01 off)*

Yes, quite right, K.S. For the listeners at home. A little more context. What had started as a simple adventure: rid the local woods of a goblin infestation, had turned into a—

HUK *(cutting Kelzu off)*

War! It had turned into a full-blown, full-scale war. All because this little bastard had opened the one door he'd been warned not to touch and warned on several occasions, if I recall.

KS-01

I can hear knocking.

HUK

Knocking? He hadn't knocked, K.S. He damn near ripped the door off its bloody hinges.

KELZU

How often do you see a small door growing out of a tree in the middle of the woods? Exactly! A door like that? It's getting opened!

HUK

And so, a regular goblin infestation turned into the unleashing of an ancient evil.

[The distant sound of knocking]

KELZU

Which, I think, we will save for next week's episode. And perhaps, we can even wrangle in a special guest to tell her side of the story.

HUK

Oh... there's someone knocking on the door here.

GRANNY GRACK *(distantly)*

Will someone answer that bloody door!

HELP WANTED (URGENTLY)

Poppy knocked on the door for what had to be the fifth or sixth time. She waited, but there was still no answer. A building as big as Sunnywood, though—you could probably knock all day and never be heard. Perhaps that was the case?

She leaned back and peered through the diamond-shaped window panes. No movement. Or none that she could see.

She considered walking around the manor. There had to be a back door, and like most homes, maybe that was the one everyone actually used?

But this wasn't a normal-sized house. Quite the contrary. It was three stories tall, ancient-looking, and if it weren't for the air of shabby disrepair about it, it might have been mistaken for the country residence of minor royalty.

A building like this should've had a doorman.

Poppy huffed and shoved her tangle of red hair out of her face. At least a doorman would open the bloody door when someone knocked, she thought.

She decided she'd give it one more go before climbing in through a window. She'd really been looking forward to a bath and some food, and rather suddenly, she decided she wasn't leaving without both.

She knocked again.

Hard.

And she'd been about to knock once more—this time with her one remaining shoe—when the door was yanked open, furiously.

'WHAT? WHAT COULD YOU POSSIBLY WANT? WE'RE TRYING TO RECORD A BLOODY RADIO SHOW IN HERE!'

In front of Poppy stood a gnome. He was beet-red with rage and barely up to her waist, with a shock of silver hair that looked like it had been electrocuted. Behind him stood a... well, there was no other way to describe it: a towering brass-metal machine man.

They were called something.

Definitely.

She'd only ever heard about them, never seen one in person.

The word came to her suddenly. 'An automaton,' she whispered. She looked at the gnome. 'That is an automaton, isn't it?'

'Hello there! I am K-S01, but you may call me K.S. This, here, is Kelzu Luckyhand. My programming forbids me from apologising for his behaviour. But I would like you to know that if not for such protocols, I would be. Apologising, I mean.'

Poppy was stunned.

The automaton could speak.

Was that normal?

She didn't know.

Poppy started to laugh.

'What are you laughing at?' spat Kelzu.

'Should I end it?' shouted a deeper, much gruffer voice from further down the hall.

The gnome scrunched up his fists and screamed, dramatically.

'My protocols don't allow for it,' said K.S. apologetically. 'But if I could, I would.'

'Oh, shut up, K.S.' The gnome stormed off, moving with surprising speed for someone shaped like a stubborn turnip.

'Have I come at a bad time?' Poppy peered past K.S. There was an old half-orc sitting at a table, surrounded by gleaming metal contraptions. He wore headphones far too small for his massive ears and looked like a grandfather who'd been forcibly rebranded as a radio show host. He waved at her. She waved back.

'And that's where we'll leave it for this week,' said the half-orc. 'We hope you've enjoyed this episode of The Sunnywood Signal, and we look forward to you joining us next week. But for now, listeners, I have a confused-looking kid standing at my door and an ever-dramatic gnome storming off in a huff, so—K.S., kill the broadcast now, please.'

'Of course, Huk.' The automaton's strange blue eye dimmed, then brightened. 'The radio broadcast has been terminated.'

'Hullo,' said the half-orc, disentangling himself from the strange metal machine. 'Are you all right?'

Poppy nodded. 'I'm here about the job, actually.'

'The job?' said Huk. 'What job?'

'Is someone down there?' shouted a frazzled sort of voice.

Huk looked up to the floor above. 'There's a kid here about a job!'

'A job? What do you mean about a j— Oh! I'll be right down. Don't let her go anywhere!'

'What job?' An old woman leaned over the balustrade and looked down at them.

'I dunno. I said the same thing.' Huk shrugged. He looked at Poppy again. 'Well?'

Poppy passed him the advertisement. 'It just says: *help wanted urgently.*' Though even as she said it, she realised how old the parchment looked. How faded the ink was.

'DO WE NEED HELP URGENTLY?' Huk shouted upstairs.

'WHAT?'

'I SAID, DO WE NEED HELP URGENTLY?'

'I HEARD YOU! I'M NOT DEAF!'

'Then why'd you say "what"?!'

Huk looked at Poppy. He stopped smiling, suddenly.

'I think the position's been filled, kid. You can sod off now, if you like.'

'Tell her she can bugger off,' the old woman shouted. 'We don't need her!'

'I already did that!' Huk shouted back. 'She's still standing here looking at me like she's daft. Are you? Are you daft?'

'A bit, yeah. If I'm being honest, I lost my shoe this morning running from a goblin army. Well, I say *lost*. I left it behind.'

Huk looked taken aback. 'You don't run from a goblin army. There's your first mistake. They get off on the chase. If you walk, they get bored. Idiot. And don't agree with someone when they call you daft.'

'Why not?'

'Because it makes them feel mean for having said it.'

'Then you shouldn't say it in the first place,' said Poppy.

'Touché, kid. Now, get. Go on. Scram.'

The frazzled woman sprinted down the staircase toward them. 'No, don't go! I was up a ladder. Cleaner got stuck in the chandelier again.'

She stumbled a little, pulling off her apron—then sort of tripped and somersaulted the rest of the way down the staircase. If the walls weren't made of carved stone, she might've gone through them, thought Poppy.

She landed like a sack of potatoes, skidding to a stop by Poppy and Huk's feet.

'Fucking hell,' gasped Poppy. 'Are you all right?'

The woman looked up at her in a daze. 'Oh yes. I'm just dandy.'

Poppy helped her up and leaned her against the wall she'd just knocked into.

'What happened?' shouted the old woman from upstairs.

'Nothing,' said Huk, wandering off into the house. 'Matron just tripped again.'

The old woman chuckled. 'Did she just?'

'The job,' said Matron, frantically. It was, Poppy was beginning to think, her default state of being. She swallowed. 'The job is still available. The position remains unfilled. If you want it, it's yours.'

Poppy was too stunned to speak.

These people, she thought, were animals.

And what's more, they hadn't even interviewed her.

'But... what about my credentials?' whispered Poppy, dumbly.

'What about them?' laughed Matron. 'If you want the job, it's yours.'

'I'd feel better if you interviewed me first.'

Matron sighed. 'Oh, fine then. But you'll have to help me up first.'

NO TAKE-BACKS

Matron's office was a thing of pure chaos. You couldn't see the desk for papers, and you couldn't see the papers for half-empty cups of tea —and that didn't even take into account the unopened mail. It wasn't so much stacked as it was *towered*. Poppy could barely see Matron through it.

'Just, I don't know, shove it to the side,' said Matron.

Poppy cleared a little window through the paper so she could see her. Matron was perched behind the mess in a fraying cardigan the colour of tea stains, her white hair pinned up in a collapsing bun that had given up hours ago. Her glasses were slightly wonky, and her left eye blinked more than her right, as if it had lost patience with the other and decided to work alone. 'You're not from around here, are you?'

'No,' said Poppy. 'I'm not.'

'I can tell.' She wrinkled her nose.

'How can you tell?'

Matron laughed. It was a tired, almost bitter sound. 'The locals don't like us much here. Even the bloody postman has it out for us.'

'That's probably because your letterbox has teeth.'

'Oh, does it? *Again?*' Matron rubbed at her head, as if she had a headache she could massage out. 'Look, I really don't think an interview is necessary. I honestly don't even know what to ask you.'

'"Am I good with the elderly?" might be a good start,' prompted Poppy.

'Well, are you?'

'I'm not sure,' said Poppy. 'I don't think so.'

'Good. I wouldn't want to turn you off them. Better that you already are. Avoids disappointment that way.'

Poppy frowned. 'Will you just hire literally anyone, then?'

'You're the first person I've interviewed for the job in a year. Occasionally, someone comes up to the house and asks about it. That's always very exciting.'

'What if I said I was a murderer?' said Poppy.

Matron shrugged. 'Could do with the skillset, I think.' She sipped from an old cup of tea. Poppy hoped it wasn't one of the cups with mould growing in it. 'Murderers usually tidy up after themselves. They're effective with their time. Good at pretending to be polite, I suppose. Are you a murderer, Poppy?'

Poppy shook her head. 'No, I'm not.'

'Shame,' said Matron. 'Would you like to see your room?'

'You can't just... just give me this job willy-nilly.'

Matron groaned. 'You're not hard work, are you? I've got enough of that as it is. I can't afford for you to be hard work too.'

'Well, no. But I just think, before you go and hire someone, you should at least make sure they're right for the job.'

She could scrub floors, change beds, even wrangle the odd enchanted cupboard if it existed—but she didn't want to feel like an afterthought. She'd had rather enough of that lately. No, she needed to know she was wanted for a reason, not just because she happened to knock on the door.

Even if it was only for a few weeks.

'Listen. Do you want the job or not?'

Poppy nodded. 'Yes, but—'

'More importantly, do you *need* this job?'

'Well, yes.'

'How badly do you need it, exactly?'

'I haven't bathed or eaten anything in the last two days,' said Poppy. She looked down at her feet. 'And I'm also missing a shoe.'

'Yes, I noticed that. So it's settled, then.' Matron smirked. 'The job is yours, and there are no take-backs.'

HER OWN ROOM

'We can do this one of two ways,' said Matron. 'You can see your room first, get settled. Bathe, perhaps? I think you ought to have a wash. Then I can show you the house and the grounds, and introduce you to the staff and the residents. Or you can do all of that first, and finish up in your room, where you'll be left undisturbed until tomorrow morning.'

Matron got up from behind her desk, her cardigan catching on a dying fern as she navigated the debris like someone who'd been doing it blindfolded for years. She looked at Poppy expectantly.

'Well, what shall it be?'

Poppy had only just gotten used to the idea that she now had a job. She still hadn't wrapped her head around the fact that it was in a nursing home in the Totswolds. She'd been hunting goblins that morning. And now?

Well, the goblins had been hunting her, really.

If she couldn't be honest with herself, who could she be honest with?

Still—

'I don't know,' she whispered. 'Does it matter?'

Matron shrugged. 'It's nice to feel like you have a choice. A sense of agency is important, especially in a job like this. And if I'm being honest, I've tried it both ways with the last two. They didn't make it to the morning. So I'm not sure it matters much. I could flip a coin if you like?'

'Why didn't the last two make it to morning?'

Poppy's attention caught on that, sharp and sudden.

'I should have a coin here somewhere, I think.'

'Matron?'

'Mmm? Oh—here we are. Crest or Claw?'

'I'll see my room and have a bath first, I think,' said Poppy, distractedly. 'Really, though, what happened to the other two?'

Matron laughed nervously. 'They didn't die, Poppy. If that's what you're getting at.'

'I wasn't,' said Poppy. 'I wasn't even remotely getting at that.'

Matron exhaled loudly. She looked, Poppy thought, like someone at the end of their tether.

'No, they just decided the job wasn't for them,' said Matron.

'How could you know that after one day?'

'My point exactly.' Matron left the office and headed down the hall.

'Now, we're on the first floor at the moment. Your room's on the second floor—the top floor, for now. The third floor is... well, let's just say it's out of action.' Matron screwed up her nose. 'Are you a farmer, Poppy?'

'A farmer?'

'It would explain the smell.'

'Oh. No... I—I tripped.' Poppy's cheeks flushed. 'One minute it's all grass, and then you take a stumble and next thing you know you're covered in cow-shit.'

'Yes,' said Matron. 'Quite so. Quite so indeed. Don't look in there. Granny's doing her brewing. The fumes will singe your eyebrows off. And she doesn't take kindly to being disturbed. Trust me.'

Poppy stepped away from the door.

It had been slightly ajar, and an ominous green mist was seeping out from underneath it. She'd only been going to glance in.

'Her brewing?' she whispered. 'Like mead or ale or something?'

'Or something, yes,' said Matron distractedly. 'Quickly now. The day's getting away from me, and I've got too much to do.' She headed for the stairs.

'Now, be careful. One of these steps doesn't like to be trodden on.'

'Sorry?'

'You will be, yes. So tread lightly.' Matron grimaced as she carefully touched each step with the tip of her shoe.

Poppy followed her lead. She felt both ridiculous and terrified at the same time.

The gnome burst back into the house, followed by his automaton, K.S.

'She moved the enchantments,' he growled, running up the stairs. 'It's in a cupboard or something now—I don't know. Move, I said, move!'

He pushed Poppy out of the way, despite the staircase being wide enough for four humans, let alone two and a gnome.

'Honestly, girl.'

'Don't worry about him,' said Matron. She'd taken to climbing the staircase normally now. 'He's just upset the radio show didn't go to plan.'

'A radio show,' repeated Poppy. 'About what?'

Matron turned to look at her. She seemed to be chewing something over and then shrugged.

'I don't know, and honestly, I'm not sure I care to. As long as it keeps them both busy and happy.'

Poppy looked up at Kelzu, who was standing at the top of the staircase now and looking down at them.

He looked, she thought, not like an elderly gnome at all, but rather a vaguely demonic child.

'And what kind of enchantment is in a cupboard now, exactly?'

Matron was on the second-last step. Poppy watched as her foot went clean through it, the marble turning soft as mud. She stumbled, but didn't fall this time.

Kelzu sniggered in front of them.

'Oh yes,' said Matron, steadying herself. 'Very funny. Well done.'

The gnome walked off whistling, followed by K.S.

Matron looked at Poppy.

'Be careful of this one. It's a Trick Step. The enchantment clearly isn't in a cupboard.' She lowered her voice. 'Unless we've got two Tricks to deal with now. Gods, let's hope not. Bad enough dealing with one.'

'Exactly how we feel,' shouted Kelzu.

There was the sound of a door slamming.

Poppy jumped the last two steps.

'They do this a lot, then?' She helped Matron free her foot.

'Only every so often. Thank you, you can let me go now. It's just practical jokes. Fun little pranks. You know how it is.' Matron smiled. It didn't reach her eyes.

Poppy bit her lip. She'd watched Matron trip down the entire marble staircase only an hour or so ago. She wasn't sure that qualified as a fun little prank. It seemed to belong in an entirely different category—one intended to seriously maim or injure. And yet, for some reason, it utterly delighted Poppy. It was so far from what she'd imagined working here would be like, she couldn't help but feel oddly buoyed by it all.

'Why are you smiling?' asked Matron.

'I just think it's brilliant,' she said.

'Right.' Matron took off her glasses and polished them on her cardigan. 'You're an optimist, are you?'

Poppy nodded. 'I'm told it's one of my worst traits.'

Matron leaned forward. 'Perhaps they won't break you after all.'

'What?'

'Or perhaps they'll just enjoy the challenge.'

Poppy laughed awkwardly.

'Now, your room, I'm afraid, isn't exactly large nor completely clean. It's become a bit of a storage space. Haven't needed to use it for staff, evidently. So your first job will be to clean it. It's your room—I don't care what you do with it. So long as you don't come out of it looking and smelling like a homeless sheep-herder. Now, what size shoe are you?'

Poppy looked down at her feet. She'd forgotten she only had one shoe.

Matron sighed, a little impatiently.

'Never mind. I'll bring you options.'

She opened a door at the end of the hall.

The room, thought Poppy, wasn't small at all. If this wasn't "exactly large" by Matron's standards, she couldn't begin to imagine how big the rest of the rooms in Sunnywood House were.

But she had been right about the mess. You could barely see the floor for things: old mops, brooms, and boxes. Moth-eaten curtains were draped across furniture. Cobwebs clung to mouldy corners of the ceiling.

'Right,' said Matron. She opened the curtains against the far wall. Light spilt into the room, catching on a cloud of dust. It made the air look full of fireflies.

'I'll leave you to it. I've got a meeting with the gardener. Wants to talk about bees, apparently. As if I have time to talk about bees. We'll worry about your introductions and your training in the morning. For now, I think, I'll leave you to get settled. I'll have the cook bring you up something for dinner. Just yell if you need anything.'

Matron paused and looked at Poppy.

'But please don't need anything.'

She pointed as she spoke.

'There's a cupboard of fresh linens just there. The cleaners are charging, so you'll be tidying the old-fashioned way. Cleaning equipment is in that cupboard.'

She turned and stormed off.

Poppy watched her go in a kind of dumbfounded haze. Matron had reached the end of the hallway before Poppy even processed what she'd said.

The cleaners are charging? What in the world?

'I can come down for dinner,' she shouted after her. 'I don't need to have it in my room!'

Matron stopped.

'Oh no, my dear. That won't be necessary,' she laughed. 'You'll have plenty of time to dine with them later, if you so choose.'

She turned to the staircase—and rather promptly screamed, stumbled, and tripped down it.

Poppy flinched with each thudding noise.

There was an ear-ringing silence that followed.

The half-orc, Huk, ducked his head out a door.

'Did we kill her this time?'

'Did we?' called Kelzu, further down the hallway.

'I'm alive,' shouted Matron. 'So don't get your bloody hopes up.'

'Are you alright?' shouted Poppy.

'Yes, I'm fine. Just brilliant.'

Kelzu and Huk both glared at her. They slammed their bedroom doors—one after the other.

Poppy nodded and shut her bedroom door.

She looked around at the mess and felt, for the briefest of moments, as if she'd just walked into a trap. And it wasn't goblins or undead rabbits she had to watch out for.

She sat down on the edge of the bed and looked around the room.

In her room.

She'd never had her own room before. Even if it was just for a few weeks, and even if it was an absolute mess.

Poppy lay down and looked up at the ceiling, smiling a little.

She wondered just what she'd gotten herself into.

And she just hoped the food, the bath, and the bed were worth it.

GRANNY GRACK DID
NOT SURRENDER

Granny Grack had had—*to be quite frank*—rather enough of this nonsense. How anyone was supposed to work under these conditions was beyond her. It had been in the terms of her agreement, for crying out loud: *a fully stocked apothecary cupboard at all times*. Granted, a still-alive fallen star was erring on the side of hard to get, but nevertheless, she needed one. And that had been the whole point of this place, hadn't it? Anything they could want or need: it was to be taken care of.

She sighed.

Granny stirred her spell. It was starting to stick, the spoon dragging along the bottom of the pot. She looked out the window. Matron and the gardener, Clay, were walking through the flowerbeds. Clay had been trying to lobby for funds to get a few beehives. He wasn't having much luck. Granny had told him not to get his hopes up. If anything was going to be purchased, it was going to be a fallen star, not some bloody bees.

But here he was, trying anyway.

Granny thought about opening the window, leaning over the balcony, and telling him, *"Not so fast."* She had a spell to finish, and

all she needed was a sodding star. But what would be the point? No
—*something was up with Matron lately.* Things had been slipping
around Sunnywood. Slipping where things had never slipped before.

And anyway, there were only so many times you could ask for
something before it became little more than begging. And Granny
refused—*point blank*—to beg.

To beg, she thought, was to give away power.

To surrender.

And Granny Grack did not surrender.

So she did the only thing she felt she had left: she called an official
meeting of the Sunnywood House Residents (not including the staff,
thank you very much), and lured them all into the library—or War
Room, as she liked to call it—under the pretence of a good tin of
biscuits and a catch-up.

Huk was the first to join her, ducking through the doorway with
the care of a man who'd once been built for battle but was now mostly
achy knees and spite. There was nothing he loved more than shortbread.

'Grack,' he said, easing himself into his favourite chair.

Granny passed him the tin of biscuits.

'We've got to do something about her,' she said—straight to the
point as ever. At her age, there was no use beating around the bush.
Better to cut them down and push right through.

'She only arrived a few hours ago.' Huk swallowed. 'These are a
bit stale, by the way. I won't be sharing them. Don't want anyone to
get sick.'

Kelzu burst into the library, cloak swirling behind him, his beard
trimmed to a fine point that practically glittered with smugness. He
was followed closely by K.S.

'We have got to do something about her.'

Granny smiled. 'Thank you, Kelzu.' She sat down on the sofa
beside Huk. Now this was more like it, she thought. Taking matters
into their own hands once more.

Kelzu leaned against the window, then turned to face them, almost theatrically. Some things never changed—and one of those things was Kelzu's love of a good entrance.

'What'd you have in mind, then?' Granny reached for the shortbread.

Huk slapped her hand away. 'They're stale. You'll get sick.'

Granny rolled her eyes and settled on a sherbet lemon instead. She always kept them in her pocket for such occasions.

'K.S., engage meeting moderator mode,' said Kelzu. He turned to face Granny and Huk. 'It seems we have a stranger among us. Living in our home. Using our water. Eating our food.'

'Meeting number eighty-five has commenced,' said K.S. 'Let the record show all who are present for it. Attendance will now be called. Granny?'

'I'm here, love.'

Kelzu sighed. 'Attendance won't be necessary, K.S.' He leaned back towards the automaton. 'And next time, if you wouldn't interrupt me mid-speech, that would be great.'

K.S. looked down at Kelzu, then back at Granny and Huk.

'Huk?'

'What?'

'I'm calling attendance. I've marked you as present. Alfred?'

'Alfred?' Granny bit into her sherbet lemon. It fizzed in her mouth. 'He's not here. He's off doing whatever it is he does.'

'Alfred?' repeated K.S. He looked up at the ceiling.

They all looked up.

A dwarven ghost with a translucent beard and a look of permanent disappointment was looking back down at them.

Alfred groaned. 'I'm here. Though why I bother trying to sneak about when you go, and blab is beyond me. Should be ashamed of yourself, you rusty old tin bucket.'

He soared down and sat—or rather, floated—on the empty seat

beside Granny. She wished he wouldn't, though. It made her shiver. And she hated to be cold.

'Does he really have to be here?' said Huk.

'Don't start,' said Granny. They'd been down this road one too many times, and she tried to catch it early now; before it turned into ectoplasm and creepy revenge hauntings. They'd had to hire an exorcist once. Cost an absolute fortune. And he'd done nothing but avoid Alfred's gaze and pretend not to see the bloody ghost at all.

'Don't start what?' said Huk, defensively.

'You know just what. Shut up and eat your shortbread.'

'I'm just saying. I don't see why he should be invited to a meeting for residents. For paying, alive guests, for whom these things actually matter.'

'Oh, come on.' Granny hit Huk in the chest. 'I said, don't start.'

'No, it's fine, Granny,' said Alfred. 'I can see I'm not wanted here.'

'About bloody time,' muttered Huk.

Granny threw her arms up. It wasn't that she hated drama and a good fight—because she really didn't. She'd made quite a lot of money and lived quite a life doing just that. But sometimes—and especially in this case—it did nothing but get in the way.

'I'll just go and hang myself from the chandelier again, then, shall I?'

Alfred soared up from the sofa and straight through the ceiling.

'At least do a better job of it this time!' Huk shouted after him.

'Oh, you really are intolerable sometimes. You know that?'

'It's just a laugh. Don't worry.'

'Let the record show,' said K.S., 'Alfred is no longer present for the meeting. The ghost has left via the ceiling, headed for the third floor; his usual haunt when he's feeling particularly sulky. Now, residents, what is the topic of discussion for which the meeting has been called?'

'What's gotten into him?' said Huk.

Kelzu shrugged. He looked at K.S. through squinted eyes.

'Are you all right, K.S.?'

'Yes, Master. I am quite all right.'

'Well, be less formal or something. I don't know. It's giving me the creeps,' said Huk.

'Certainly, Huk. Less formal. It's been noted.'

'Right... where were we?' said Kelzu.

'The topic of discussion for today's meeting, sir.'

'It will be regarding the new staff member, I should think,' said Granny. She clasped her hands on her lap. She wished she had her needles with her. She could think better when she was knitting, and her fingers had a way to keep busy. It was like pacing—but for the mind.

'And how we deal with her,' added Kelzu.

'I'd prefer not to murder anyone, if it's possible. I don't have the joints for it. Not anymore. We're out of biscuits, Gran.' Huk passed her the empty tin.

She rummaged through her bag and took out the backup snacks.

'We're not murdering anyone, love. Those days are behind us. It's why we're here and not out there. They're raisin scones—you'll just have to make do, I'm afraid.'

Huk screwed up his nose. He took them, though.

'I'm not sure we should rule murder out just yet,' said Kelzu. 'She might well be an insurgent. We don't know, do we? She was hardly vetted. Or worse still—she could be incompetent.'

'I hate incompetence. There's truly nothing I hate more.' Huk swallowed a scone in one. 'These would be better with butter.'

Granny took a block of butter from her bag and handed it to him.

'The thing is, right—this girl is being paid,' said Granny. 'And paid *our* money. I think we ought to have some say in who that should be. We've already got Matron—I don't know why she feels the need for backup. We've a cook. A gardener. The cleaners. She's got more than enough help.'

'Mhm,' agreed Kelzu. 'It's true–Huk, I don't think you should be eating butter like that.'

The half-orc was alternating entire mouthfuls of butter with entire scones.

'It masks the taste of the raisins,' he said with a shrug.

Granny sighed. She'd just been getting to her point, too. 'What was I saying?'

'It's our money,' prompted Kelzu.

'Oh, right—yes. Well, the thing is: it is *our* money she's using. And I feel the funds could be better spent elsewhere. Apothecary supplies, perhaps.'

She needed that star, right or wrong.

'We could do with an extension to the armoury too. My walk-in wardrobe isn't cutting it anymore,' said Huk. His shopping habits for weapons and armour hadn't changed, despite no longer needing them.

'And this girl—this smelly, wandering-in-off-the-streets girl—she's standing in the way of all that.' Granny stood up. She passed Huk a flask of whisky to wash down the scones. He always did this—he'd choke before he slowed down enough to chew anything.

'So, my lads... where do we start?'

THESE FOUR WARM WALLS

It had taken her all day and all night, but Poppy had gotten the room clean in the end. She'd swept, dusted, mopped, and scrubbed. It was, she thought, unfortunately satisfying work. A few times, she'd caught herself smiling and had to tell herself to stop. She was an adventurer. She'd do well to remember it.

But the months she'd spent out there in the world—whether she wanted to admit it or not—had been some of the coldest, dampest, most miserable days of her life. These warm four walls felt like a gift.

She was twenty-three, and she'd never had a room to herself. Not really. At the orphanage, she'd slept in a hallway cupboard most nights; just wide enough to lie down if she didn't stretch her legs. It wasn't a room, technically, but no one else had claimed it, so it was hers.

A door that closed. A bed that was hers alone. These things still felt like magic.

She'd always told herself she didn't need a family. But the truth was, maybe she was just waiting to find the kind that wanted her back.

She'd made her bed up with fresh, crisp linens and tucked the edges in tight. The once-dusty, scuffed floors now shone with polish. All that was left, finally, was a bath.

The ensuite had been a mess, too, of course. It more than likely hadn't been used in years—perhaps decades. Mushrooms were growing in the claw-foot bathtub—the glowing kind—and a strange slime that moved about in the toilet bowl when you weren't looking directly at it. But it didn't matter. It was all cleaned soon enough.

The bath water ran brown and murky at first, until it eventually steamed hot and crystal clear. It smelled faintly of lavender, a remnant of the magic from the ether-heating, Poppy figured. The technology was rare and expensive, normally reserved for noble estates or high-end city hotels. She'd only ever read about it in books.

Sunnywood, despite its peeling ceilings and old stone façade, was a surprisingly modern home. Even the lights were ether-fuelled, glowing softly from pipes in the walls like veins of slow lightning.

She removed her clothes and slipped into the bath, and every part of her relaxed. She chuckled to herself and felt a little deranged and giddy from the simple pleasure of it all.

It was strange to think that only that very morning, she'd nearly been killed by a roving band of goblins. Stranger still, she felt as if she were missing something by being here, at Sunnywood—and not out there, in the world, making a name for herself.

Poppy woke some hours later.

The water, somehow, was still hot and steaming.

It was pitch black outside.

Poppy sat there, disoriented for a moment, before she remembered where she was. A dull, glowing light emanated from the ether-pipes in the walls—just enough to see by.

She dried herself—her skin wrinkly and papery from having soaked for far too long—and then crawled into bed.

She laughed again.

Unable to contain her joy, and too tired and too relaxed to feel any kind of guilt about it.

'You are, I think, the most comfortable bed I've ever slept in,' she whispered.

Poppy fell asleep with a smile and did not wake once.

At least, that is, until the early hours of the morning: Matron was knocking on her door.

'I hope you're decent.' The door opened, and Matron walked in backwards. 'Is it safe to turn around?'

Poppy sat up, squinting against the sudden harshness of the ether-lights.

'Has something happened?'

'No, not that I know of,' said Matron. She gave the room a cursory once-over. 'You've done well with the cleaning. I barely recognise it.'

She set a tray down on the edge of Poppy's bed. It was laden with still-sizzling bacon and eggs (sunny-side up, sprinkled with chives and fresh-cracked pepper), alongside large batons of sourdough fried in butter. It looked to be perfectly plain, quite fucking delicious.

'That's for me?' asked Poppy.

She could barely believe it.

'I'd be knocking on someone else's door if it wasn't.' Matron placed a pair of shoes by the desk near the window and hung several sets of uniforms in the wardrobe.

'Leave your washing on the floor and your door open. The cleaners will be in. They'll have a field day with your farming attire.'

Poppy nodded, crunching on perfectly crisp bacon. She smirked —realising then that Matron was the kind of person who preferred to call her stained and filthy excuse for clothes farming attire, instead of just saying they were covered in cow-shit.

Matron frowned and looked behind her.

'What? Why are you looking at me like that? You do like bacon and eggs, don't you?'

'Of course,' said Poppy. 'I'm not an idiot.'

'Well, forgive me, but you rather look it at the moment.' Matron fussed over the room, then turned to face her.

'Right. You're all good then?'

'Yes,' said Poppy. 'I think so. Why?'

'Made it through the night okay?'

'I fell asleep in the bath. It stays hot.'

'Right. I'll leave you to get ready. Don't get used to this, by the way. I will not be serving you breakfast in bed again, so don't for a second think I will.'

Matron checked her pocket watch. Its glow lit up her tense, pursed lips.

'I expect to see you in the foyer at 5 a.m. sharp for the breakfast shift.'

'What's the time now?' asked Poppy, around a mouthful of toast.

'4:55 a.m.'

And with that, Matron turned on her heels and was gone.

'But that's in five minutes!' Poppy shouted after her.

There was no answer.

EPISODE 3

Excerpt from the transcript of
The Sunnywood Signal.

Episode 3: *"The Myth of the Glorious Life"*
Transcribed by KS-01.
Broadcast on The Upper Susshingham Radio 102.3EM

HUK

There's something they never tell you about adventure, you know.

KELZU

That it ruins your knees?

HUK

That too. But no—it's that after you've stormed a castle, outwitted a Lich, and galloped halfway across the kingdom on a horse with trust issues—

KELZU

—Named Clive—

HUK

—Named Clive, yes. After all that, the thing you want most in the world—

KELZU

A feast? Soft kisses from a stranger? A statue in your honour?

HUK

A lie in.

KELZU

...Oh. Yes. Gods, yes.

HUK

You dream of it, out there. A warm bed. No rocks in your back. No cursed leeches in your socks. Just linen. And a pillow that doesn't smell like sweat, blood and regret.

ALFRED (SPECIAL GUEST)

I was under the impression adventuring was meant to be glamorous?

KELZU

It is, Alfie, old boy. Just... retrospectively. In the moment, it's mostly cuts and bruises, and someone else's blood on your boots.

HUK

But the bed? The bed is real.

KELZU

The bed is good.

THE RESIDENTS ARE CREATURES OF HABIT

Poppy launched herself out of bed and dressed as quickly as she could. The uniform was uncomfortable and itchy. She splashed cold water on her face, and, in the bathroom mirror, noticed—not her reflection—but that the glowing mushrooms in the bathtub had grown back. She lifted the toilet seat, and that strange moving slime was back too, though it retreated down the drain, spooked by the sudden interruption.

I'll have to fix this, thought Poppy, and properly this time.

'Don't go getting too comfortable,' she muttered. 'I'll be dealing with you later.'

The toilet bowl trembled atop the tiled floor.

The shoes Matron had left for her were a full two sizes too big, but they were better than the alternative. Poppy left the room at a sprint, ran back for the last piece of bacon, and then made her way downstairs. She forgot the Trick Step and went stumbling—but managed to catch herself just in time.

Matron was standing in the foyer with a clipboard. She frowned. 'Well, don't rush about. I don't tolerate franticness. And I refuse to

engage with someone who is…' she looked Poppy up and down, '…
frazzled.'

This was, thought Poppy, a bit bloody rich considering how
Matron had behaved when they'd first met. Yesterday, she'd been
scattered, exhausted and very possibly mid-nervous breakdown. Now
here she was, all crisp cuffs and clipped authority—stern as a
headmistress.

'Sorry.' Poppy straightened her jacket. The collar itched against
her neck something fierce. 'I didn't want to be late.'

'You already are,' said Matron, and turned sharply through the
foyer into the dining hall. She began opening curtains and turning
up the ether-powered rune lights.

'Now, the residents are early to bed and early to rise. We've about
fifteen minutes before they start to wander in, so it's all hands on
deck.'

She tossed Poppy an apron and stalked off into the hall.

Poppy tried—hopelessly—to get it to knot behind her back as
she followed.

'The tables need setting—two over there, one over here, and
another here. Our residents—whether they like to admit it or not—
are creatures of habit. Huk likes the morning sun, so he sits by this
window in winter, and that one over there in summer. Kelzu, as a
rule, sits wherever Huk sits. They're tied at the hip. Except for when
they fall out, which is often—but never for long. In that case, they sit
opposite each other rather than beside each other. Granny prefers to
sit alone. She likes to read and enjoy her morning solitude. She sits—
what are you doing?'

Poppy had stopped in the middle of the room, arms awkwardly
lifted behind her. 'I can't get the sodding apron to knot.'

'Here,' said Matron, sweeping over. She cinched it tightly around
Poppy's waist. Too tightly. Poppy let out a small sound—something
between a yes and a cry.

Matron handed her a stack of shiny white plates. Perhaps because it was early, or perhaps because the apron had just cut off her circulation, Poppy sort of just stood there, frozen.

Matron sighed. 'The tables by the window, Poppy. You put the plates on them.'

'Right, yes. Of course.' Poppy swallowed. She would have. Truly. She was about to, in fact—

Except she'd just seen the ghost of a dwarf.

It had floated through a wall, humming.

'It's just that,' she said slowly, 'and I could be losing my mind here—but there is a ghost. Right there.'

'Oh, don't worry about him,' said Matron, waving a hand dismissively. 'That's only Alfred. He's like the damp in the laundry cupboard—impossible to get rid of and has been here since day dot.'

'Morning!' said Alfred cheerily. He leaned toward Poppy. 'I saw you sleeping last night. One hell of a snorer.'

Poppy swallowed hard.

What kind of retirement home had a ghost, exactly? She could look past the angry gnome with the brass automaton and the old woman casting tripping spells on staircases.

But a *ghost*?

She felt like she ought to be running for a ghost-killing sword. Or at least preparing some kind of spectral trap. A ghost should be contained, shouldn't it?

'Crossword or news first?' said Matron.

'What?' said Poppy.

'Neither,' said Alfred. 'Page five, if you will. I've heard there's a new troll bank opening in town and I should like to read about it.'

Matron flicked through a newspaper and slammed it down in front of him. She looked at Poppy. 'You'll have to set him a table too. He gets upset if he isn't served food.'

'I'll have French toast this morning. Black coffee. Freshly squeezed juice of the day. And an omelette.' Alfred pulled out a pair of reading glasses and looked down his nose at the paper.

Matron rolled her eyes. 'Hasn't been a resident in thirty-five years,' she whispered. 'But the wee bastard paid enough to stay here several lifetimes, so...' She shrugged. 'What can you do?'

'Four lifetimes, to be exact. Dwarven lifetimes at that.' Alfred peered over the top of his glasses. 'Breakfast now, if you please.'

'You'd better go and get it,' said Matron to Poppy. She checked her pocket watch. 'Service starts in ten. I'll finish setting up here—you can start bringing in the food.'

'The food. Yes. Right.' Poppy turned and made for the nearest door. Then stopped.

'Poppy?' called Matron.

'Mmm?'

'Kitchen's that way.'

Of course it was.

A DRAGON IN THE PANTRY

The kitchen was quiet and calm and—at the present moment—blessedly empty. Poppy leaned against the wall, closed her eyes, and tried to catch her breath.

It was just a ghost.

A newspaper-reading, glasses-wearing ghost.

It wasn't a big deal.

She'd fought kappas and goblins. She'd watched a man turn into a dog. A unicorn had cornered her—its horn dripping with the blood of her fellow adventurer. (She had passed out at that point and conveniently woken up after it had all been sorted out.) But still. A ghost?

The thing was, thought Poppy, expecting to see a ghost and having one appear out of a wall to demand a four-course breakfast with freshly squeezed juice and black coffee—well, that was something else entirely, now wasn't it?

'They haven't broken you already, have they?'

Poppy opened her eyes.

A man stood in the doorway, watching her with mild curiosity. He had well-kept black hair and the first signs of age creeping into the corners of his eyes. Not old. Not young. Just that uncomfortable sort of middle.

'The last two she hired never made it to the breakfast shift,' he added. He began to chop onions at a speed Poppy hadn't thought possible. One moment, a whole onion; the next, finely diced and stirred into a pan of sizzling butter. 'There's a back door through there, if you want to do a runner.' He pointed with his knife and smirked in a way that struck Poppy as infuriatingly smug.

She decided instantly that she'd stay—just to prove him wrong.

She straightened up and held out her hand. 'I'm Poppy.'

'Hello, Poppy.' He glanced at her hand and then ignored it, returning to his chopping.

'I'm the new carer. Well—I think I am. Matron hasn't really explained anything yet.'

He scoffed. 'I bet she hasn't. Look, put your hand down. I'm not going to shake it. I'm busy. My name's Hiro.'

He tasted a sauce, made a face, and promptly chucked the contents out the open window.

'You can call me Chef, if you like. But never 'cook.' You call me 'cook', and I'll throw a knife at your head.'

'Okay,' Poppy nodded. She pulled at her collar. 'Sorry, but... why?'

Hiro closed the window and returned to his bench. 'It caramelised too much. Would've thrown off the whole dish.'

'No, I meant—why not call you 'cook'?'

'Because I'll throw a knife at your head,' he said again, much more slowly. Then, suddenly dropping the blade onto the chopping board with a thud, he turned. 'I didn't apprentice under the world's finest chefs in the finest palaces just to be degraded to a title like cook, understood?'

Poppy shrugged. 'Yes, Chef.'

Hiro grunted. He opened the oven and pulled out a tray of steaming fruit buns that glistened and smelled like cinnamon.

'There's a service trolley in the pantry—just through there. Grab it, won't you?'

Poppy opened the pantry door—

—and was promptly knocked flat on her back by what could only be described as a dragon.

She screamed. Loudly. But it wasn't the scream of a damsel; it was the battle cry of someone thoroughly sick of surprises.

'Back—get back!' she shouted, kicking at the beast furiously.

Dragons were something adventurers worked up to. They came after you'd graduated from goblins, orcs, and bugbears. You didn't just get ambushed by one in a kitchen pantry.

Poppy grabbed one of Hiro's knives from the kitchen counter and started swinging it wildly, ready for the inevitable lunge.

A small part of her—deep under the terror and adrenaline—realised the dragon was roughly the size of a dog. A large dog, yes, but still. A dog.

Hiro darted around the bench and grabbed the dragon by its collar.

'Yes, brilliant idea,' Poppy panted. 'You hold it down—I'll slice its throat.'

'You will *not*,' said Hiro. 'Does he look deadly to you?'

The dragon whined impatiently. Licking at Hiro's face.

'He's basically a dog with scales and wings. He's harmless. Put the knife down before you hurt yourself.'

Poppy hesitated. 'And you're sure he won't kill me?'

'He might lick you to death, but that's about it. Now put my knife down.'

Poppy lowered it. 'Why's it so small then?'

'*He*, not it—his name's Bernard,' Hiro said firmly. 'And he's not small. He's fully grown.'

'What kind of dragon is he?'

'Well, he's not a dragon. He's a book-wyrm.'

'A book-wyrm?'

The wyrm was now sitting under Hiro's legs, panting happily and puffing little clouds of steam.

'His name is Bernard?' she asked, disbelieving.

Hiro nodded. 'He helps tend the stove when he's not on guard duty.' He scratched Bernard's head. The creature leaned into it, nearly knocking him over. 'His sparker's faulty, though. Most of the time, he just leaks gas, no flame. So we have to light him manually. Bit of a faff, but it makes him feel important.'

'Matron didn't mention Bernard,' said Poppy, quietly. She pulled out a chair and sat down at the kitchen table.

'She didn't mention Alfred either, did she?'

'No,' said Poppy. 'She didn't.'

'Maybe she figured it'd be better if you saw for yourself. Less chance of you legging it before signing the paperwork.'

'And what is the job, exactly?'

Hiro wheeled the trolley out of the pantry and began loading trays of food beneath the steaming heat lamps.

'Service is starting. Why don't you go find out?'

Poppy took the trolley and began to wheel it carefully toward the door.

'Oh—and Poppy,' Hiro called.

She stopped. Turned.

'Don't you ever, under any circumstances, touch my knives again. Do you understand?'

Poppy nodded. She wasn't entirely sure if she liked the chef. He was too forward. And he struck her as someone who spent far too much time alone in his kitchen, with no one but the dragon for company.

But then again, if she couldn't handle an irritable chef, a pet wyrm, and a ghost with a breakfast order, how could she possibly survive anything out there on a real adventure?

A HAPPY GHOST IS LESS WORK THAN AN ANGRY ONE

When Poppy returned to the dining hall, Matron was nowhere to be found, but there was another resident seated at a table. A kind-looking old lady was staring out the window at the garden and the sunrise beyond. She had long grey hair tied in a bun and reading glasses on a chain around her neck. She looked, thought Poppy, like the kind of person you expected to see in a retirement home. Unlike the half-orc or the gnome with his towering automaton, this resident looked how residents ought to look: she looked old.

Poppy smiled at her.

She didn't smile back.

But that was fine. She wasn't wearing her glasses, and her eyes looked a little milky. She likely just hadn't seen her smile.

'Good morning,' said Poppy, pulling the trolley to a stop beside her. 'You must be... Granny?'

'And you must be the new help,' said Granny Grack, dryly. She gave Poppy a slow, precise once-over. The examination was intense and exacting; it made Poppy want to barrel-roll straight out the window. 'You've met Bernard, I see?'

Poppy laughed awkwardly. She caught her reflection in the

window and patted her hair down. 'Yes, though I'm not sure I'd describe it as meeting him. More like being attacked by him. Tea, coffee, or juice?'

'He's only a big squishy idiot. Makes the mistake of liking everyone he meets. Tea. I don't tolerate coffee. It doesn't amuse me, and nor does juice.'

Poppy went to pour her a cup. Her hands had started to tremble under Granny's steely gaze. It was, she thought, a hundred times more terrifying than an army of goblins charging at you with swords.

'What are you doing?' said Granny, sharply.

'Pouring you a cup of tea?'

'I can pour my own cup, thank you. I'm not an invalid. Leave the teapot.'

Poppy set the kettle down nervously. She only had the one— Gods knew what she was supposed to do if someone else wanted tea. 'And for breakfast?'

'Should I just guess the menu this morning then?'

Poppy thought what was on offer was fairly bloody obvious, given the trolley of food on display in front of her. She pointed at the dishes. 'Well, there's porridge, fruit buns, bacon, eggs—scrambled or fried—crumpets with the usual condiments. And whatever this is,' she stirred a steaming pot with a spoon, 'I think it's baked beans. But it doesn't look like any baked beans I've ever had.'

Granny ignored her after that.

Poppy left her with crumpets, some bacon, and eggs. She figured that, between all that, Granny would find something she liked. The morning went on like this for the next few hours. Granny eventually left, having drunk an entire pot of tea, but without touching a single bite of food.

Alfred, Poppy was learning, was about the most annoying person she'd ever met—dead or alive. She'd be halfway through clearing a table when he'd ask—well, demand was more appropriate—that she top up his coffee and turn his page.

Poppy did this without saying a word, because Matron had returned and was watching her every move like a hawk. She'd been serving Huk—the half-orc—his truly unhinged, heaping mountain of bacon when the ghost had said, 'I'll have some of that. And I'd like to read the paper again. Back to front this time. Front to back didn't scratch the itch.'

Poppy looked at Huk and whispered, 'Is he always like this?'

Huk nodded, mouth full of bacon. 'He's a knob.'

Poppy smiled.

Huk smiled back—then seemed to remember himself and turned his full concentration back to his breakfast. The half-orc, at least, wasn't openly hostile; not like Granny or Alfred. She was beginning to suspect that, so long as he was supplied with a steady intake of food, he would continue to regard her with complete and utter indifference.

She made a mental note: Huk can be won over with food. Preferably greasy.

'I'll have a top-up on my coffee too, if you don't mind,' said Alfred. 'I'd prefer a fresh pot. You've had that there too long. It'll have gone stale.'

Poppy turned the page of the paper—perhaps a little more viciously than necessary—and opened it. 'What do you care for current events anyway?'

'You don't care about what's going on in the world?'

'I mean, of course I care. But,' she skimmed the article, 'do I care what the price of Rune-Stones means for the economy of Upper Susshingham? No. No, I'm sorry, I don't.'

'And that's why *you* work at a retirement home, and *I'm* an esteemed guest of one,' said Alfred. He smiled—not unkindly. 'Now, don't forget my coffee.'

Poppy returned to the kitchen and emptied the coffee pot into the sink. The sun had fully risen, and it felt like she'd done nothing all morning but turn the bastard's pages. She wanted to scream.

'He can't even drink it,' she muttered to herself. The coffee just sat there, growing cold. How did he even know—or care—if it tasted stale?

She ground more beans, filled the pot, and poured in boiling water. She tried and failed to dodge Bernard's attempts at affection and was promptly knocked sideways into the wall. The coffee pot went skidding across the kitchen floor.

'Oh, fuck it.'

Hiro poked his head out of the pantry. 'All going well?'

'Yes, it's grand,' she said, viciously. 'They're all lovely.'

'Lovely?' He leaned against the pantry door. 'I've heard them described as many things. But never lovely.' He grinned. 'You survived a breakfast shift, though. That's more than anyone else has done.'

Poppy groaned. Maybe she should run out the back door.

'If he wasn't already dead, I think I'd kill him,' she muttered.

Hiro laughed. It was the first time she'd heard him laugh. It was a good sound—warm and honest. The kind of sound that made the sharp edges of her morning feel a little less jagged.

Maybe Hiro, she thought, could become a friend. Or at the very least, someone to vent to when she needed it.

'Honestly,' she said, 'I'm serious. There has to be a way to kill a ghost, right?'

Matron appeared in the doorway. Her face was stern, and her upper lip fixed into a thin line. 'There isn't,' she said, flatly. 'We've tried. And I suggest you don't bring it up again. It took months to stop him from being all sulky and spooky about the place. A happy ghost is less work than an angry one. Trust me.'

Poppy nodded. She had the sudden, almost undeniable urge to stand ramrod straight and salute. 'Yes, Matron.'

'Mr Luckyhand hasn't come down for breakfast. When you're done doing... whatever it is you're doing here, could I trouble you to check on him? And take something up.'

'Yes, Matron. Sorry.'

Matron narrowed her eyes. 'Sorry for what?'

But she'd already turned and was gone before Poppy could answer.

She looked at Hiro, but he only shrugged and vanished back into the pantry.

Poppy loaded a tray with breakfast things and set off for Mr Luckyhand's room.

She might've survived the breakfast shift, she thought—but it'd be a miracle if she were still here by the end of the week.

And yet...

There was a plan. A threadbare one, but still.

She hadn't come to Sunnywood because she wanted to work in a retirement home full of lunatics, ghosts, and bacon-hoarding half-orcs. She was here because she needed money. Real coin. Enough to buy gear that wouldn't fall apart at the first sign of frost. Enough to make it—finally—to the Mistling Mountains.

She'd heard about them from travellers on the road. Seasoned adventurers with scars and stories and that quietly mad glint in their eyes. The Mistling Mountains. A place of wild magic, old riddles, and untold treasure. Everyone said that if you were serious about making a name for yourself, you'd end up there eventually.

Poppy didn't want to end up there. She wanted to *begin* there.

And for that, she needed to save. Gods, no one ever warned her how expensive adventuring could be. Rations. Repairs. Bribes. Licences. The cost of entry was steep, and all you had to offer was *everything* you had. It was the kind of life where the line between "hero" and "hobo with a sword" blurred by the day.

So she'd stick it out at Sunnywood. For longer than a few weeks, perhaps. For as long as it took. She'd save enough and get out.

And one day—if all went to plan—she'd find her way to the Mistling Mountains.

THE WAR ROOM

Granny wasn't snooping. She was performing reconnaissance. There was a difference. Snooping was nosy and pathetic; an act reserved for curtain-twitchers and bored children. Recon, though? That was Warcraft. And Sunnywood was full of people the world once feared. That made it a target. So yes, Granny had good reason to keep tabs on the help, especially when they arrived with a sword, no references, and a frankly suspicious amount of rope.

There was a slime in Poppy's toilet.

That slime was Granny's.

It was sentient: her eyes where her eyes couldn't go. She'd tasked Alfred that morning with keeping Poppy busy whilst she went back to her own room and set about getting to work. In some ways, Granny found she enjoyed having a new staff member. Once she got past the infuriating idea that she was surplus to needs, taking their money and getting in the way of her finishing a spell five years in the making, it was, she hated to admit, rather nice to have someone to actively root against.

She got by with occasionally tripping Matron, small tricksy spells and the like. But it was losing its appeal and, at times, it felt a little too much like biting the hand that fed you; something that didn't sit quite right with Granny.

Of course, she wasn't going to go rifling through the girl's things by hand. That would be beneath her—and besides, if she got caught, she'd never hear the end of it. No, the slime was better. The girl would never know. And even if she did—what would she accuse her of? Toilet espionage? The slime didn't ask questions. Didn't fumble. And if there was anything in her bag that proved the girl was a threat —well, Granny Grack was going to find it.

She sat down in her armchair, pushing aside her balls of wool and knitting needles. She closed her eyes, and when she opened them next, Granny was inside a toilet inside of the girl's room at the end of the hall. 'Now, this is more like it,' she whispered.

Granny, as the slime, crawled out of the toilet bowl and slinked along the floor, and then she set about rummaging through the rest of Poppy's room.

There was a trail of water left in its wake. It was unfortunate, really, that the slime had to live in the toilet. But you couldn't very well ask someone to leave the sink or the bath full of water so that your spying beastie wouldn't dry up and die. When they'd been out on the road, it hadn't been a problem; there was always a lake or a river or a conjured floating orb of water to store the slime in, but, well, in a residential setting, one had to get mundanely inventive.

The girl was trouble, though, of that Granny was sure. She had to be. And if she wasn't trouble, well, then she'd just have to make sure she *became* trouble. The slime shrank and slipped into the girl's bag. It rifled through the usual detritus that littered any bag. Daggers, long ones, short ones. Caltrops, ball-bearings. Rope. A half-eaten pack of rations. Just your standard adventuring kit. The kind you could buy at any general store. The kind all adventurers fresh into the world and having flown the nest go out to buy.

Nothing. Just a basic adventurer's kit. Granny hissed through her teeth. So she really was just some green-footed wannabe out for coin and purpose.

Boring.

Unless that was what she wanted them to think…

The slime slipped out of the bag and looked under the bed.

Nothing.

Nothing.

Nothing.

'Uggghhh,' groaned Granny. People were so dull these days. She found herself thinking it more and more often of late. She'd wondered if it was the world that had changed or if it was her. Because it never felt like this when she was out and about.

And then it hit her.

Granny opened her eyes. She saw her own room and could hear Huk's tell-tale floorboard thumping outside her door. She crossed the room quicker than her knees normally allowed and dragged him in.

'Well?' she said.

Huk frowned. '*Well*, what?'

'What did you think?'

'She seems normal enough.' Huk shrugged. 'She served me as much bacon as I wanted, too. That was nice.'

'That's the thing, though, isn't it. She does seem normal.'

'Yeah.' Huk frowned. 'That's what I just said.'

'But no one seems normal to us. I was just rummaging through her bag, and do you know what I found?'

'You were rummaging through her bag?' Huk sat down on Granny's armchair with a grin.

'I found weapons, Huk. Daggers, ropes, rations, a bedroll! Even a compass.'

Huk shrugged. 'So, lots of adventurers have all that gear.'

'Exactly!' Granny nearly jumped with the excitement of it. 'Lots of *adventurers*, Huk. Not people. Not normal people. What we consider to be normal isn't, well, normal at all. And this, this *Poppy*, she's no carer. She's a spy. Kelzu was right. We're dealing with an insurgent here. I'm sure of it.'

Huk laughed.

Granny shot him a hardened, deadly kind of look.

He stopped. He knew better than to laugh at her when she was like this. 'You're being serious? Oh come on, Grack. She's not a spy. What would she even be spying on? In case you hadn't noticed, we're old and boring now.'

'We still have enemies, Huklin. We're not totally irrelevant, thank you very much. Why else do you think we have a guard dragon?'

Huk looked to be trying his very level best not to grin at that.

'Where is the little bastard anyway?' Granny folded her arms. 'He was supposed to help me this morning.'

'Who? Kelzu or the dragon?'

Granny looked down her nose at him. 'Kelzu, of course.'

'Having a lie-in, I suspect.'

Granny groaned. Kelzu had a knack for sleeping through all the important things. It was, she thought, half the reason Gnomes lived for such an infuriatingly long time. All they did was sleep. 'You go and wake him. I'll begin setting up the war-room.'

Huk sighed. 'Fine, but if there's no—'

'—cake, yes, I know.' Granny waved her hands dismissively. 'Go and wake him.'

'And I won't tolerate —'

'—Anything with fruit in. Honestly, who do you think I am? I'll have Hiro whip one of his chocolate things up.'

'Two!' said Huk. 'Two chocolate things.'

'Two is a bit excessive, love. You're not bulking anymore. Without the fighting, it'll become fat, not muscle.' Huk had stopped at Granny's door. 'We're too late,' he said. 'Your spy has just gone into Kelzu's room.'

'Well, fuck,' swore Granny.

LUCKYHAND'S LOOTLAND

Poppy entered Mr Luckyhand's room and nearly collapsed from the shock of it.

She stepped back out into the hallway, just to check. Just to make sure she wasn't losing her damn mind.

Then she stepped back in again.

Nope.

This was, she thought, about the most insane thing she had ever seen.

She ducked out once more. Just once more. She had to be certain. Had to convince herself that what was happening here was real.

The hallway was normal. Just a regular old hallway. Stone brick walls. Polished wooden floors. Carpet runners. Potted plants. Huk and Granny watching her through a half-open door.

Poppy swallowed. 'Am I losing my mind, or is his room...?'

'It's not really a room,' said Huk.

'No, I can see that. What exactly is it then?'

'It's Lootland. Luckyhand's Lootland. You've never heard of it? It used to be our home before Sun—'

Granny smacked Huk on the back of the head and slammed the door shut.

'Lootland,' Poppy repeated.

She was almost certain she could still see Granny's eye peering at her through the keyhole.

She stepped back inside Kelzu's room—and promptly spilt half the breakfast tray down her front as she spun around in a state of catatonic amazement.

Because this wasn't a room, Huk had been right about that.

It was... vast. Sound echoed in its vastness. Her own breathing bounced back at her, louder than it had any right to be. The space didn't just stretch, it spiralled and corkscrewed off into the distance.

There were aisles, like in a shop. Endless shelves stacked with all manner of objects. Things that glowed, shimmered, floated. Not a single speck of dust. Potions in bottles shaped like teardrops. Weapons hung on velvet pegs. Cloaks that seemed to twitch when you looked directly at them. A fireplace flickered beside a squashy couch, hemmed in by bookshelves that wound upwards and sideways in defiance of gravity.

Some shelves had ladders. Others, spiralling staircases. One had a floating platform drifting slowly up and down, carrying a small potted fern.

Poppy set the tray down beside a bowl of eyeballs. They all turned to stare at her.

'Hello,' she whispered.

They blinked—then merged into one massive eyeball, the size of a crystal ball, which lolled gently in the bowl.

Poppy stumbled back, knocking into a wall of armour. Some suits gleamed so brightly she had to shield her eyes. One of them was steaming.

There was a noise then. It sounded like both a single footstep and a thunderous stampede—like an alarm.

She followed the sound through the maze of shelves, passing

stranger things by the second: a shelf of jam jars, each holding a storm cloud; a sword that hummed with its own eerie lullaby; a taxidermy duck wearing a crown and radiating faint menace.

At last, she found the source of the sound: the gnome's automaton, standing guard beside Mr Luckyhand, who was curled in bed with a pillow clamped over his head. The automaton emitted a high-pitched, glass-shattering hum on a relentless loop.

Mr Luckyhand cracked one eye open at her, then groaned and scrunched it shut again.

Poppy hesitated. 'Breakfast is served. I left it... on a table... somewhere,' she called. 'If you wouldn't mind pointing me back to the exit, that would be grand. I think I've lost the house.'

The gnome groaned louder.

He sat up and threw the pillow at the automaton, which didn't flinch.

'Are you awake now, sir?' it asked, red eye gleaming. 'May I stop the morning alarm protocol and bring you your breakfast?'

'Now you'll stop it, will you?' shouted Kelzu.

'Yes, sir. Morning alarm protocols can be safely disarmed once you have made SIGNIFICANT EFFORTS TO STOP ONESELF SLEEPING. As you are now sitting up and have discarded your pillow, processes dictate you are no longer in danger of falling back to sleep.'

The automaton's eye faded from bright red back to light blue.

'I could murder you.'

'You could not. You have TRIED.'

'Maybe I should try HARDER.'

The gnome rummaged for his glasses, jammed them on, and squinted at Poppy.

'And what are you doing here, then?'

'I'm Poppy, Mr Luckyhand. Matron sent me up with your breakfast, but, um, I got a little... lost?'

'Ughhh, gods. Don't ever call me Mr Luckyhand again. It makes me feel old. It's Kelzu.' He peered at her. 'Did my breakfast get lost too?'

'No, I—'

'Placed it on a coffee table in aisle three. Then wandered down aisles five, twelve and fourteen. You touched a copy of Living Maps and left a fingerprint smudge on the Ever-Gleaming Armour.' Two beams of light scanned Poppy. 'Despite touching the inventory, you have not stolen. YET.'

'Go and get my breakfast, K.S.,' Kelzu muttered.

The automaton nodded and lumbered off, metal joints clanking.

'Never mind him,' Kelzu said. 'I had K.S. built back when I ran the store. It's just old habits, only for him they're hard-coded. He's been yelling more than usual, though. Probably got a bloody spider in his rune-board.' He rubbed his eyes and shoved a tangled mess of grey hair behind his ears. 'Anyway—how's your first day been?'

'Different,' said Poppy.

'I'd expect as much. Pass me my slippers, would you? The floor's freezing.'

She found them beside a pile of scrunched-up paper—plans and half-baked ideas for his radio show, she noted—and helped him out of bed. His slippers were pointed velvet things, ridiculously soft, like holding a hug.

'You're going to ask,' said Kelzu. He looked at her as though he already knew what she was thinking.

Poppy flushed. 'Well, I mean... how? Just... how?'

'How do I fit all this in here, behind that door out there?'

She nodded. 'Bend your big toe down. I can't get it on. There. That's better.'

'Well, the thing is, it's not behind the door at all. That door's just in front of all this, here.'

'I don't get it.'

'No,' said Kelzu. 'And very few do.'

From somewhere in the distance, they heard the thunderous clank of K.S. returning.

Poppy opened her mouth to ask another question, but shut it when Kelzu gave her a look.

'What?'

'What's the deal with the morning alarm?'

'It's remnants from days past. I set it years ago—before you were a twinkle in your parents' eyes, and before they were a twinkle in theirs. But I can't, for the life of me, remember the bloody password.' He slumped into a perfectly gnome-sized armchair.

Poppy stood nearby, feeling like a giraffe in a dollhouse.

'I think if I ever got a lie-in,' Kelzu muttered, 'I might die from happiness.'

'Matron got me up before five this morning,' said Poppy.

'Gods, she makes me sick.' Kelzu smiled.

Poppy smiled back.

'Oh, don't do that,' he said.

'Do what?'

'Make me like you. It's going to make getting rid of you too hard.'

'Get rid of me?'

'Mmm. Feed you to Trevor. Hang you by the neck from the staircase so you look like a chandelier. Or just poison you blind and send you walking. We haven't decided yet.'

A silence followed. Not the comfortable kind.

Poppy coughed a nervous half-laugh. 'And why do you want to get rid of me?'

'You're surplus to needs.' He grinned, unsettlingly.

It was, Poppy thought, a grin with just a little too many teeth.

'I didn't know you were a joker.'

'Oh, my dear,' said Kelzu, suddenly very serious, 'there's a great deal you don't know about me. Or, indeed, about us.'

YOU MIGHT JUST MAKE IT

Later that morning, when the breakfast shift was done and the dishes were washed, Matron led Poppy out of the manor and into the grounds. She was a stern woman, Poppy was learning. The frazzled Matron who'd been tripped down the stairs and had practically begged her to take the job was gone; and in her place was someone formidable. She seemed, thought Poppy, like the kind of person who had no time for sleep.

'You get half an hour for lunch. Your hours are breakfast to dinner. Though you will remain on call all night.' Matron held the front doors open for Poppy. She tapped her feet whenever she had to stand still; it made Poppy feel like she had to jog to keep up. Matron sighed. 'Quickly, Poppy, if you don't mind. I have to organise Hiro's absurd grocery demands before he puts the orders in.'

Poppy had already been hurrying. If she hurried any further, she was liable to meet herself coming down the stairs. It didn't help that her shoes—two sizes too big—had started to eat at her socks, and her collar (still infuriatingly itchy around her neck) had begun to cause a rash.

Matron pushed both front doors wide open and latched them back, letting the cool spring breeze rush into the hallway.

'So,' she continued, 'if the residents need us, they have Call-Stones. Though they're strongly encouraged to use them only in emergencies. And no, retrieving Huk a tin of biscuits does not constitute an emergency, no matter how much he presses you for them. You have Sundays off to do as you like. You'll be paid weekly on Saturdays—watch your step, that stone was alive last week.'

Poppy jumped a little over the stone path set into the grass. 'What do you mean it was—never mind. I see it now.' The rock got up and hobbled away slowly, like a tortoise.

'Infuriating, honestly,' said Matron. 'But I can never catch her in the act, so I just have to put up with it.'

'Granny does this?' said Poppy.

'Mmm.'

'The residents—they are...'

Matron stopped and turned to face Poppy. Her expression was set and stone-like. 'They are what?' she prompted.

'Well, they're different. Kelzu threatened to poison me this morning. Though apparently they were tossing up hanging me from the balustrade or feeding me to Trevor.'

'And yet,' Matron smiled—a small smile: just the corners of her lips. 'You're still here?'

Poppy frowned. 'But he was joking. Right? And I guess... I mean, I really do need this job.'

'Good,' said Matron. She turned and headed off between the hedge-rows. 'Very good. You might just make it through the first week after all.'

'Who is Trevor, anyway?'

Matron's brisk pace faltered a little. 'He's none of your concern. Now, the daily schedule at Sunnywood, although varied, rarely changes. Breakfast, followed by rest. Morning activities for those who participate. Lunch, often served throughout the house and in the garden, followed by rest. Afternoon activities for those who participate. Dinner is served in the dining room and never in personal quarters. Forced socialisation for at least one meal a day is mandatory. Nightly checks and medicine checklists, followed by lights out at ten —though lights out is not enforced, only encouraged. I'll have a schedule and roster made up for you by the end of the day, as well as an advance for your first week's wages. I think, given everything, you seem likely to still be here come the end of the week, don't you agree?'

Poppy nodded. Her head was spinning a little.

'I suggest you use this advance to buy something rather more suitable to wear. The uniform is old, and if I'm being perfectly honest, it doesn't suit you in the slightest. And your shoes are fit for a clown. Much too large.' Matron cleared her throat. 'Maybe an advance of two weeks might be in order. You could buy yourself some soap and pyjamas, then too. The smell of that farm clings to you, Poppy.'

Poppy felt like she'd both been slapped across the face and hugged.

'I did bathe,' she said, defensively. 'All night, really. And I'm not a farmer.'

But then, tripping and landing in cow-shit whilst trying to outrun some goblins was hardly any better. Not that there was anything wrong with being a farmer, of course. It's just that, well, she wasn't one.

'Of course. But another scrub won't hurt.' Matron's glare was unflinching. 'Sensible shoes and whatever you would like to wear should suffice. Just ensure it looks clean and presentable, and it'll be —oh no, no—no!' Matron stalked off in a sudden fury. 'I told you petunias and pansies, Clay. Does this look like petunias and pansies to you? And I said to keep them behind the garden edges, not... not... every kind of flower and certainly not everywhere.'

Poppy watched as Matron cut across the flower bed toward the gardener, who was busy trying to gather his things—and by the look of it, thought Poppy, starting to grin—and run off on Matron. When it became clear he wouldn't be able to make it away in time, though, he stood up and smiled at her, sheepishly.

'Oh, Clay,' groaned Matron. 'Down the hill, too? Really?'

Poppy joined them both and nearly gasped in amazement. The entire hillside was blossoming with wildflowers—all at once, like time had sped up. She felt something nudge her shoe and stepped aside as a foxglove sprang up around her legs.

It was brilliant.

It was beyond brilliant. It was—

'An eyesore. What an absolute bloody eyesore,' said Matron. She groaned again. 'It looks plain unruly. I mean, honestly, Clay. At least see to it that the borders around the beds are kept well-maintained. That way we can have the illusion of a garden, and not some frivolous wild meadow.' Matron sighed. 'Poppy, this is Sunnywood's groundsman: Clay. Clay, this is our new carer: Poppy. He'll help you prepare the cut flowers for the flower arranging before lunch. Meet me in the library when you're done.'

Matron stalked off, leaving Poppy and Clay to look at one another wordlessly.

TAKE A SEAT, POPPY, DEAR

'I like the wildflowers everywhere,' said Poppy. 'They look nice.'

Clay smiled. 'I only do it to annoy her. It makes me happy when she's mad.'

Poppy had noticed this. The residents seemed only to tolerate Matron out of necessity. Even the chef, Hiro, didn't seem so keen on her.

'Does everyone not like Matron, then?'

'I don't *not* like her,' said Clay, thoughtfully. 'But I don't much care for her, either.'

'What's wrong with her?'

'Nothing's wrong with her. She's a perfectly normal person.'

That's one hell of a glowing recommendation, thought Poppy. 'She is a bit... mercurial, I'll give you that.' She'd hoped that if she started the conversation, perhaps Clay would fill in the gaps.

But he just shrugged and knelt on the ground. He placed his fingers into the earth, and all around them, the flowers began to recede to their garden beds. Paths of lush green grass unfolded in every direction. Though the hill, Poppy noticed, remained covered in wildflowers.

She laughed. 'You're a green witch?'

Clay scowled, the magic of the moment gone in an instant. 'I am no such thing.' He turned his back on Poppy and began to collect his gardening tools in a rush.

'I'm sorry, I didn't mean to upset you,' said Poppy. She knelt to help Clay gather his things—old pruners, well-oiled and timber-handled, polished with use. There was a leather wrap loaded with glass vials, too. She passed them to Clay.

He took them, hesitantly, as if she might bite.

He was, thought Poppy, an incredibly strange man. And if he grew things with magic, then wasn't that the very definition of a green witch?

'What's wrong with being a green witch, anyway?'

'They're far too pompous. Think themselves better than everyone else just because they studied at some fancy botanical university in the capital. And I am *not* that.'

'Right,' Poppy nodded. 'It's just that, you can still be and do a thing even if you didn't study in a fancy school for it. It doesn't diminish your skill by comparison.'

Clay groaned. 'Oh gods, you're not one of those new-age hopelessly optimistic types, are you?'

Poppy changed the subject. 'So,' she said, 'where do we start?'

Clay passed her some scissors and a basket. 'Don't take anything a bee has claimed. And stay away from the snapdragons—they're particularly snappy this morning.' They watched as white and purple and pink flowers all leaned at once toward a fly and lashed out, grasping and fighting in competition for it. 'I'll be here if you need me.'

Poppy held the basket and scissors in her hand. She looked around at the gardens and then at Clay. 'And won't I be here too?'

Clay wrinkled his nose. 'Do you have to be? You could pick flowers from over there instead.'

Poppy rolled her eyes and began, carelessly, to pick flowers at random. 'You know, you're all quite rude here. It's like none of you were taught manners.'

A snapdragon lashed out and tried to take a bite out of her finger. She flinched away and then cut it from the ground viciously. Even the flowers, she thought, were hostile.

They fell into a kind of companionable silence, which—although tense at first—soon became menial and meditative enough that, as time passed, so did the mood.

'How long have you worked here, anyway?' asked Poppy.

Clay shrugged. 'Since I was a kid. My grandfather was the grounds caretaker. He taught me the ways of gardening—Sunnywood gardening.'

'And Sunnywood gardening is different to normal gardening, I take it?'

'Oh yes,' said Clay. 'We don't do vegetables, for one.'

'Vegetables are bad?'

'Incredibly so.'

'Right,' said Poppy. She went back to her flower-cutting. The morning—up until that point—had felt so bizarrely hectic and stressful that it was odd to feel so at peace, and yet so abruptly, violently bored.

Occasionally, one of them would be bitten by a snapdragon, or a particular flower would catch their eye, but for the most part, Clay, it seemed, preferred to work in silence. They watched as Bernard, the book-wyrm, bounced around the garden like an overexcited dog. He chased after butterflies, hurling himself into the air after them and immediately falling over in a somersaulting crash. The early morning sun reflected off his scales in a cascade of rainbows.

Poppy laughed as he lay there on his back, rolling around and snapping at anything that moved—flowers, bees, butterflies.

'He really hates them,' said Clay. 'Butterflies, I mean. I think it's because they can fly and he can't.'

Poppy didn't think it was anything like that. It seemed to her that

Bernard was just having fun—a book-wyrm doing book-wyrm things. But seeing as she knew nothing about Bernard—or indeed, about book-wyrms, really—she kept the opinion to herself.

She was still watching Bernard when something else twitched in the corner of her eye, a flicker of long ears behind a clump of yarrow. For a heartbeat, she thought it was a normal rabbit, until it hopped into a patch of sun and she caught the pale glint of exposed ribcage beneath its fur. One of its back legs dragged behind, stiff and badly reattached. It paused, staring at her with a milky, unfocused eye.

Before she could speak, Bernard spotted it and launched himself forward with a triumphant screech. The rabbit bolted—surprisingly fast for something half-stitched together—and disappeared into the wildflower hill.

Poppy blinked. 'Did you see that?'

'See what?' asked Clay, not even glancing up from the soil.

'...Nothing,' she said, because she no longer trusted her own eyes. She snipped another stem, letting the quiet settle again. But the uneasy feeling didn't go away.

'Can I ask you something, Clay?' The question had been needling her for a while. The residents, she was beginning to realise, were no normal, run-of-the-mill people. They were different.

'I'd rather you didn't,' said Clay. He turned the earth over with his bare hands. 'But I think you're going to anyway.'

She was. 'Kelzu threatened to murder me this morning. I told Matron about it. She didn't seem bothered by it. Which makes me think it was a joke. But...'

'But?'

'But it didn't feel like a joke.'

'I'd lock your bedroom door if I were you.'

Poppy threw a flower at him. 'See, I can't tell if you're joking now.'

'I'm not. Lock your door. Properly.'

'What kind of place is this, Clay? Like, actually, really?'

'It's Sunnywood House.'

'What does that mean?'

'You stay here long enough, you'll learn for yourself.'

Poppy rolled her eyes.

'Put a chair under your door handle too. Just in case.'

Once she'd filled two full baskets with cut flowers, she left Clay to his gardening and headed back to the manor.

She found the residents making their way to the library. They all held vases and jars; some still held half-dead, wilted flowers, others were empty and cleaned. The library had been set up with two long tables, with containers full of pruners, twine, and jugs of fresh water. Matron was busy helping Kelzu up into a chair, and Hiro was setting out a tray of tea-cakes and biscuits. Huk followed him with the wide eyes of an overeager and particularly hungry dog.

Poppy set the baskets of cut flowers down: one on each table.

They all looked at her in varying degrees of curiosity... and, in Granny and Kelzu's case, she couldn't help but notice: open hostility.

Matron looked over the flowers.

She scrunched up her nose a little at them.

'The snapdragons are still bitey,' said Poppy, defensively.

She didn't know why, but she wanted to impress Matron.

'I have some paperwork to get through,' said Matron. 'I'll be in my office if you need me.' And with that, she turned and left the library, leaving Poppy alone with the residents.

It took her all of about five seconds to realise this was bad. Quite terrifyingly bad.

Granny patted the empty seat beside her. 'Take a seat, Poppy, dear.' She said this with the air of someone about to begin an interrogation.

'Right,' said Hiro. 'I'd best be off too. Begin prepping dinner. Poppy, make sure Huk eats no more than four cream rocks. Yes, four is more than fair, Huk. Any more and you'll have a heart attack.'

Poppy looked at Hiro, eyes wide and suddenly pleading. 'You can't go too.'

But Hiro hadn't heard her—or perhaps he'd pretended not to.

Huk cracked his knuckles.

Kelzu sniggered.

'So,' said Granny Grack. 'Down to business, then.'

GAME ON

'Who are you and what are your intentions here?' said Granny.

'My intentions?'

'There's a reason we can't keep staff,' said Kelzu. 'It's because we root out the weak.'

'Matron might hold the interviews, but it's our money she's paying you with. So we figure it's up to us to conduct the real tests. See if you have what it takes.' Granny leaned over the table and grabbed a pair of scissors.

Poppy's heart was in her throat, but she straightened her spine anyway. She wasn't going to crack—not in front of them. 'What it takes?'

'Do you always repeat everything that's said to you?'

'What?'

'You do then? She does. Look at her. I think she might be daft.'

'She's a nosy parker, is what she is,' said Kelzu, quietly. He was busy knotting together some lavender. 'K.S. caught her wandering my room this morning. Touching things and snooping around.'

'I wasn't snooping at all,' said Poppy. 'I was helping you put your slippers on.'

Kelzu's face flushed immediately. 'Don't be ridiculous. I put on my own slippers, thank you very much.'

'Are you a thief, kid?' said Huk, through a mouthful of cream. 'I don't like thieves. Slippery little buggers, they are.'

'I am not a thief,' said Poppy, but her voice wavered and sounded doubtful.

She hated that. Hated how small it came out. Like maybe they were right about her.

'You look like a thief.'

'What's that supposed to mean? And I don't reckon thieves look like anything—not if they're any good.'

'She has a point,' said Granny. She'd begun to arrange flowers in her vase in a slapdash kind of way. 'Who do you work for, then?'

'I work for you, apparently,' said Poppy. 'Seeing as you're paying my wages.'

'No, really,' said Kelzu. 'Who are you spying for? Are you working for Floonby?'

'That's a good point, I hadn't thought about that,' said Granny.

'What the fuck is a Floonby?' said Poppy.

Huk laughed. He was on his sixth cream rock.

She got up and took the plate from him. He stopped laughing.

'I'm not working for anyone but you lot,' said Poppy. 'I'm not a thief. I'm not a spy. Why you think anyone would want to spy on you at all is beyond me. I'm Poppy. Just Poppy. I'm from Upper Susshingham. I'm an adventurer, currently in between jobs... and adventuring parties... and I'm a little broke.' She heard herself losing steam, but couldn't quite stop it. And there it was, she thought, all her mediocrity laid bare. 'So that's why I'm here. All right?'

They were all silent then.

You could hear a pin drop.

That is, until they started to laugh.

A part of her shrank, whilst the rest got angry.

Poppy wasn't sure if she wanted to strangle them or run. But one thing was certain: she had never been so embarrassed and insulted in her life.

'So you're an adventurer, then?' said Huk.

'*You?*' said Granny. 'Are you sure? Quite sure?'

'What was your last job, then?' said Kelzu.

'Dealing with pixies in a bakery?' asked Huk.

Granny laughed. 'Fire-mice in the palace garden?'

'No,' said Poppy, viciously. She stood up from behind the table. 'It was a goblin infestation in the woods, thank you.'

They laughed again—louder this time—and she clenched her fists to keep from shaking. She could still hear the goblins scream, the squelch of her boots in the mud. It hadn't been funny then.

Poppy wanted to find a very large and very dark hole to crawl into.

'So you're not very good, then?' said Huk. He'd started on the biscuits now that Poppy had taken the cream rocks.

'Well, I'm new at it,' said Poppy, defensively. 'You're not supposed to be good at something new.'

Kelzu shrugged. 'I don't know—'

Granny kicked Kelzu off his chair. Poppy saw her do it under the table.

Matron returned, holding a clipboard and a pile of papers. The residents, upon seeing her, all changed. Shifting in inconspicuous ways that were, to Poppy, as noticeable as if someone had flicked a switch. They hunched over, where before they had sat up straight. Kelzu crawled back into his seat and didn't say a word. Flowers were arranged with a deep, concentrated kind of focus. And when Granny spoke next, it wasn't with a threatening cackle but rather with a kindly—if not suspiciously stereotypical—old lady voice.

'Pass me a ribbon, love.'

Poppy passed her one, thinking all the while that she'd been right. These residents were anything but normal. Something was, indeed, going on here. And above all else, she was beginning to understand why no one had kept the job as carer at Sunnywood House for very long.

But the thing about Poppy was this: she was stubborn.

She didn't know how or when to give up.

And deep down, despite the laughter, the insults, the condescension—she still believed there was something within herself worth seeing. Worth trusting. She just had to prove it.

Goblins in the woods.

Werewolves in the mists.

Will-o'-the-wisps in the dead of night.

And, of course, as much as she hated to admit it: pixies in a bakery.

All of them had one thing in common: they were, to Poppy, something she wouldn't allow to beat her.

She looked at Granny and smiled.

Granny did not smile back. She just frowned; an arching of the eyebrow, a challenge behind the eyes.

Well, thought Poppy, you're on, old woman.

'Your flower arrangement,' she whispered, so that Matron wouldn't hear, 'looks like absolute dog-shit.'

Granny's eyebrow went higher. But she didn't answer. That, Poppy decided, was a win.

She needed this job. Needed the money and the food and the bed, and she'd be damned if she was going to let a bunch of rude old bastards get in the way of that.

If they wanted a game, then game on it was.

STRIKE ONE

The next day, Granny Grack was looking for Huk and Kelzu.

They hadn't been at breakfast, like she'd told them to be, and they weren't in Lootland or Huk's room either. It was, she thought, utterly typical—and yet, after all these years, it never failed to make her blood boil. It didn't help that she'd been up all night, planning and stress-knitting.

Granny was, to be quite frank, in one hell of a temper.

Why was it always up to her to sort these things out?

She knocked on the door of Matron's office. Well, thumped on it was probably more accurate. Tried the doorknob. Locked, of course. Probably jammed a chair under it, just like the other silly girl. Never mind. Granny had her slime and ways of getting into things that would make a bank robber blush.

'We need to talk,' she shouted through the keyhole. 'Now.'

There was, of course, no answer.

Granny sighed, knelt on one knee (a skill she was immensely proud of; Huk's own knees had disowned him years ago), and found her handkerchief. She unfolded it, and a much smaller, pocket-sized slime blinked up at her.

'Open the bloody thing,' she told it. 'Go on.'

The slime slinked off the cloth and under the door. Granny closed her eyes so she could see through its vision, just as it reached the wall and began its slimy ascent toward the doorknob.

Matron cleared her throat behind her.

Granny opened her eyes. The slime, suddenly blind, flopped off the doorknob and hit the floor with a wet slap.

'Miss Grack,' said Matron.

'Matron,' said Granny, smoothing her skirt. 'I was looking for you.'

'Yes. I can see that.'

'I have questions.'

'I'd expect nothing less,' said Matron. She sounded tired, even though it was only morning.

'You look haggard,' Granny said. 'Up all night?'

'Yes. As were you, I daresay.'

'Impossible to sleep when a spell you've been cooking for five years is ready for the final ingredient you don't have,' Granny muttered. 'A spell that might finally let me walk a mile without needing to bloody sit down after. And then to top it all off, our home has been invaded by strangers.'

'A stranger,' corrected Matron.

'No,' said Granny. 'I said strangers, and I meant it.' She narrowed her eyes in a look that had once withered armies. Infuriatingly, Matron looked merely amused.

'What do you want?'

'A freshly caught fallen star, still alive. And for that girl to be gone.'

'I'll add it to the list,' Matron said dryly, stepping past Granny to unlock her door.

'You won't.'

'No, of course I won't. Do you know how much a fallen star costs? Freshly caught and still alive?'

'How much are you paying Poppy?' countered Granny.

'She could work here until she's as old as you are and still not come remotely close to the going rate.'

'Fine. No star. I'll get it another way.'

Matron hesitated. 'Wait. You're giving up just like that?'

'No. I can just see you're going to be absolutely no help.'

'What's the spell for, exactly?' Matron folded her arms. 'Because so help me, if you're messing with that staircase again—'

'I'd be very careful about your next words,' said Granny coldly. 'We have a replacement now, remember. You're suddenly not so... indispensable.'

'Is that a threat?'

Granny shrugged. 'If you feel threatened, that's not my business. You need to ask yourself why that is.'

Matron shook her head and slammed the door in her face.

Granny did not take this well. She was not the kind of woman one slammed doors on.

Especially not when her knees had spent the past week creaking like haunted floorboards. She needed that spell. She needed that star. And Matron could stuff her 'budget' where the sun didn't shine.

'That,' she yelled at the door, 'was strike one!'

'Oh, fuck off,' came Matron's voice from the other side.

Granny chuckled. It had been far too long since someone had told her that. She rather missed it. It was exhilarating. It made you feel alive.

'Before I do, you know, fuck off—can I ask: have you seen Huk and Kelzu?'

'They're in the basement.'

'Thank you, love.'

Granny found them: they were, indeed, in the basement. Though it no longer looked like a basement. All the junk it usually contained had been dumped atop the stairs near the front door, and the room itself was spotless.

Kelzu was walking the perimeter with a twitching measuring tape that refused to behave. Huk was bashing the controls of a microphone while muttering curses at a metal panel.

'Stupid, stupid hunk of shit.'

K.S. was the only one who acknowledged her. 'Hello, Granny.'

'Morning. I trust you reminded them of our breakfast strategy meeting?'

'I did. Unfortunately, its priority was overruled. The studio must be completed for this week's episode.' He leaned down, modulator crackling at full volume: 'I did encourage them to inform you, but, well... you know how they can be.'

'You're a dear,' said Granny, patting his arm. 'Am I to overthrow our tyrannical carer alone, then?'

Huk ignored her. He was conveniently deaf when it suited him.

'She's hardly tyrannical,' said Kelzu, fiddling with his tape. 'Now that I know she's a shit adventurer, I actually feel kind of sorry for her.'

'I meant Matron,' snapped Granny.

Huk grunted. 'You're not starting on Matron again, are you?'

'Yes. I am. Because I tell you what, Huklin—something is up. I wouldn't trust her as far as I could kick her.'

Both Huk and Kelzu groaned.

'What?' snapped Granny.

'If it's not Poppy, it's Matron,' said Kelzu.

'If it's not Hiro, it's Clay,' added Huk.

'If it's not Trevor, it's Bernard,' said Kelzu, hands on hips.

Granny muttered that trusting the wrong people was how you ended up dead; especially once your joints started aching and your magic fizzled like a spent firework.

She wanted to kick them both through the nearest wall.

'It's okay to say you miss it, you know,' said Kelzu.

'I most certainly do not know what you're talking about.'

'The enemies,' said K.S. 'You miss having them.'

'You need therapy,' said Huk. 'Anger management, maybe?' Then he saw the look on Granny's face and immediately busied himself with the microphone leads.

'That's a good idea,' said Kelzu brightly. 'Therapy. We could do a whole episode about how adventuring left its mark on us. Physically. Emotionally. K.S., jot that down!'

If it hadn't proved them right, Granny might've kicked the smug little bastard into next week.

She stormed back upstairs, boiling with rage, and forgot to double-tap the balustrade.

The tricksy staircase spell activated. Her feet gave way, and she was unceremoniously launched from the bottom step where she landed arse-first on the hardwood floor.

She groaned.

Something had to change around here.

And she'd be damned if it was going to be her. Not when she was this close to getting it all back.

PEAS AND DRAGONS

'They think I'm some kind of spy,' said Poppy. She was shelling fresh peas into a bowl, as instructed by Hiro, who was currently attempting to bathe Bernard in the kitchen sink. 'Honestly. They do. Reckon I'm working for someone and reporting back. Which— seriously, Hiro—if I had someone else paying me, do you think I'd still be here putting up with them? I'd have to be mad.'

She laughed as she said it, but the joke didn't quite land in her own chest. She was here because she had nowhere else to be, and wasn't that the real madness?

Hiro laughed. It was a glorious sound: light and bubbling.

'They tried to lock me out of the kitchen when I first started.'

'They didn't?' Poppy reached for another pod. She was far more invested in talking than shelling; at this rate, it was going to take her a full week to get through the lot. 'What'd you do?'

'Threatened to stab them, of course.' Hiro shrugged and pushed up his soap-sodden sleeves. Bernard whined.

'Oh, shh. It's just warm water, you big coward.'

'Of course you did,' said Poppy. 'No, but really. There's this weird slime in the pipes, and I swear I woke up last night and it was watching me. I've about had enough.'

'Well, don't let them hear you say that,' said Hiro. 'It sounds too much like giving up, they'll think they're getting close to cracking you.'

'They bloody are,' said Poppy. She'd been at Sunnywood House for nearly a week now, and things hadn't improved. On the contrary, they'd gotten steadily worse. Her arm was bandaged, she had a black eye, and the staircase now had two tricksy steps. The library, meanwhile, had books that punched you. How she was supposed to know that without warning was beyond her. But still, Matron had asked—with a dismissive wave of her hand—'Well, what did you expect? To be hugged?'

So, Poppy had taken to hiding out in Hiro's kitchen whenever she could. As long as she made herself useful, he let her stay and vent about the residents; occasionally, he even joined in. This, to Poppy, was glorious. They'd become almost-sort-of friends, and Poppy rather treasured it.

He hadn't laughed in her face or asked what she was doing here or called her daft—and that counted for more than she wanted to admit.

'But no,' said Hiro. 'I didn't do anything. Didn't have to. Not once they'd tried my cooking.'

Poppy rolled her eyes and threw pea after pea into the bowl. 'I can't cook, though.'

'Well, good. I should bloody hope not. That's my job.' Hiro squeezed the soapy water from Bernard's downy fur, working towards his neck where the scales began. Bernard looked like a puppy, a kitten, and a duckling all rolled into one—if those things had been bred for mild chaos and smelled faintly of singed parchment. His down-like fur faded into pale scales around his snout and feet. Poppy would've said he looked a bit like a chicken, but she didn't want Hiro to hit her.

'Pass me that towel, won't you?'

'So what am I supposed to do?' said Poppy.

'Make yourself indispensable,' Hiro said with a shrug. 'Make getting rid of you impossible. I dunno.'

The infuriating thing, though, was that no one, including Hiro, would tell her who the residents actually were. Sure, she knew their names. That wasn't the issue. The issue was... well, something else. Truth be told, Poppy wasn't even sure what she meant by that. But she knew something was off. Bone-deep certainty. She'd pressed Hiro on it a few times, but he was never direct with his answers. More often than not, he just closed up.

Who was Granny before she, you know, got old and retired? That earned her a shrug and a question about whether the chocolate cake was too dense. (It wasn't. It was fucking delicious.)

And why did Huk have an entire walk-in wardrobe full of swords and armour?

Because he likes them, how the hell am I supposed to know?

And that was barely scratching the surface. Kelzu's room was bigger than was physically possible and contained an entire store; an actual, full-blown shop, bursting with all kinds of nonsense. How? And more importantly: Why?

Eventually, Poppy had stopped asking Hiro. But she couldn't stop thinking about it. It was an itch she couldn't scratch. There was something in her, something clawing to make sense of the people around her; as if by understanding them, it might help her understand her place here, too.

And of course, she knew about magic. She wasn't daft, and these old bastards hadn't invented it. But there was just so much more of it here. And no one would explain why. On top of that, it seemed to her that, although they were all technically elderly, none of them really needed to be in a home.

Didn't they have families to go back to? Grandchildren to sneak sweets to and spoil with too many gifts?

It defied everything Poppy thought she knew about old people.

The only thing about the residents that made any kind of sense… was how much sense they didn't make.

Hiro sighed. 'The towel, Poppy. This century, if you don't mind.'

Poppy threw it at him. 'Hiro, how long have you worked here?'

'Why?' Both Hiro and Bernard stopped and looked at her. The dragon was shivering, eyes the size of tea saucers.

'Just wondering,' she said, turning her attention back to the peas. Nonchalance. That was the tactic. Pretend not to care, and maybe he'd open up.

'Four years, I think,' said Hiro, resuming his drying. 'And no, Poppy. I won't be tricked into answering anything. I've told you once, and I won't tell you again: whatever questions you've got, the answers aren't mine to give. You'll have to take it up with the residents. Or Matron.'

Poppy groaned.

'You can groan all you like. I'm not getting involved in anyone's business but my own.'

'What questions?' said Matron.

She was standing behind them, in the kitchen, arms full of papers and folders.

Poppy still wasn't sure whether she ought to be afraid of Matron or not, so she kept her mouth shut. Matron had this uncanny ability to diminish you. Not in a rude or condescending way—no, it was subtler than that. Just this way of making you feel about three inches tall. And yet, somehow, this was the same woman who'd practically begged Poppy to take the job a week ago.

'I was just curious,' Poppy muttered. 'About the residents.'

'Curious about what?'

'I don't know. Their life before Sunnywood, I guess.'

'Well, ask them. I'm sure they'd love to tell you all about it.'

Poppy nearly fell off the kitchen bench. The idea of asking any of the residents anything—anything beyond tea, coffee, or juice—felt suicidal.

'I'd prefer it if you didn't sit on the kitchen benches, Poppy,' said Matron. 'It's unhygienic. Your farmer smell will leach into the timber.'

Poppy slid off the bench. Washing a book-wyrm in the sink didn't seem terribly hygienic either, but she bit her tongue and ignored the farmer comment altogether.

Matron handed her a small folder.

'What's this?'

'Your contract, timetable, and an official list of duties in a handy-dandy manual. There's a guide to Sunnywood inside: activities, amenities, helpful notes. I'd have given it all to you earlier, but I wanted to make sure you were right for the job. And I think you are, Poppy, don't you?'

Poppy made a kind of strangled, panicked noise.

Matron must have considered it a yes. 'So, as promised, here's the advance on your pay.'

She offered Poppy a surprisingly heavy coin purse.

Poppy reached for it—but Matron pulled it back.

'The contract first, if you don't mind.'

Poppy looked down at it. It wasn't in any language she recognised. Probably Trollish. Or Osmunkish. One of those. They did love their contracts. She signed it without hesitation. She needed the money, and that was that.

'Brilliant. Now see to it that you're looking more presentable from now on, please. Shoes that fit. A shirt that doesn't give you hives. A sweater without holes. Some good-quality heavy-duty soap–'

'–You've already told me all this,' Poppy cut in.

'Well, yes. But it bears repeating, I think. And some perfume wouldn't go astray either. And,'—she tapped the file—'please be back by six for dinner.'

'Back by six? But I'm not going anywhere.'

Poppy opened the folder. Dozens of pages. Her timetable was a thick parchment card, no bigger than her palm, with writing that shimmered and moved.

At the moment, it read:

1:35 pm: Dining room clean-up (post-lunch)
Then the ink ballooned and shifted:
2 pm–6 pm: Extended break & store collection rounds

'Store collection rounds?' she asked.

But Matron was already gone; her shoes clicking out into the lobby and up the stairs.

Poppy flipped to a page labelled 'Shop Day'. It detailed her responsibilities: escort any residents who wanted to go into town, assist them however necessary, collect supplies for Sunnywood: groceries, laundry goods, oddities. And then she had to buy her own things and still be back for dinner.

Poppy chewed her lip. The dishes were still a mess. The sink still had a dragon in it.

Alfred ducked his head through the wall behind her. His ghostly beard was neatly plaited, his hair combed.

'I'll be coming. I have a shopping list. And I want to visit the new Troll bank.'

Bernard launched out of the sink.

'Don't you dare!' Hiro shouted—but it was too late.

The book-wyrm exploded out in a frenzy of water and soap, did a manic lap of the kitchen, then launched himself at Poppy. He knocked her flat, smothered her with dripping dragon fur, and proceeded to lick her face with his very hot tongue.

Poppy shoved him off and looked up at Hiro. 'I cannot be expected to take them into town by myself, can I? They'll murder me —I'll never return.'

Hiro rolled his eyes. 'You'll be fine.'

'No, seriously,' said Poppy. 'They'll drown me in a puddle or something. Just for a laugh. Vicious bastards. The lot of them.'

She grinned when she said it, as if it were a joke, and felt the familiar drop in her stomach—the fear that followed her everywhere, the old certainty that sooner or later she would only make things worse.

Hiro considered this far too long.

He sighed. 'I'll get the wagon. You finish drying Bernard.'

SHERBET LEMONS
AND GREATSWORDS

Two o'clock came, and Poppy waited by the front door for anyone who wished to join her. She hoped—prayed, even—that they were all too busy napping or knitting or floating through walls or doing whatever it was they did when no one was looking.

But then Granny Grack descended the stairs with a look of such steely determination that Poppy instinctively braced for impact.

'You're taking us on the rounds, then?' said Granny, elbow-deep in her handbag, rummaging with the intensity of someone trying to catch a rat. 'And will *that* devil be joining us?'

Poppy tried not to sigh. This did not bode well for the afternoon.

'Sorry,' she said, 'but who's the devil in question?'

'You know damn well who.'

'I really don't,' said Poppy, looking about for someone—anyone. She'd have settled for Alfred. She'd been at Sunnywood for a week now, and this was perhaps the most terrifying Granny had ever been —and that was *really* saying something.

'Her, of course. *Matron*,' spat Granny.

'Oh.' Poppy laughed, awkwardly. Relief flickered through her. At least the loathing wasn't directed at her anymore. That alone felt like dodging a fireball.

'No, she's got me doing the excursion today, I'm afraid.'

'She's been ordering you about, then? Typical.'

Poppy shifted. 'Well... she is my boss, so... yes? Is everything all right, Granny? It's just that—'

'—What?' snapped Granny. 'It's just that what?'

Gods. It was like being barked at by a very small, very dangerous terrier. 'Nothing,' muttered Poppy.

They stood there in the foyer awkwardly. Granny continued rummaging in her handbag, muttering angrily to herself. Poppy noticed a rather large pile of junk on the front step, spilling into the garden. She told herself: Don't ask. Don't ask. Don't—

'What are you looking for, anyway?' she asked.

Granny froze. Sighed. 'None of your business.' Then, softer: 'My sherbet lemons. I can't travel without them.'

Poppy checked her pocket. Bernard was partial to hard-boiled sweets, so Hiro had given her a handful to keep the wyrm occupied. She held them out. 'They're not sherbet lemons, but—

Granny snatched them, rolled her eyes, and popped one into her mouth.

'Thank you,' said Granny quietly, just as Poppy blurted: 'Why's there shit everywhere, do you know?'

Granny gestured vaguely at the clutter outside. 'The boys have turned the basement into a recording studio.'

'Are they starting a band?' Poppy asked, half-sarcastically. She knew it was for the radio show.

'Gods.' Granny snorted. 'Imagine them two singing.'

'No, thanks. What's the radio show about, anyway?'

Granny looked at her. Really looked—like she was trying to see through her skin and into the skull.

Poppy felt her spine go cold.

'You really don't have a clue, do you?'

'Generally? No.'

'It hasn't clicked?'

'Well, maybe if everyone stopped dancing around it,' snapped Poppy, 'I'd be in with a chance.'

'So you have an idea, then?'

That this isn't a retirement home but some kind of magical asylum, Poppy thought. But she bit her tongue. 'I know this place, and you lot aren't exactly... run of the mill. Just, no one will tell me how, exactly.'

Granny smiled, a gleam in her eye. 'Run of the mill. How diplomatic.'

But you're not going to tell me, Poppy thought bitterly, because keeping me in the dark is more fun; like a cat playing with its dinner.

Kelzu came thumping down the stairs, his automaton trailing behind him. He looked utterly ridiculous in a velvet robe of imperial purple, stitched with gold. It trailed behind him like royalty on laundry day.

'I have a shopping list a mile long,' he said. 'I hope Hiro is hitching the trailer?'

'The trailer?' asked Poppy. 'What do you need a trailer for?'

'Radio gear,' Kelzu snapped, his upper lip twitching. 'I've special-ordered enough equipment to fit out a proper studio. It will be over my dead body, Poppy—' he spat her name like it had a bitter aftertaste '—that you interrupt this weekend's episode.'

'You've packed supplies for the journey, I hope?' said Huk, appearing from around the corner, nonchalantly eating a biscuit. He was, Poppy noticed, carrying a sheathed greatsword.

'Supplies?' she echoed. Her head had begun to spin; its default setting when faced with multiple residents at once.

'Food,' said Granny. She produced a cake tin from her bag and thrust it at Huk. 'Honestly, girl. You've got to be more prepared.'

'We're only heading into the village,' said Poppy. 'It's an hour's walk. Half that in a wagon.'

'Why do you look like a drowned rat, anyway?' said Granny.

'Bernard was having a bath,' said Poppy flatly. She scanned the driveway, desperate for Hiro and his wagon. One-on-one, she could hold her own with these people. But all of them at once? It felt less like escorting residents and more like leading a small, well-armed cult on a field trip.

'And why do you have a sword?'

'Never leave the house without one,' Huk said, around a mouthful of biscuit. 'You won't catch me unprepared.'

Poppy considered taking up smoking. Or drinking. Or both.

At last, Hiro pulled the wagon around, complete with trailer. It was one of those modern monstrosities: no horse, just steam and gears and pistons chugging along with indecent enthusiasm. Just looking at it made Poppy slightly nauseous.

They all clambered aboard. Bernard leapt into the front seat and sat between Poppy and Hiro, tongue lolling contentedly. Granny climbed in behind with her handbag, and Alfred floated beside her, clutching a list. K.S. settled himself into the trailer like a dignitary in exile.

If it hadn't been so comical, Poppy might have cried. It would be a miracle if they weren't run out of the village with pitchforks.

'Don't worry,' said Hiro, as if reading her mind. 'Alfred can't go any further than the property's boundary.'

'Watch it,' said Huk, leaning forward. 'He always tries to come. And it happens every time.'

'He just wants to be part of the group,' said Granny, sympathetically.

The pistons hissed. The engine trembled. The wagon jolted forward—and with a *shlurp* of displaced air, Alfred was abruptly yanked out of the wagon, hurled backwards through the sky, and vanished in the direction of Sunnywood.

Poppy's mouth fell open.

She stared after the ghost, her chest tightening with something she didn't particularly want to name. Sympathy, maybe.

She knew what it felt like to be the outsider.

PLAN OF ATTACK

The clockwork wagon would take some getting used to, but Poppy found that if she didn't think about it—and just stared out at the horizon—it wasn't too bad. It could have been worse. At Sunnywood, she was realising, it could always be worse.

The afternoon sun was warm and golden. The breeze was fresh but not cold. A perfect day, really. She wondered how the residents might ruin it.

'Right,' said Hiro. He pulled the wagon to a stop outside a grocery store. The whole town was lined with bunting and flower pots hanging beneath the lamp-posts. Even just parking the wagon here felt like they were breaking some kind of law.

'I'm off to have words with the grocer. I'll meet you lot back here by 5:30, and not a minute later. I will leave you all behind, and don't think for a second that I won't.'

Granny chuckled. She'd lost her foul mood somewhere along the way. 'You wouldn't.'

'I bloody would,' said Hiro. 'I'm a chef, not a carer. You think I care about you lot?'

They all smiled. Even K.S., lounging in his trailer, seemed to smile. Maybe that was the trick with them, she thought. Tell them how you really feel, and only then will they accept you.

Poppy climbed carefully out of the wagon, taking care not to put pressure on her bandaged arm. It was still painfully sore from when she'd landed on it funny coming down the stairs. Bernard leapt down beside her and immediately rolled onto his back in the dust.

'Don't let him do that,' Hiro groaned. 'We just gave the wee bastard a bath. Come on, up! STOP IT!'

Kelzu stood up on the seat and stretched his back. Hiro lifted him down without being asked, and with the same casual familiarity one might use with a particularly fussy toddler. He turned to Huk. 'You alright, big man? Or are your knees playing up?'

'I'll be fine, thank you,' said Huk, jumping out of the wagon with not even a groan.

Poppy watched them scatter off into town and marvelled at how easy it was to forget they were, well... generally quite old. The sheer rage they inspired usually counteracted that.

Hiro caught her eye and mouthed: Good luck.

But Poppy didn't think she needed luck. With Hiro off doing his own shopping, it left only a few items on Matron's list and a bit on her own. If she were being honest, Poppy found herself almost thankful for the break.

'So, where to first?' said Granny, sliding her arm firmly through Poppy's.

And just like that, her optimism crashed and burned.

'I do need some new handkerchiefs,' Granny continued cheerfully, 'and I thought we might stop by the tavern for a drink or three. And if there's time left over, we could treat ourselves to a look in the Apothecary. They always have such nice things in there.'

Poppy looked down at Granny's arm, hooked through her own like some kind of venomous snake in a floral cardigan.

'So what shall it be?' said Granny.

'Sorry—what?'

'Our plan of attack. The key to any successful adventure, my dear, is a plan of attack. So, where to first?'

Poppy died a little inside. She unfolded the parchment Matron had given her.

'Well, I have to pick up two arcane capacitors for the heaters,' she read aloud, 'then some new clothes for me, shoes and the like... and I wanted to...'

'Yes?'

'...Laundry supplies,' finished Poppy.

'You want laundry supplies?'

'Well. No.' Poppy didn't need laundry supplies. Nor did Matron. She'd only panicked, because what she'd really wanted to say was *I want to look at the Adventurers' Job Board again*. It was staring at her right now, through the window of the tavern across the street. But she couldn't very well do that if Granny was hanging off her arm.

Granny followed her gaze and then, without warning, punched her in the arm. Surprisingly hard.

'You bloody animal. Well, come on then.'

And just like that, she began dragging Poppy toward the tavern.

Matron had warned her ahead of time: Granny wasn't allowed near alcohol. Especially not a building dedicated to the stuff.

'No, no, no,' said Poppy, trying to resist. But Granny was unstoppable. Like a bull. Or like K.S., when Kelzu told him to guard something.

'No—we can't. We've only got a few hours to get all this done—'

'All the more reason to get stuck in early,' said Granny.

Poppy managed to wriggle out of the tavern ambush by suggesting, with as much persuasive charm as she could muster, that they knock out a few errands first. Surprisingly, Granny agreed, though with the patronising tone of someone letting a toddler choose the bedtime story before inevitably ignoring it.

They set off through town, and for a few precious minutes, Poppy was convinced she was in control.

Their first stop was the arcane supply shop—a dim, copper-scented space that smelled like burnt ozone and disappointment. Behind the counter stood a goblin who looked as if he were held together by eyebrow hair and pure resentment.

'Two capacitors,' Granny said, rapping her knuckles on the wood. 'And none of that refurbished shite.'

Poppy handed over the coin Matron had given her. The goblin sniffed at it suspiciously, then—reluctantly—passed her a cloth bag. Inside were two dull brass cylinders, humming faintly with restrained power.

'Lovely,' said Granny, with a smile sharp enough to cut stone.

Next: clothes. Specifically: shoes.

The boutique was aggressively cheerful; too much lavender and gingham. A sales assistant greeted them like she'd been personally threatened into being enthusiastic.

'She needs boots,' said Granny. 'Leather ones. Not bloody canvas.'

'I hate these,' Poppy muttered, sitting awkwardly as Granny shoved a boot violently onto her foot.

'Shut up,' Granny snapped. 'They're good, sturdy travelling boots.'

'They look ridiculous.'

Granny stood back and inspected her. The boots had absurdly bright red laces.

'They're perfect,' Granny said. 'We'll take them.'

Poppy didn't argue. She just felt vaguely itchy all over, like someone was trying to stuff her into a shape she didn't quite belong to.

They emerged back onto the street, arms full of bags, dignity in tatters—just as a sharp scream echoed faintly up from a nearby grate.

Poppy stopped. 'Did you hear that?'

Granny didn't pause. 'No.'

Poppy lingered. The grate was small and rusted, easy to overlook

—but something about it made the hair on her arms prickle. The scream had sounded too distant to be local. Too deep to be human.

And yet... already she found herself doubting she'd heard anything at all. Probably just gurgling pipes. Or rats. Big old screaming rats.

They passed the Troll Bank on the corner—the one Alfred had been so excited about. It looked harmless enough: clean marble steps, polished glass, neat gold-and-green signage. The sort of place you wouldn't look at twice.

Granny paused outside the Apothecary only to find the door boarded shut and the windows blocked with newspaper. Her whole face puckered. 'Bugger me sideways. Of all the bloody weeks—' She pressed her nose to the newspaper. 'Typical. You work five years toward something and the moment you need the one bloody thing, the bastard's shuttered up like it's plague season.'

'Is this for your brewing, then?' asked Poppy.

Granny turned to look at her. 'What do you know about my brewing?'

'Only that Matron told me to stay away from it if I valued my eyebrows and my life. What are you making, exactly?'

'What I'm making,' said Granny, severely. 'Is none of your bloody business.'

Several nearby shops were closed. One was completely boarded up. Another had FINAL SALE – NO RETURNS scrawled across the window in frantic chalk.

The street, Poppy thought, felt a little... off.

They continued on to their final stop: the sweet shop.

It smelled like sugar and nostalgia, and for a blessed moment, it was peaceful. Poppy thought maybe—just maybe—Granny would get her sherbet lemons and the day would end without incident.

Then the man in front of them turned, and Poppy realised immediately that she wouldn't be so lucky. The man looked far too much like a weasel for her liking. Beady eyes. Pointed nose. The sort of smile that suggested he charged for his unsolicited opinions.

'I'm afraid I've just bought the lot,' he said, tapping the counter with one long fingernail. 'Every last one.'

'What are you talking about?' Granny frowned and looked at Poppy. 'What's he talking about?'

'The sweets,' he said slowly. 'They're all mine. I'm terribly sorry.'

Granny's mouth dropped open. 'You bastard.'

The shopkeeper looked dumbfounded, holding a bulging bag of coins. 'Everything?' he asked. 'Even the liquorice bombs no one likes?'

'Everything,' said the weasel man. 'Even the liquorice bombs.'

'And where am I supposed to get my sherbert lemons now, then? They're practically medicinal, you know?'

But both the shopkeeper and the weasel man ignored her. They were going over the finer points of what buying *everything* entailed.

Granny rolled her eyes and stormed out of the shop.

'We're going to the tavern *now*, Poppy. Unless Mr Entitled in there has bought ALL OF THE FUCKING ALE AS WELL!' she shouted the last bit, for the weasel man's benefit.

Poppy didn't argue. She was too busy trying to keep up with Granny's vengeful march across the square—thinking that somehow she'd left the house with just errands, and now felt instead as if she was escorting a war crime to the local pub.

EPISODE 4

Excerpt from the transcript of
The Sunnywood Signal.

Episode 4: *"The Curse-Off at Copperhill"*
Transcribed by KS-01.
Broadcast on The Upper Susshingham Radio 102.3EM

HUK

Right, so to set the scene—there's a pub, right? Normal pub. Ale, pork scratchings, cursed immortal necromancer in the corner.

KELZU

And Granny. Don't forget Granny. She was three pints in and furious.

HUK

Because Steve, he was the necromancer—

KELZU

He had a fancy title, something like Lord Mortane, King of The Bone Court or some such bullshit—

HUK

—Called her "a third-rate enchantress with a perm like a wilted sunflower."

KS-01

Which prompted the first of thirty-seven curses that evening.

KELZU

I still can't eat pork scratchings.

HUK

And Steve? He can't say the word "Tuesday" without shitting himself.

KS-01

That is an exaggeration—

KELZU

No one cares, K.S.! Point is—never underestimate Granny when she's half-cut and full of spite.

HUK

Oh, and fun fact: this is why Copperhill no longer has a mayor. And we think Steve might have actually died not long after that.

WHERE ADVENTURERS
GO TO DIE

Poppy could barely see Granny behind the two giant flagons of ale. She watched her take a never-ending gulp, and then, when she was done, Granny burped loud enough for the whole tavern to hear. She raised her tankard in cheers.

'Delicious,' she crowed. 'Absolutely bloody scrumptious. Granny shall have another!'

'No, you bloody won't,' said Poppy. 'And keep your voice down.'

Granny reached for Poppy's own tankard and began to sip it at a much more reasonable pace.

That was fine by Poppy. She didn't drink. She thought all it was good for was poor decisions and headaches. She glanced at the Adventuring Board—because how could she not? Hard to believe she'd been here only a week ago. She'd been in worse shape then, sure, but still full of hope.

Her next adventure.

Finally, finding a party she fit into.

Strangers who might one day become like family.

And now she was back here, and what? She was a carer. In a retirement home. For a pack of mad old bastards.

She felt embarrassed. Ashamed, even. Her idea of how life was meant to go cast a long, cold shadow—and she was wilting under it.

It wasn't a good feeling, sitting there in that tavern with Granny, beside that board full of her dreams. It made her itchy in a way she couldn't name. Like her insides were starting to burn, it made her feel like she'd given up.

She watched a group of people about her age stood in front of the board, laughing and pushing each other around.

'A necromancer,' she heard one of them say.

So that farm with the undead rabbits hadn't been sorted out yet, Poppy thought. And every part of her longed to get up, to ask if they needed help. Another member, perhaps. Another friend. But she'd struggled lately to see herself as anything other than a deadweight.

Granny kicked her under the table. Hard.

'Ow.' Poppy kicked her back—just as hard—but missed and got the table leg.

The whole thing lurched beneath them, and Granny's empty tankard clattered across the pavers. It felt as if everyone in the tavern turned to look—though Granny didn't notice.

'What are you staring at?' Granny leaned across the table, squinting toward the Adventuring Board. She looked back at Poppy and smirked. 'Ohh, I see.'

Poppy's stomach fell—hard and heavy into the back of her spine. 'See what?'

'Which one is it? The tall lanky one or the short stocky one?'

Poppy rolled her eyes. Her face felt hot and stingy.

'Or the girl then? She really is rather pretty, isn't she?'

'I wasn't looking at them,' said Poppy, louder than she meant to.

'Why not?' said Granny, grinning. 'I am. Why don't you go say hello? Go on.'

'I'd rather chew off my own arm.'

'What's the worst that can happen—you make a fool of yourself?

Go make some friends.' And then, for good measure, Granny shoved Poppy off her seat.

'I can't just go over there and strike up a conversation,' hissed Poppy. 'I'm not—I can't—they'll think I'm deranged.'

'Oh, what a load of tosh,' said Granny. 'Look, I'll come with you.'

'No,' said Poppy, much more forcefully than she meant to. 'You just—you stay here.'

Granny grinned, and Poppy thought she might have preferred it before—when she was an outsider, an enemy insurgent to be rid of. Because if this was what getting along looked like, then she wanted no part of it.

'Fuck's sake,' Poppy muttered.

She walked slowly toward the board and the adventurers. They were all huddled around it, whispering conspiratorially. Poppy glanced back at Granny. She gave her a thumbs up and was now somehow halfway through an entire jug of ale. Tankards be damned. How she'd gotten another drink so fast was beyond her. But she looked, Poppy thought, like she was trying to drink as much as she could in the shortest amount of time. And if she kept up at this rate, there'd be no ale left in the building, and Poppy would be dragging her through the streets by her legs back to the wagon.

'Tell them you're an adventurer, just like them!' Granny shouted.

Poppy's insides crawled up her throat.

But thankfully, the adventurers hadn't heard—too wrapped up in their own world to take any notice. They were crowding the board so tightly she could barely see what jobs had even been posted.

There, in the bottom left-hand corner, was the notice about the farmer and the undead rabbits.

Poppy smiled. It had been updated.

The farmer's young daughter, it turned out, was the necromancer responsible.

Tutelage required for a gifted toddler, the notice read.

In the interest of full disclosure, she is—of course—a budding but terrifyingly prolific necromancer. This is perfectly acceptable, provided she is kept away from things that are already dead.

Please note: I would appreciate it if the next applicant did **not** suggest knocking my own daughter on the head.

One of the adventurers snorted. 'It's glorified babysitting.'

They laughed—and, without thinking, Poppy laughed too.

That was her first mistake.

They stopped and turned.

'Zombie killer, then, are you?' one of them asked.

She didn't know what to say. She'd never killed a zombie. In fact, she'd never even seen one, and truth be told, she had no real desire to even if they were an adventurer's bread and butter.

One of them raised an eyebrow.

Poppy swallowed. Say something. Say anything. Ask them about their weapons, their last job. Ask if they want a new member. You're a good...

Well, she didn't know what she was good at.

And that was half the problem.

Actually, it was most of the problem.

Gods, Poppy, just say something.

But they wandered off toward the bar, and Poppy stood there awkwardly.

She turned and saw Granny halfway through her third jug.

'No.' Poppy ran back and clawed the ale from her hands. 'That's enough.'

'It went well, did it?' asked Granny. She wiped her mouth on her sleeve. She had a beer-foam moustache.

'Astoundingly well,' said Poppy, deadpan. She realised, with no small amount of irritation, that Granny had only been distracting her so she could get a proper drink in.

The tavern door opened, and Huk, Kelzu, and K.S. walked in.

The locals all looked, but no one said anything. It was too much like the beginning of a bad joke.

Granny waved them over.

Kelzu ordered a whiskey. Huk got an orange juice.

'Young Poppy and I were just checking out the scenery,' said Granny. She belched.

'We were not,' said Poppy. '*You* were. I was looking at the Adventurers' Job Board.'

'There's not an adventure worth taking in these parts,' said Kelzu dismissively.

'This is where adventurers go to die,' said Huk.

'And not in the fun way,' added Granny.

They all laughed, like it was some great inside joke Poppy wasn't in on. It irritated her more than she expected. She couldn't say why exactly, but it made her feel defensive.

'Actually,' she said, 'I saw an interesting job on there a few days ago. About a farmer dealing with the undead, not far from here.'

She decided to leave out the bit about the necromancer being a toddler. And the undead in question being rabbits.

That got their attention.

Granny sipped her ale, now suspiciously thoughtful. 'How far from here?'

Poppy shrugged and took the jug from her again. 'Not far. Still within the village limits.'

'No,' said Kelzu. 'I know that look, and it's no. We promised, Grack. We made a pact. No more getting involved. No more sticking our beaks in where they don't belong.'

'I wasn't looking any kind of way, thank you very much,' snapped Granny.

'You were,' said Huk. 'Your eyes glaze over when you're making plans.'

'This is historically ACCURATE,' added K.S. 'In addition to an elevated heart rate, you scrunch up your hands before making a decision that usually ENDANGERS the party.'

Kelzu laughed and tapped his automaton fondly. 'She does, doesn't she? You know, I've never noticed that before.'

Granny looked down at her lap—where both fists sat scrunched—and scowled.

'What would you have done, anyway?' said Poppy. And then, as the rest of what they'd said sank in: 'And what do you mean you made a pact about getting involved? With necromancers? Or in general?'

Huk looked pointedly at Granny. 'Well? Which is it?'

Kelzu laughed, but Granny looked suddenly furious.

'You shut your mouth, Huklin Eldaruk, before I shut it for you—and don't think for a minute I won't.' She pushed herself up from the table. 'Now, if you'll excuse me, I have things to do and people to see.'

Kelzu stopped laughing. 'Oh come on, don't be like that. We were just having some fun.'

Poppy looked between them, eyebrows raised.

No one said a word. It felt to Poppy like Huk was staring right through her.

'Well? Go on. Spill it.'

Huk shrugged. Kelzu gave her a sympathetic kind of smile.

'It's not our story to tell, kid. If you want to know, you'll have to ask her.'

Poppy sighed. She was getting fed up with feeling ten steps behind everyone else. It was like they'd all made a pact—residents *and* staff—to keep everything from her. And what pissed her off more than that... was how much she wanted to know.

But they all danced around her with deflections and half-truths. It made it impossible to do anything but want to hit them with a great big stick.

Granny knocked on the window from the street outside, peering in at them.

'Well? Are you coming or not?' she shouted.

Poppy pointed to herself. 'Are you talking to me? Is she talking to me?'

Huk laughed. 'She's definitely not talking to us, kid.'

'It'll be a week before she's talking to us,' said Kelzu, though he didn't sound all that worried.

Poppy sighed and got up from the table. She'd almost made it out of the tavern when she turned and jogged back inside.

When she left again, it was with a slip of parchment folded in her pocket: a job request for help with a toddler who just so happened to be a necromancer.

Some adventures, she figured, you didn't need a party for.

Some adventures, you could take on your own.

CAREFUL, THEY'RE SHARP

They all piled into the clockwork wagon once more. The sun was low on the horizon, and its golden light caught the dust in the air. The residents yawned and groaned, and Poppy found herself doing the same. Together with Hiro, she helped load the shopping into the wagon. Hiro, it seemed, had noticed right away that something was off. He glanced at Granny Grack, then at Kelzu and Huk, in between hauling boxes.

He looked at Poppy, eyebrows creased. 'What did I miss?' he whispered.

'They had a fight, I think? I don't know,' Poppy replied, just as quietly. 'Something to do with a necromancer—'

'A necromancer?' Hiro cut in, a little too loudly.

'Keep your voice down.' Poppy looked at the others, but they hadn't seemed to notice—or were, at least, pretending not to. 'And then there was something about not wanting to get involved anymore. But I think at some point, Granny was involved with one. A necromancer, I mean. But they wouldn't tell me any more than that.'

Hiro helped Bernard jump into the wagon.

'What did they do, Hiro? Before they, you know… got old?'

Hiro chuckled.

'What?' said Poppy. 'What are you smirking at?'

'They didn't just stop being who they were because they grew old. They're still them.'

'I know. I didn't mean it like that.'

And she hadn't. But it still stung, the thought that one day she might be someone the world stopped noticing. That she'd get stuck somewhere, forget what she was good at—if she was good at anything at all. Hiro looked at Poppy, then at Granny. He shook his head.

Poppy got the message. Not here. Not now.

'Let's get a move on. The gods above and below won't be able to save us from Matron if we're late for dinner.'

The clockwork wagon rumbled along hedgerows and across fields of wildflowers; something Poppy was beginning to suspect Clay, the gardener, might be behind. The sun glowed softly, catching in the steam from the engine and on the tips of the wheat in the far-off fields.

Poppy looked over the job notice she'd taken from the board earlier. She wasn't sure why she'd taken it—not really. It wasn't anything like the kind of adventure she'd imagined. But it felt like the sort of thing she could do. It might even be nice. Helping a farmer and his child. And undead farm animals? That was something she figured she ought to see at least once in her life.

Behind her, Kelzu and Huk were snoring—Huk leaning on K.S., Kelzu on Huk. Granny Grack glanced from them to Poppy and smiled.

'You know,' she said quietly, 'I like them quite a bit more when they're asleep.'

Poppy smiled. 'How long have you known each other, exactly?'

Granny laughed. 'Far too many years, I suspect.'

'How'd you meet?'

'That, my dear, is a tale too long for a night this short.' Granny squeezed her knee lightly and tapped it in a final sort of way. 'If you're still here at the end of the week, perhaps I'll tell it to you.'

Poppy stuffed the job notice in her pocket and smiled, looking out at the wildflowers and the valley beyond.

'I'd like that,' she said. And she found she truly would.

So that's what I'll do, she thought. I'll earn the advance Matron paid me. Help this farmer. Help his terrifyingly talented kid. And maybe, if I do all that without buggering it up—

Maybe I'm not such a lost cause after all. And in the meantime, if I have to strap this lot to a chair and threaten to chop off their toes one by one to hear their stories, then so help me: I will.

It was dinner time. The residents had all been served, and Hiro had set a table for the staff—though the spot Poppy had assumed was for Clay was, in fact, for Bernard.

It was a roast dinner. The kind of roast Poppy had never had, but always dreamed of. The vegetables weren't wilted mush but just tender enough, and they tasted like what they were meant to taste like—carrots like carrots, peas like peas.

And the potatoes—oh gods, the potatoes—were crispy little fluffy pockets of pure joy. The bread came in thick slabs, dripping with herby butter that melted down her wrists.

Poppy glanced up now and then. The residents were happy. The dining room buzzed with the soft thrum of laughter and conversation. She'd just been about to lick her plate and load up on seconds when she caught Matron's eye.

She was frowning at her.

'What?' said Poppy, mouth full.

'You're eating like someone's about to snatch away your plate.'

Poppy swallowed. 'Sorry.'

Hiro laughed. 'Bernard eats with better table manners.'

The dragon had his own chair. Hiro had tied a napkin around his neck—it looked like a bandana—and he was slowly, but meticulously, working his way through an entire roast chicken.

'It's really good,' Poppy shrugged, and started to laugh. 'Like, *really* good.'

Hiro beamed. 'Did they not have roasts where you're from?'

'Something like that,' said Poppy.

She thought of home. Of never quite enough to go around. Milk diluted with water. Butter scraped so thinly it chipped the glaze off the dish. And in this last year, out on the road, even less than that.

If her wage at Sunnywood consisted of Sunday roasts alone, she wasn't sure she'd mind.

'Well, save some room for dessert,' said Hiro. 'I've been experimenting with cream and pastry. I'd like your thoughts.'

Her thoughts were simple: at that moment, she could quite happily die there. It was marvellous what a full stomach and a seat under your arse did for your mood. The last few days, in hindsight, hadn't seemed so bad. In fact, things had begun to feel... well, rather brilliant.

Poppy watched Huk and Kelzu eat in fits and starts, more focused on the strange brass contraption they'd bought in town. It sat gleaming on the table, covered in dials and crowned by two odd coils.

'Is their radio show popular?' asked Poppy, picking bits of chicken from between her teeth. 'Like, do lots of people tune in?'

Matron shrugged. 'They're only a few episodes in. And the format's a bloody mess. The timelines don't make any sense.'

Poppy watched them speaking into the device. A metal rod at its core began to glow faintly red.

'So... no, then?'

'I don't know, Poppy,' said Matron, with a touch too much exasperation than the question deserved. 'I don't get involved any more than I have to. My advice? Do the same. Don't ask them questions. You'll just get answers you don't like.'

Poppy didn't know which was worse: that the residents were hiding things, or that they thought she couldn't handle the truth.

Hiro returned with a tray loaded with pastries. They were intricate little things: delicate, jam-covered shields of biscuit and swords of twirled pastry with whipped-cream hilts. There were tiny goblin slices, which sounded disgusting, but were the most delicious thing Poppy had ever eaten. She felt like a child celebrating her birthday, Yuletide, and Solstice Eve all in one.

In hindsight, Poppy would think to herself that this was when she should have run.

In her experience, when things felt too good to be true, they usually were.

'I'm torn between calling them Cream Daggers or Pointy Puffs,' said Hiro. He placed one on Bernard's plate. The dragon waited for him to cut it into bite-sized chunks.

'Careful, though,' Hiro added. 'They've got a sharp edge.'

Alfred appeared suddenly in the centre of the table. The ghost looked furious, and more than usual.

'I won't stand for it! I won't! We had an agreement!'

Matron sighed. Her pastry was halfway to her mouth. 'If I recall, Alfred, I told you not to be absurd, and you flew off in a tiff. I'd hardly call that an agreement.'

'It's torment! It's just plain insensitive, is what it is!'

Matron bit into her pastry. 'Yes, that's it. Go have another tiff and bugger off.'

'What is it?' Poppy whispered to Hiro.

Hiro shook his head. Don't ask.

Matron raised a hand. 'Don't, Poppy. Please. Trust me. Don't get him started.' She looked back at Alfred. 'Honestly, Alfred. You're lucky I don't organise another exorcism. A proper one this time.'

'You can't even organise an exterminator. So I think I'm safe from your exorcisms. Enjoy your cream puffs—I hope you choke.'

Poppy watched as Alfred soared up through the ceiling with a melodramatic shriek.

Matron sighed and put down her pastry. 'I've lost my appetite.'

Poppy reached across the table. 'I'll finish it, then. Feels a shame to let it go to waste.'

Poppy sat back, full and—gods help her—happy. Not content, not secure, but... almost like she belonged here. It was dangerous, that feeling. Every time she got used to something, the world had a habit of taking it away.

There was a loud thumping overhead, then.

The rune-stone chandeliers shook. The floors trembled.

Plates shuddered across the table.

The dining hall fell quiet.

'What was that?' Poppy whispered.

The ceiling rumbled again.

Matron stood up sharply. 'Alfred,' she called. 'When you said 'exterminator'... did you mean—'

And at that precise moment, something stepped into the room—something Poppy never expected to see, at least not inside of a retirement home in the Totswolds of Upper Susshingham.

A giant spider filled the doorway, hunched and twitching, its legs long enough to scrape both floor and ceiling. Its carapace shimmered like obsidian wrapped in cobwebs. Eight eyes blinked in perfect unison, glassy and jet-black, each one reflecting a warped echo of the dining room and the terror frozen inside it.

Poppy accidentally sliced her lip on the pastry sword.

'I told you to be careful,' said Hiro with a sigh. 'They're sharp.'

'Oh, fuck it,' muttered Matron, and threw her napkin down on the table.

The giant spider roared.

Poppy hadn't known they could do that.
And she wished, even now, that she'd never learned it.

FIND A TABLE.
HIDE UNDER IT.

'Kelzu, your bloody spider has escaped again,' said Granny. She barely looked up from her knitting.

Kelzu and Huk looked up from their recording machine, then at one another—and whirled into action.

It wasn't, Poppy thought, the kind of action the situation deserved. They started rushing around the contraption, flicking switches and pressing buttons. Both grabbed a microphone.

'Hello, Trevor,' said Kelzu cheerily. He'd said this as if Trevor were a small feral cat, not a giant spider.

'You best do something, Kelzu,' warned Matron. She grabbed Poppy's wrist, hard. 'And you best do it quickly.'

Granny smirked over her glasses. 'Never fear, Matron. Our girl here, Poppy, is an adventurer. She'll have it all sorted in a jiffy, no doubt.'

She held up her knitting. It was a sweater. The hole where the neck went was all wrong.

Matron turned to Poppy. 'Find a table. Hide under it. If you can make it to a cupboard, even better. Shut the door and don't come out until it's over.'

Poppy dropped to the floor and crawled. Trevor the spider charged into the dining hall. Chairs went flying. The table she'd just been under was hurled through the window, glass raining down like sharp confetti.

'There's a giant spider in the house,' whispered Poppy. She dragged herself under another table and hugged one of the legs. Bernard scrambled under the table with her, head jammed beneath her arm.

She'd known something wasn't right. Had known it for days now. The way they dodged her questions. Sunnywood made the impossible feel like an ordinary Tuesday. But every time she tried to press, they danced around her like it was a game.

And she'd started to believe maybe the problem was her. That she was slow, or dense, or missing something everyone else had already grasped.

But now?

Now there was a bloody spider the size of a wagon hanging from the ceiling, and no one—not a single soul—seemed particularly surprised.

'What the fuck is going on?'

The dragon whimpered.

'Welcome, listeners, to The Sunnywood Signal,' said Huk.

'Now that,' said Kelzu, laughing gleefully, 'that is good. Last week, we talked about one of our first adventures. But today? Let's talk about what's happening right now. Normally that's nothing terribly exciting—though, of course, we did just recently welcome a new staff member to Sunnywood.'

'Poppy, where are you?' said Huk.

She made a noise. Somewhere between I'm here and a terrified gurgle.

'Hiding beneath a table,' Kelzu said into the mic. 'Do you think she has what it takes to survive life here, at Sunnywood House, Huk?'

'Well, she is a budding, self-proclaimed adventurer. Why don't we ask her what she thinks?'

A spider leg stabbed down through the table above Poppy.

She screamed.

Bernard bolted.

'But today,' said Huk, 'we thought we'd explore the eternal question: what happens to adventurers after the quest is done? Do they lay down their swords—or do the giant spiders of their past come back to haunt them?'

'Oh, what a load of complete and utter tosh,' muttered Granny.

'Trevor really has gotten big,' said Huk, as if the sheer size of the spider had only just sunk in. 'I mean, look at the size of him.'

Kelzu turned off the recorder. 'Huk, buddy, you've got to stay professional. If you break mid-recording again, it throws the whole thing off—'

'It's on the ceiling, lads,' said Granny. She ducked under the table to look at Poppy. 'Now, I'm not very good. I can't knit straight for a start, so keep that in mind: but do you think it's nice?' She spread the half-formed sweater across her chest. 'You like the colours?'

Poppy tried to speak, but the noise that came out barely qualified as language.

'Who let him out this time?' shouted Hiro. He was standing in the hallway with a meat cleaver in one hand and a pot lid held like a shield in the other.

Matron, Poppy noticed, had shut herself inside the broom cupboard.

'*Again?*' said Poppy. 'This has happened before?'

'Oh yes,' said Granny distractedly. 'But you don't think it's a bit... frumpy?'

'Yeah. Frumpy,' Poppy croaked. Her mind was starting to work now. The spider was called Trevor. Matron had said he wasn't her concern. Well, he bloody well was now. In fact, at this exact moment, he was her *only* concern.

'Well, who fed him last?' shouted Kelzu. 'He looks starved. Poor lad's all legs and no abdomen.'

'He's your bloody pet!' Matron shouted from behind the cupboard door.

'I don't see why I should have to organise his food too,' said Hiro.

'The fact he has the entire third floor is bad enough!' Matron continued.

Poppy looked past Granny, up at the ceiling: the giant spider was in the corner now, defying gravity and looking down at them all. Its fangs were dripping. Venom or saliva, it didn't seem to matter a great deal. Either way, it looked like drool, and it wasn't what you wanted to see from a spider that was three times taller than you.

'Who names a giant spider Trevor?' said Poppy.

She had been eating jam-filled pastries ten minutes ago. Now this.

K.S. had picked up Kelzu like an overprotective parent.

'Perhaps we should just kill the blasted thing?' said Huk. 'What do you say, Zu? Knock it in half and get back to our recording?'

Granny stopped knitting. 'Have you forgotten your bad knee and brittle wrists, or are you just daft?'

'Like you can talk,' said Huk. 'You wouldn't remember how to cast a battle spell if it up and bit you on the arse.'

'What did you just say?'

'You heard me.'

'This is madness,' Poppy hissed. She launched herself toward the hallway, half running, half crawling. 'Absolute fucking madness.'

Matron peeked out of the cupboard, frazzled. 'They only argue every few weeks. It's not that common, I promise. And Trevor's usually happy upstairs. When he's fed. Don't let this put you off the job. Please.'

She sounded frazzled again, and she looked, thought Poppy, like the Matron who'd begged her to take the job on the first day.

Nothing at all like the stern no-nonsense woman she'd been ever since. Poppy wondered which was the lie.

'What kind of nursing home is this?' said Poppy.

'Seriously?' Hiro gave her a look like she'd just asked what two plus two was. 'You really haven't put this together?'

Matron sighed. 'Don't start this now, Hiro. We're in the middle of something here.'

'What? I'm worried she might not be all there. You're hiding in a cupboard, and there's a giant spider in the dining hall. If she can't figure it out now, then there's no hope.'

He turned to Poppy.

'What kind of nursing home? This is Sunnywood House, you prize donkey. You know—retired adventurers, legends of the realm, all of that? Do you live under a bloody rock? Honestly, we thought you'd have clocked it weeks ago by now.'

Poppy stared up at Trevor again. 'Yeah… no, that checks out.'

And she wasn't stupid, of course, she'd guessed.

Bits of it.

Okay, well, more than bits, really—the truth had been tapping her on the shoulder for days, she'd just kept brushing it off as nonsense because the whole picture had always stayed just out of reach; obscured not by clever lies, but by something quieter. It was hard to put the pieces together when you were busy helping someone into their slippers. Or rubbing ointment into their bunions. Or watching them argue over crossword clues and custard recipes.

How could she have seen them as legends, when they'd spent half the week arguing about jam, for godsake?

And every time she asked a question, the answers came half-wrapped in riddles, or else not at all. And if she pushed? They closed ranks. Smiled. Changed the subject.

She hadn't been stupid. Just… too close to see them for who they really were.

There was a tremendous crash behind them.

The floorboards shook.

'I'm alright!' Huk shouted. 'The great big bastard just caught me off guard!'

'It used to be famous,' muttered Matron. 'Adventurers are a dying breed. Hardly any of them make it to retirement. HUK, DON'T LEAP OFF THE TABLES—'

Poppy turned just in time to see Huk take a running jump. The spider no sooner flung him off, throwing him against the wall.

Matron rubbed her temples. 'Look, I'll understand if you want to leave. No hard feelings. You can keep the two weeks' pay. You've lasted longer than anyone else.'

That line again. Like it was something to be proud of. Like she should feel lucky just to still be standing. She stared at Matron and felt that flicker again—the smallest shift in her voice, something warmer than dismissal. Maybe... maybe they were all just scared to let her in. Or scared of what she'd do with the truth.

And for a moment—just a moment—Poppy thought maybe she meant something else, too.

That maybe she didn't want her to go.

That maybe she *was* wanted here.

She didn't realise until much later that what she'd taken for care had been something else entirely. But right now, she was grinning. Poppy looked from the spider—its fangs were twitching in a way that made your knees buckle—to Matron.

She was too full of pastry and adrenaline and a wild, impossible hope to do anything other than laugh.

'Leave?' she grinned. 'Why would I want to leave? Five minutes ago, I was eating the most delicious thing I've ever eaten in my entire life.'

She was thinking out loud again. She had a habit of doing that when stressed. The last adventuring party she'd joined had eventually started taping her mouth shut.

'Why the fuck would I want to leave?'

Adventurers. A whole house full of them.

And not just any kind.

The kind they told stories about. The kind she'd grown up wanting to be.

SOMETHING MORE

'I mean, should we help?' said Poppy.

Hiro laughed.

Matron shook her head. 'Gods, no. I'm staying in my cupboard, thanks.'

Huk stood up and dusted himself off. He looked, Poppy thought, suddenly furious, and the fury wasn't directed at Trevor, but at Granny.

'Don't,' he shouted at her.

'I didn't do anything.' Granny held up her hands. She'd finally stopped knitting, which was a relief, because it was starting to make Poppy feel a little sick. It wasn't right to sit so calmly in the middle of chaos like this.

'You've got that look,' spat Huk.

'I don't know what you're talking about,' said Granny, pushing her chair under the table—even though the table was currently being eaten away by spider venom.

'Oh, piss off.'

Granny sighed. 'I'm off to bed, now, I think. Should I put Trevor back in his room before I go, or would you like to be thrown through a window first?'

Kelzu, still cradled in K.S.'s arms, turned on his microphone.

'And just like that,' he said, 'we reach that point. All of us do. And if you, dear listener, try your hand at a life of adventure, you too will come to this moment—the moment where you must ask: have the giant spiders gotten smarter, stronger, bigger... or have I just gotten older, slower, weaker?'

He turned the microphone off and gave Huk a cheerful thumbs-up. 'Brilliant, yeah?'

The fury bled from Huk's body in an instant. Poppy saw it in his shoulders, his face. He looked, all of a sudden, very old—and very tired. Without a word, he stormed past them, out of the dining hall and up the stairs.

Granny raised her hand. She made a few complicated motions in the air, and the space between her fingers began to glow. She sent a ripple of magic shimmering toward the giant spider. It hit Trevor square in the abdomen.

He turned, looking ten times angrier.

His fangs dripped venom that sizzled on the floorboards as he came charging towards them, legs skittering like blades.

But as he neared them, he began to shrink.

No longer twice as tall as a horse or as wide as a small house, the magic twirled around him like a storm, spinning and folding Trevor until he was the size of a coin.

Poppy thought she might just shit herself at the sheer brilliance of it. She had never, ever in her life seen magic like that.

'Kelzu,' said Granny sharply.

'Mm?'

'Fix this.'

'Fix what?'

'You know full well what. Now, go on and make it right.'

Kelzu climbed down from K.S.'s arms, grabbed an empty bowl from one of the few intact tables, and trapped Trevor beneath it.

'There,' he said.

Granny smacked him upside the head. 'Not the spider, you blithering fucking idiot—*Huk*. Go and make things right with Huk. Think about what you just said. Think about it for longer than a second and tell me you haven't hurt him.'

'You're the one who said he had a bad knee and weak wrists.'

'Because he *does*. But it's another thing entirely to be reminded of what you used to be capable of. Now go apologise. I'll handle your bloody spider.'

Kelzu sighed. 'Fine. Just don't—'

'I'm not going to hurt him. Now go.'

Poppy waited until Kelzu and K.S. had thudded up the stairs before slipping back into the dining hall.

It was absolute chaos.

There was one good table left. The floor had been eaten through in places, and she could see the basement peeking up between charred and venom-burned boards.

Granny had transferred Trevor onto a plate. 'Put Trevor back where he belongs, won't you, love? He'll be growing back to full size shortly, and I don't have it in me to shrink him again.'

Hiro took the plate and sprinted off with the now coin-sized spider.

Granny sat down heavily. 'Takes it out of me now,' she muttered. Her voice was thin and trembling. 'I'd have been able to shrink a whole clutter of the bastards, not that long ago. Now it's just the one.'

'You never told me you were a battlemage,' said Poppy. Her voice carried an edge of awe; dangerously close to reverence.

Granny looked different now. Not softer: just sharper. Clearer. The world had tilted and snapped into focus.

Adventurers.

Of course, she was intolerable half the time. *Of course*. You didn't live that kind of life and wind up here without being a handful. It wouldn't have been right.

'No,' said Granny, 'I don't suppose I did.'

'And you were an adventurer?'

'You know,' said Granny, rubbing her hands together, 'I never much liked that term. Makes it sound far grander than it was—when really it's just going without a bath for a week, running out of tea, and never getting a proper night's sleep because you're too busy trying not to die.'

'Trying not to die,' Poppy repeated, as if it were poetry.

She meant to stay calm. She really did. But it took all her willpower not to leap in the air and run screaming in a circle.

Because Sunnywood wasn't *just* a job, maybe it never had been. Maybe—if she played things right—it could be something more. She wasn't sure what, exactly. But she was going to pay attention. Watch their hands when they worked magic. Be it spells, swords, or inventing. And she'd ask questions when they forgot *not* to answer.

She'd learn. One way or another. Whether they liked it or not.

She didn't need to be their favourite. She just needed to be there.

'Why is she smiling like that?' Granny asked flatly.

Matron shrugged. 'I dunno, I expected her to barrel-roll out a window at the first sight of Trevor.' She took Poppy by the shoulders and gently spun her toward the stairs. 'Go to bed, Poppy, please. It's been a big day, and you're making me worry we've broken you.'

'I'm not broken,' Poppy said, adamantly. 'I just think it's all a bit brilliant.'

'Yes,' said Matron, brows knitting. 'That's exactly what I mean. Now, off you go.'

'What about the mess? I can help clean up.'

Matron gave her a look: lips pursed so tightly they could've devoured each other. Poppy couldn't tell if it meant she was impressed or concerned. Possibly both.

'I'll fix it.'

Poppy shrugged and turned to go.

She reached the top of the stairs—dodging the two tricksy ones without thinking—and realised something peculiar.

She was already getting better at this.

When she glanced back, Matron was still watching her.

THE CLEANERS

Poppy opened her bedroom door before Matron had a chance to knock the following morning. She wore a fresh pair of pants and a button-up linen shirt. She'd cut her hair herself over the basin—it was a little blunt, but a definite improvement on the wild, scraggly mess she'd spent the week pushing behind her ears. At least she could run a comb through it now. She felt like a different person.

Matron's mouth fell open.

'Good morning,' said Poppy. She pushed past her and headed down the hall.

'Morning,' said Matron, dumbly.

'I checked my timetable in the manual you gave me. Looks like we've got cleaning duty before breakfast.'

'Well, yes,' said Matron. She managed to reconnect her jaw and straighten her coat. 'But don't sound happy about it, please. It's too early for me to be questioning anyone's sanity but my own.'

'Right, of course.' Poppy lowered her voice. 'Bloody cleaning. Couldn't think of anything worse.'

'Better. Much, much better.'

Matron turned off at the end of the hallway. 'You're heading the wrong way, Poppy. We keep the cleaners in here.' She stopped in front of a small door. They'd have to hunch to get through it. It was, Poppy realised, gnome-sized—perfect for Kelzu, or even Bernard at a stretch.

'You keep the cleaners in a tiny room?' Poppy asked. It was such a strange way to phrase it; it left her feeling slightly off balance. The gloves were off now. She knew the truth about Sunnywood, and the rest was rushing in to fill the blanks. She only hoped there weren't actual people locked behind that door.

'Certainly,' said Matron. She unlocked it with a brass key from her belt. 'Now don't look at me like that. It's not what it sounds like.'

They both ducked inside. The room was barely the size of a wardrobe. Matron fumbled for the light switch, and ether crackled in the rune-light sconces until the room was washed in a pale, moon-like glow.

'These are the cleaners?' said Poppy, relieved.

They weren't people at all, just clockwork animals, each set into its own tiny alcove and plugged into the wall via a braided brass hose.

'They were given to Sunnywood as part payment for Kelzu's room. Marvellous things. Gnomish-made—you won't find better anywhere else,' said Matron. She hunched towards a small lever at the end of the room. 'They do have trouble distinguishing between guests and mess sometimes, though, so I like to get them out and tidying before everyone wakes for breakfast.'

Poppy knelt to take a closer look. They were about waist-height, made of gleaming silver and brass. Beneath their plating, she could see delicate filigrees of clockwork and magic. Two glowing crystal eyes apiece. A single wheel where legs ought to be.

'They are, I think, the cutest things I've ever seen.'

'They're determined little sods, is what they are. So whatever you do, don't get in their way. They see in black and white: mess and order.'

'Do they have names?'

'Names?' Matron looked genuinely offended. 'Don't be ridiculous. Now look here and pay attention. This lever disconnects the arcane chargers. When they're back in place, you flick it again. It's simple.'

She showed Poppy the activation protocol, where the service kits were: replacement wheel treads, joint oil, mop heads, and duster attachments. 'There's a small rune on each chest plate. Can you see?'

Poppy could. It was the same rune K.S. had on his own chest plate.

'You press that, and they'll wake up.'

Poppy hesitated, suddenly worried they'd mistake her for a mess. 'Should I press—?'

'—That's why you're here,' sighed Matron.

Their metal chests were warm, not burn-your-hand hot, but just warm enough to surprise you. She pressed the rune—a small carved crystal—and the cleaners looked up, eyes glowing. They rolled forward from their alcoves in eerie synchrony. Poppy nearly tripped.

'They'll follow you like sheep until you give the command,' said Matron. 'So lead them out into the hall, if you don't mind.'

Once back in the hallway, the cleaners lined up in perfect formation. Tiny soldiers ready for war.

'You know,' said Poppy, 'if they weren't so adorable, I think I'd be shitting myself.'

'You shit yourself near one of them, and you won't find them adorable for long,' said Matron. 'Now, the command.' She clapped twice. The cleaners turned to her in unison. 'Hop to it.'

They spun into motion. One stretched up to dust cobwebs, then shrank again to wipe a smudge from Poppy's shirt before she had time to decide if it was a hostile move or not.

'You've got twenty minutes for breakfast. I'll see you in the basement when you're done,' Matron called, heading for the stairs. 'You'll be happy to know Hiro's trialling something with cinnamon and butter.'

Poppy was already off down the corridor. 'You know, it is kind of hard to believe no one wanted this job.'

'You've only been here a week. You've been tripped down the stairs, punched by a book, and attacked by a giant spider. I find it extremely believable. Frankly, I'm amazed you're still here.'

'Yeah, but I'd do anything for good food.'

'That is becoming increasingly evident. Oh, and Poppy?'

'Mmm?'

'Tell Hiro I've let the cleaners loose. They get... excitable in the kitchen.'

I BOLT IT, POPPY

Hiro was already hard at work. Poppy thought she'd risen early, but he looked as if he'd already been up for hours. Bernard was asleep on his back in front of the stove, legs twitching. Alfred hovered over a bubbling pot, looking smug.

The air smelled of butter and cinnamon. The benches were lined with pastries, both sweet and savoury.

'Morning,' said Poppy. She pulled up a seat and reached for a bun.

Hiro slapped her hand with a wooden spoon. 'Not that batch. The good ones are over there.'

'What's wrong with these?'

They looked perfect. They looked, she thought, good enough to declare war over.

'He does this,' said Alfred. 'Gets into these moods where nothing's good enough.'

'Rules, Alfie,' said Hiro. 'Don't forget the rules.'

Alfred sighed. He watched the pot boil over without blinking. 'Oh look,' he said flatly, 'it's boiling.' Then he sniggered and floated through the wall.

Poppy grabbed a bun from the 'good' tray and took a bite. She gagged and spat it out just as Hiro turned his back.

'You look different. What have you done?'

'Cut my hair.'

'It looks clean too. You look... not grimy.'

'Wow, thanks,' she said dryly. Poppy tried another piece. It was *still* awful. 'Hiro?'

'Mm?'

'This was the good batch, right?'

'Yeah?'

She couldn't swallow it. 'They taste like shit.'

Hiro frowned, took a bite, and immediately hurled the whole tray at the wall. 'I'm going to kill that fucking ghost.'

Poppy reached for a sausage. She figured that, at least, was a safe bet. 'Well, I think we've all learned something valuable here this morning. I've learned you have one hell of a temper, and you've learned not to let Alfred in the kitchen anymore.'

Hiro sniffed the rest of the buns. 'That little blue floating fucker.'

'Do you think Granny would teach me to shrink a giant spider?'

'Try this one,' said Hiro, holding out a bun.

'You try it.'

'Ohhhh,' cried Hiro. 'Now, look! You doubt my cooking—'

'I don't doubt your cooking, it's just...' he looked borderline heartbroken. 'Oh, fine, give it here.' She took a bite and... she relaxed. It was soft and sweet and buttery.

She took another bite.

'Well?'

'Good,' she exhaled. 'Really good.'

'Just good?'

'Delicious, then. Happy?'

'No. You said it was good first. If you'd meant 'delicious,' you'd have said it. What's wrong with them, then, do you think?'

Poppy shrugged. 'I don't know? More cinnamon, maybe. Anyway, do you think Granny would? Teach me, I mean?

'More cinnamon? Really. Are you sure?'

'No? I don't know. Yes?' She threw an apple at him. 'I'm talking here. *Listen*. Gods, man. Because I was thinking if she taught me how to shrink things, like a giant spider, that would come in handy, wouldn't it? I could do all sorts then. If I knew magic.'

She'd tried magic, of course. Everyone does once. A few months ago, she'd found a spell book in a second-hand shop—more accurately, stolen it, since she hadn't had the coin. She tucked it under her shirt and into the back of her pants. The spell book caught fire before she even made it out the door. The shopkeeper had helped put it out, realised she'd stolen it and then booted her flaming arse into the street.

She could still feel the burn if she thought about it too long.

One of the cleaners rolled into the kitchen, then. It stopped and looked around. It seemed, to Poppy, as if it were having trouble deciding on where it ought to start.

There were buns all over the floor, after all.

Hiro went to the sink and grabbed a tea towel. He was still muttering about cinnamon, and then, when he saw the cleaner, he screamed: a terrified shriek of a scream. 'Watch out, Poppy. Quick!'

'Oh, yeah. Right.' Poppy took a sip of her coffee. 'Sorry. Matron said to tell you the cleaners were out this morning.'

'Well, don't just sit there, grab a fucking knife or something.'

Poppy frowned. 'First of all, calm down. And you told me you'd kill me if I ever touched your knives again.'

'Calm down? Are you mental? You should have told me first thing. I bolt the door shut on cleaning days.' He looked at the cleaner and then at the door. 'I BOLT IT, POPPY. I FUCKING BOLT IT.'

'Gods, man. You'll have a heart attack. They're just wee little fellas anyway.' She finished her coffee and watched as the cleaner wheeled around the floor, mopping and sweeping as it went. Hiro ran around the other side of the table and scrambled for the rolling pin.

'I suppose, when you think about it,' continued Poppy. 'Granny would know more than just how to make things shrink. You don't think she could move stuff with her mind, do you?'

Hiro threw the rolling pin at the cleaner. It missed by a long shot, but it did nearly hit Bernard, who yelped from the shock of it and ran towards Poppy for emotional support. She looked at Hiro. 'You really need to get a grip. He's just sweeping your floors.'

Poppy took a small fruit bun and left the kitchens to go and find Matron.

'Where are you going?' shouted Hiro.

'To start work, I guess. You should probably do the same. Your oven's just caught fire, by the way.'

'POPPY DON'T LEAVE ME IN HERE WITH IT!'

But Poppy was still thinking about magic lessons with Granny. She'd ask her today, she decided, if she were in an agreeable mood. She thought of all the things she might learn. Flight, whether by an enchanted coat or a broomstick: she'd heard both were possible. Invisibility. Mind control. Mind reading. Teleportation. Super speed. Her list of questions was suddenly, hopelessly, endless. Was any of it possible—and if not, *why* not? Oh, and a good offensive spell, too. She'd be needing one of them up her sleeve. A witch-bolt perhaps: the big explosive kind you could set a whole forest alight with, if you needed to.

WHAT'S FOR
BREAKFAST THEN?

Poppy and Matron had carried a bunch of old furniture up from the basement—carefully stepping around the half-assembled radio equipment Kelzu and Huk were setting up down there—to replace what had been destroyed the night before. Between the cleaners and a few well-placed rugs, you'd barely know a giant spider had rampaged through the place. Though the table leg was still embedded in the ceiling, the scorch marks across one wall, and the divots in the floorboards had all taken considerable coaxing. Still, the cleaners had done their best. Only the smell of singed curtains and smashed jam tarts remained; stubborn, cloying, and utterly impervious to lavender polish.

Outside the tall arched windows, the sky had lightened into a rosy pink. The trees beyond were dipped in gold. The cleaners moved through the room in perfect single file, heading back to their charging stations. One paused to straighten a tablecloth, then zoomed off to join the others.

Poppy watched them go, eyes wide with something close to awe.

'They're dead clever, aren't they?'

Matron jogged after them. 'Four... five... six? Where's Six? We're missing one.' She frowned.

'What are you looking at me for?' said Poppy.

'I reckon it's gotten stuck in Trevor's webs again. You'll have to fetch it. It'll be by the staircase. Six loves the staircase.'

'And you're certain Trevor can't get out again?'

'I triple-checked the locks last night.'

'It's just... he's escaped once already. And I don't fancy meeting him again. Not alone, anyway.'

Matron waved a hand dismissively. 'Take Hiro with you, then. I don't care.'

Poppy considered this. Hiro would be perfectly useless if Trevor were out—but at least he was loud, and she could probably outrun him.

She wandered back through the house toward the kitchen. She'd begun to notice things now; not just the oddities, but the pattern. The logic behind the lunacy. Things that hadn't struck her before as anything beyond weird now made a strange kind of sense.

A pet book-wyrm. (People around here usually settled for dogs, cats, or a lumpgull—maybe a grubkin if they were feeling adventurous.) A sword on display above every other lintel. A mantelpiece bearing a clockwork gun, freshly polished and bolted to the wall. Granny's strictly no visitors brewing room. It wasn't full of mead or ale, was it? Well... maybe. Poppy thought back to Granny's world-class drinking skills at the tavern. But she'd bet all her teeth spells were brewing in there, too.

She thought of them all in turn. Kelzu, a world-class inventor—she assumed—capable of building creatures like K.S. and the cleaners. Huk, with his holstered greatsword. He'd been a fighter. She was sure of it. She wondered if he might teach her to hold a sword properly. She still hadn't figured it out. Did the thumb go on the hilt or around it? Feet apart or planted? One in front, one behind?

Her head buzzed with questions. But more than that: a strange, warm hope had begun to bloom. That they might teach her. Not formally. Not with lesson plans. But in bits and pieces—between arguments and breakfast tables and botched radio broadcasts. That Sunnywood might become her *school*. A place to learn not how to care for old people, but how to survive out there. How to face down monsters, sword or spell in hand.

She took the job notice from her pocket. Looked it over. Wiped her thumb across the heavy copperplate font. The farmer and his necromancer child seemed as good a place as any to start.

And that's when, distracted and full of hope, Poppy strolled into the kitchen.

She stepped on something soft. Squishy. She looked down.

Red oozed from beneath her shoe.

'Hiro?'

It was a jam-ball. Not blood. That was good. But she didn't feel relieved.

The kitchen was a war zone. Tables overturned. Knives embedded in the walls. Flour spread from one end of the floor to the other. A pot had boiled dry and was sizzling angrily on the hob. Everything was in the wrong place. Nothing was moving.

The silence was the worst part. That echoing, eerie kind that rings in your ears.

'Hiro?' she called again. 'Are you in here?'

A faint whirring.

Cleaner Number Six zipped past her—and smacked straight into a wall. It fell over and spun helplessly on its back like a flipped beetle. Poppy froze.

It had no head.

Its two adorable crystal eyes were not attached to its body.

The pantry door burst open. Bernard tumbled out, clearly thrilled. Hiro staggered behind him, looking anything but. He was flour-dusted, bruised, and seconds away from a mental break.

'I killed the bastard thing,' Hiro said, voice oddly proud.

'Fuck,' Poppy muttered, staring at the carnage. 'And... sorry. What did you do that for?'

'I didn't have much of a choice, did I? It was rampaging through my kitchen.'

Poppy found the cleaner's head lying next to an overturned dish of sausages. Tragic waste. She picked it up. 'You chopped off its head?'

'Yes,' said Hiro, straightening his shirt. 'Yes, I suppose I did.'

'And do you do that often? Chop things' heads off?'

'I'm a chef, Poppy. Not a butcher. But in this case, I'd say it was deserved.'

Poppy sat down. 'Fucking hell.'

They surveyed the destruction. The headless cleaner spun a few more useless circles before finally stopping, dead. Bernard crept closer to sniff it. The cleaner jolted and sparked—sending the little dragon skidding backwards into the spice rack. Spices crashed to the floor.

Hiro didn't flinch.

'You don't think,' Poppy said carefully, 'you might have overreacted?'

'No,' said Hiro. 'It got what it deserved.'

Poppy blinked. 'So... what's for breakfast then?'

EGGS ON TOAST

Ten minutes later, Poppy watched Hiro hyperventilate into a brown paper bag. The adrenaline had worn off, leaving sharp, shallow breaths.

She didn't know where to look—every time things got serious, she got the urge to laugh and meeting his eyes felt like asking for trouble.

'It'll be alright. Don't worry.'

'I ripped its head off,' Hiro gasped.

'I know you did.' It was really quite impressive when she thought about it.

He stopped breathing into the bag and stared at her. 'I RIPPED ITS FUCKING HEAD OFF, POPPY.'

'I know, mate. I know.' She wasn't laughing, which felt like an achievement, but the grin had taken hold.

It was getting late. The residents would be down soon, and Matron—well, she'd be wondering where they were. And what were they going to tell her? The truth was out of the question, but Poppy wasn't about to lie, either. She couldn't afford to lose her job.

Sunnywood, she was convinced, was where she needed to be. She hadn't even made it through an entire month yet—she couldn't get the sack. Not now. Not when she had so much to learn, and more comfortable nights ahead in her own room, with her own bath and toilet. She wasn't risking that. Not for anyone.

'Look, Hiro—'

He'd gone back to panting into the bag. Bernard watched the rising and falling paper like a bemused spaniel.

'What do we tell Matron?' she asked, immediately regretting it. The bag was going to explode.

Right. He needed to get a grip.

Poppy groaned. 'Alright. I'll go and get Kelzu. The cleaners were his before they were Matron's, he'll know what to do.' She glanced at the decapitated cleaner's head now sitting in a bowl of flour. 'And you—pull yourself together. Organise breakfast. Make something, anything. Eggs on toast, maybe? Everyone loves eggs on toast.'

Hiro's breathing slowed. He nodded. 'Eggs on toast?'

'Eggs on toast,' repeated Poppy. 'I'll wake Kelzu.'

She sprinted out. Halfway to the staircase, Matron intercepted her.

'Did you find it?'

'Find what?' said Poppy, a little more defensively than she meant to.

'Not your manners, by the sound of it. The cleaner. Was it on the third floor?'

'Oh. No,' Poppy said. 'It wasn't on the third floor.'

She wasn't lying. She was... lightly rearranging the truth.

'It'll turn up,' she said, attempting breezily, and turned for the stairs.

'Where are you off to? Breakfast starts shortly.'

'I'm waking Kelzu. Hiro's cinnamon rolls failed. He's in a state. I wouldn't go in the kitchen unless you want a knife flung at your head.'

Matron sighed. 'Typical chef. The good ones always have the shortest fuse.'

Poppy laughed awkwardly—and for much longer than necessary. Matron frowned.

'He is making an alternative, I hope?'

'Eggs on toast.'

'Eggs on toast?' Matron arched a brow.

'He had a fancier name for it,' Poppy lied. 'But eggs on toast are eggs on toast, I reckon.'

She bolted up the stairs, down the hall, and burst into Kelzu's room without waiting.

But it wasn't Kelzu's room.

No endless aisles, no contraptions. Just a tiny, dust-coated bedroom that looked as if it had been untouched for years.

She shut the door. Opened it again. No change.

'He's not there.'

Poppy spun. Huk stood in the hallway.

'He's gone. Left last night.'

'What do you mean, gone?' People, in her experience, didn't usually take their bedrooms with them when they left.

Huk shrugged. 'Who knows? Your guess is as good as mine. He takes his wagon and off he trots. Sometimes he's gone for days. Sometimes for months.'

'His... wagon?'

'His wagon, aye. It's his room. Same thing. He just swaps the doors.'

Poppy nodded. Then immediately shook her head. 'Nope. I'm lost.'

Huk sighed. 'Kelzu Luckyhand's Lootland. It's his shop and his home, which is inside an enchanted wagon. The wagon is all stretched-out space, with shelves full of everything: armour, potions, spellbooks. He parks the wagon here so that the Sunnywood door opens into it. But when he leaves, the room resets.'

Poppy blinked. This explanation left her with more questions than answers.

'But he can't leave. I need him.'

'That's usually when he buggers off,' Huk muttered. 'Only thing he's good at.'

'That's absolutely no use to me.'

'What do you need help with?' he asked.

Poppy chewed a fingernail, spat the end, and sighed. 'Doesn't matter.'

'Kelzu can help you, but I can't?' Huk bristled. 'I'm quite capable too, you know.'

'I don't think so, Huk,' she said gently, patting his shoulder.

'I single-handedly killed the Great Beast of the Barren-Below,' Huk snapped. 'Whatever it is—trust me, Poppy. I can help.'

'I can't help with this,' said Huk.

Poppy watched him survey the kitchen carnage. It looked less like a mess and more like the sight of an explosion: overturned tables, knives in walls, flour everywhere like snowfall from hell. Bernard lay with his head on an upside-down mixing bowl, looking thoroughly traumatised. Hiro was busy slicing bread, as if toast soldiers might somehow restore order.

The cleaner's severed head lay in a pool of hissing alchemical liquid, slowly eating through the tiles.

'I thought Kelzu might fix it,' said Poppy. 'They're his automatons.'

Huk nodded, knelt beside the twitching body, and gave Hiro an approving smile. 'Dreadful little bastards, aren't they?'

Hiro nodded, eyes still fixed on the bread.

'You did this?'

'It was wrecking my kitchen,' Hiro muttered, plating some sizzling sunny-side-up eggs. 'I didn't have a choice.'

Poppy nudged Huk. 'Don't look impressed. He had a mental break and chopped the thing's head off. We could all do that. You're supposed to be fixing it, not admiring his bloody handiwork.'

Hiro smirked.

Huk lifted the cleaner's severed head. 'I wouldn't even know where to start.'

'Morning, my loves,' said Granny.

Poppy jumped. 'Fucking hell—where'd you come from?'

'My room, dear.' Granny surveyed the kitchen. 'What's happened here, then?'

Before Poppy could answer, Hiro did: 'Poppy forgot to mention the cleaners were out. One got into my kitchen. I dealt with it.'

'What?' Poppy stared at him. 'Don't make this my fault.'

'Well... it kind of is.'

'Matron doesn't know?' asked Huk.

Granny winced. 'Oh, Poppy, you are in trouble. She does love her little brass servants.'

'Me?' Poppy spluttered.

'It's better to accept blame where you can,' said Huk. He squeezed her shoulder. 'You just look weak otherwise. Take it on the chin, kid, and move on.'

'I WOULD take it on the chin if I were the one who chopped its head off!'

'Chopped off whose head?' said Matron.

They froze.

She strode toward the kitchen. 'What's going on?'

'Oh, fuck it,' muttered Poppy.

'Now you've done it,' whispered Granny.

'Can you do something?' Poppy begged.

'Like what?'

'I don't know! Anything!'

Matron stepped inside. 'Is everything all right?'

Granny sighed. 'Fine. Ready yourselves.'

She performed several hand gestures, then a string of phlegmy coughs.

Darkness—not smoke, but something thicker—poured out of her mouth and rolled across the floor. It looked dramatic. It also did absolutely nothing. Matron kept coming; the kitchen still looked bombed.

'Whatever you're doing,' Poppy hissed, 'it's not working.'

Granny tried to widen her mouth. The darkness slowed to a sad drizzle. 'Bit slower than normal.'

Huk sighed. 'Casters think spells fix everything.' He shouldered past Poppy and intercepted Matron by the elbow. 'I've had ideas for the garden. Clay's right: we ought to keep bees.'

Matron stared at his hand. 'What are you doing?'

'Leading you out to the garden.'

'Poppy?' Matron called. 'Are you sure things are alright?'

Everyone stared at Poppy. Bernard whimpered.

She shot Hiro a murderous look. 'Yeah,' she said tightly. 'All fine.'

'Grack's been telling old stories,' Huk said, smoothly guiding Matron away. 'She even started a darkness spell.' He rolled his eyes as he escorted her out. 'Now, about my bees—ember-bees, specifically...'

The front door closed behind them.

Granny's spell finally surged, darkness billowing like a broken chimney. 'This is more what I meant. Fills a whole room. Confuses the enemy.'

'Well, you can stop now—she's gone,' said Poppy.

'It stops when it stops,' Granny wheezed. 'Like a cold.'

'Right.' Poppy grabbed the food trolley. 'I'll start taking all this out, then. You stay here with Granny. Try not to cut *her* head off, won't you?'

Hiro made a face and clapped sarcastically. 'Oh yes. Very funny.'

BABYSITTING A GREAT EVIL

Breakfast had been relatively uneventful, given the circumstances.

Alfred had been his usual annoying self and requested—well, demanded was probably more accurate—that Poppy turn his pages far more frequently.

'It's interesting, this new troll bank. They've been popping up all over the Greater Tottingfields. Started, I think, in Mannington. Can you imagine trolls in Mannington?'

Poppy shrugged. 'Wouldn't know. Never been.'

Alfred continued to drone as Poppy wiped down the benches.

At the table by the window, Clay had joined Matron and Huk, talking excitedly—and at great length—about the kinds of bees they might keep, and which wildflowers would provide the best pollen.

Granny, meanwhile, had stopped coughing darkness and was now requesting yoghurt and porridge instead of eggs on toast. 'Throat's far too sore,' she said.

'Page, Poppy,' barked Alfred.

She turned the page, dumped his cold, untouched coffee into a pot plant, and topped it up with a fresh brew.

'And would you look at this,' said Alfred, pointing at an article about recent business closures. 'To anyone else, these would seem completely unconnected. But to the trained eye—'

He floated a few inches off his chair, as he often did when excited.

Poppy sat beside him and stole a piece of toast. 'What kind of adventurer were you, before you... you know, carked it?'

Alfred looked up. 'I wasn't an adventurer. Gods, no. I was an estate agent.'

'An estate agent?'

'Yes,' he said, frowning at her. 'I bought and sold land. Often on behalf of others. You do know what an estate agent is, don't you?'

Poppy chewed her crust and zoned out. It was something of a miracle, she thought, that Sunnywood had ended up with such a boring ghost. Normally, she'd have slipped away at the first chance she got—but today, the kitchen still felt awkward and tense.

She couldn't believe Hiro had tried to blame her for what happened. It made her blood boil just thinking about it. And as for the cleaner—she'd had to help hide its remains in the pantry, under several sacks of potatoes. It felt like being an accomplice to murder.

She hated it.

They'd agreed to pretend Cleaner Six had simply gone missing at least until Kelzu got back.

'Well?' said Alfred, watching her.

'Sorry,' said Poppy. 'It's your voice, I think.'

'My voice?'

'Mmm. It's bedtime story stuff. Makes you feel sleepy.'

'What a polite way to say you don't give a shit.'

Poppy smirked. 'I didn't say that.' She started clearing his breakfast things.

Alfred rolled his eyes and went back to his paper.

At the window, Matron and Clay got up to head into the garden, leaving Huk at the table.

'You done with breakfast?' she asked.

Huk nodded, yawning. 'Thought that would never end.'

'I take it you don't actually want to keep bees, then?'

'No. I hate the bastard things.'

'Well, thank you. I don't know what I'd have done otherwise.'

Huk shrugged. 'I didn't do anything, really.'

'You did. Kept me in a job, probably.'

There was a pause. Not awkward—just companionable.

Huk looked out at the dew-drenched grass and the hills beyond. 'It's nice here, isn't it?'

'It is, I think, the nicest place I've ever been,' said Poppy.

'But boring,' said Huk. He turned to her. 'So boring.'

'You think it's boring?'

He nodded. 'At first, that was my favourite part. I'd never had time to be bored. I loved it—the lie-ins, the food, the lack of monsters. No dark, slimy caverns. No sleeping on rocks around a campfire that never quite reached the edges of things. But I think I've had enough now.'

'You miss the monsters and the caves?'

'A little, yeah. Well, I miss how they made you feel.'

'Cold and scared?'

'Alive, Poppy. They made me feel alive.'

She grinned. She'd never felt more alive than when she was being chased by goblins or hunted by a werewolf. 'It's a crying shame I'm just so, so shit at it.'

'Yeah,' said Huk, 'but we're all shit in the beginning.'

Poppy thought this over. Not just the words, but the way he said them. Like maybe he meant it. Like maybe he believed it still counted.

A bright idea took hold—hot, nerve-tingling, and impossible to ignore.

'You know what, Huk?'

'What?'

'We should go on an adventure. Together.'

Huk stared at her, trying to tell if she was joking. When he realised she wasn't—he laughed.

'What's so funny? I mean it. We could accept a job together. Granny and Kelzu could come. You could teach me stuff—how to hold a sword properly. Which mushrooms won't kill you. How to actually use a healing potion—'

'Stop,' said Huk, laughing harder now. 'Please. You'll kill me.'

'So that's a yes, then? Or maybe, at least?'

'I can't do those things anymore, kid. You heard what Kelzu said last night. I'm too old for it now. Too old, slow and weak.'

'That's not —'

'—I wouldn't be here if I could be out there, Poppy. I didn't mean—I—I can't. I just can't.'

'But you *could*. We could. Together. It would be fun, right?'

Huk smiled—a sad, far-off kind of smile. 'Of course it would be fun.'

'Well then. It's settled.'

She pulled the job notice from her back pocket—the one she'd taken when they were in town. She handed it to Huk.

He looked confused. Then he sighed and held it at arm's length.

'Bloody eyesight's not what it used to be.'

He fished out a pair of glasses and squinted at the parchment.

'This doesn't sound like an adventure,' he said. 'This sounds like babysitting a great evil before it becomes the great evil.' He looked up. 'A necromancing toddler, though. Who would've thought?

'It's settled,' said Poppy. She clapped her hands on her lap with what felt like finality.

When Huk looked up, she was already skipping off.

'I didn't agree to this!' he shouted after her. 'That wasn't a yes!'

Poppy turned, walking backwards now and grinning like a devil.

'This, Huk, is going to be fucking brilliant.'

EPISODE 5

Excerpt from the transcript of
The Sunnywood Signal.

Episode 5: *"Hindsight & Hiccups"*
Transcribed by KS-01.
Broadcast on The Upper Susshingham Radio 102.3EM

[Muffled sound of tea being poured]

HUK

Don't you ever miss it, Zu?

KELZU

Miss what?

HUK

The noise. The chaos. The way the world felt like it was just a little too big, and you were the only thing standing between it and disaster.

KELZU

We're not still talking about the banshee here, are we?

HUK

Sometimes I think we've gotten too good at being old.

KELZU

Speak for yourself. I've never been good at it.

HUK

You know what I mean. All this remembering. All these stories. Maybe we've been looking back so hard that we've forgotten there might still be a few stories ahead.

KELZU

What are you on about, man?

HUK

I'm just saying—Sunnywood doesn't feel like a retirement home anymore. Not lately.

KELZU

It doesn't...? Should we perhaps have this conversation off-air, Huk?

HUK

Maybe next week, we could talk about something else. Something newer.

[KS-01 begins softly playing the outro music]

THE MOUSE PROBLEM

Poppy stood at the bottom of a tree-lined driveway, staring at a small cottage in the distance.

She had no clue, if she was honest, whether she was at the right house. She squinted against the sun. It had to be the place—the next one was two hills over, and she was not climbing any more fences.

There were limits, even to *her* optimism.

She wondered, not for the first time that afternoon, if she should've brought a weapon. Not a big, thumping one—just something small. Something reassuring.

But then again, what would she do with it? She was here to see a kid. Not some wicked old hag. A toddler. *Just* a toddler.

It's just that this one had a knack for bringing things back from the dead and controlling them.

Poppy sighed. That didn't make her feel better at all.

She chewed her lip, steadied her nerves, and started down the drive. Like everything in the Totswolds, it was perfectly kept—all brambles and stacked-stone fences, old oaks, and green fields spiralling in every direction.

A rabbit crossed the path ahead. It stopped and sniffed the air.

Its eyes, Poppy noticed, were milky white. There was a gaping hole in its belly, with bits of ribcage showing through.

At least she had the right place. Not a comforting thought.

Maybe she should have brought someone. Maybe she should've listened to Huk. But she'd waited all day for this. Helped Hiro clean the kitchen. Supervised arts and crafts—which was really just listening to Huk shout at a canvas for not looking any good and hearing Granny mutter about how dreadful the knitting pattern was —whilst Matron locked herself in the office to do whatever it was that Matron did. Then finally, her free time arrived.

And now, here she was.

Standing in front of a charming—if slightly tragic—cottage.

There was the sound of footsteps, both heavy and light.

There was laughter and shouting.

Poppy waited. Obviously, they were a little busy.

She stepped back and peered through the window.

The cottage was an utter mess, toys and clothes strewn everywhere; beyond the lounge, she spotted a kitchen where dirty dishes teetered in stacks that defied common sense. She knocked again.

'It's open!' a man shouted. 'Just—just come in!'

Poppy took a breath. Right. Here goes nothing. First proper adventure. First one alone, anyway.

She really should've brought a knife. Why hadn't she brought a knife?

She pushed open the door.

The smell hit her like a punch. Her eyes watered. Her throat burned.

Rot. Covered, hopelessly, with lavender and incense.

'Fucking hell,' she coughed, pinching her nose. 'Hello?'

A man—surprisingly young—popped his head into the hallway. He frowned at her. His hair was a mop of chaos, and the bags under his eyes were deep enough to store groceries.

'You're not from the church, are you?' he asked. 'I don't have the energy for religion today.'

'No. I'm here about the job.'

She pulled a crumpled piece of parchment from her back pocket and flattened it.

He stared at her like she'd grown another head.

'The one about your kid?' she said.

A burst of laughter echoed through the house. A child ran past him, down the hallway and out the back door—followed by a small army of dead mice. Some were complete skeletons. Some still had scraggly fur and sloughing flesh.

Poppy felt... slightly better about the smell. At least it was mice and not people.

'You're seriously here about the job?'

She nodded. Held out her hand. 'I'm Poppy.'

'I'm Markus. And that monster—'

He shouted the last bit. It made her jump. But he was grinning, and the child burst into even louder giggles.

'That monster is Janey,' Markus added. Then, more serious: 'You're not here to kill her, are you?'

'What? No!'

'You'd be surprised how often that happens. Want a cup of tea?'

He led her into the kitchen, then paused in dismay. It really was a disaster zone—towers of dishes everywhere.

At least he looked mildly embarrassed, thought Poppy.

'Full disclosure,' he said. 'We're out of cups. Been using bowls. And if I'm being honest, I don't know why we don't use bowls more often. They fit more.'

'What happens when you run out of bowls?'

'I try not to think that far ahead.'

He tripped on a toy and started rummaging through cupboards all at once. If Poppy didn't feel so sorry for him, she might've laughed.

He was very clearly in over his head and had been for quite some time. The problem with that, she thought, is that one day treading water starts to feel impossible, and the moment you stop: you drown. She knew that feeling. It was what had driven her here in the first place.

'I'll probably move on to shoes or buckets,' he said. 'Cross that bridge when I come to it.'

He glanced out the kitchen window. 'Oh bugger.'

And then he was gone—sprinting outside.

'Be right back!' he shouted. 'She's in a tree. No idea how a five-year-old gets up a tree that fast.'

Poppy watched him vanish down the garden.

Janey was indeed up a tree—a big old oak. She looked delighted up there, teddy in one hand, a dead mouse on her shoulder, and another perched on her head.

Poppy grimaced. The kitchen reminded her of Hiro's—post-cleaner decapitation.

She found two filthy mugs with mould in them, scrubbed them out, and popped the kettle on.

She would not drink tea out of a bowl, and this man would not be reduced to shoes and buckets. Not on her watch.

By the time Markus returned, Janey was crying on his hip.

Poppy had made tea, found a tin of semi-edible biscuits, and even cleared the table.

Markus stared at her like she'd conjured it from thin air.

'Is it too early to say you're hired? You're hired. Please take the job. What was your name again?'

'Poppy.'

'Please, Poppy,' he said, bouncing Janey gently.

Janey blinked at her with burning curiosity.

It occurred to Poppy that people handed out jobs far too easily in this part of the world. First Matron, and now Markus.

She narrowed her eyes.

'Say please, Poppy,' said Markus.

Janey grinned a gap-toothed grin. 'Please, Hoppy.'

'I need help,' said Markus. 'Serious help. I can't do this on my own. I've tried, and I'm awful at it. If we keep going like this, she'll end up raising herself from the dead.'

Poppy sipped her tea. 'She seems happy enough. You can't be that bad at it.'

'She's five. All five-year-olds are happy. But she won't be five forever.'

Poppy looked at Janey. The girl was spectacularly cheerful. She clung to her father's thumb and watched intently as her skeleton mouse scampered across the table to steal her a biscuit.

'How long has she been able to do this?'

'The whole reanimate the dead thing?'

'I was going to say steal biscuits with her skeleton friend, but, yes.'

Markus grinned. 'Oh, she's an accomplished thief.'

Janey laughed—a glorious back-of-the-throat giggle.

'I'm a really really goooood feef.'

'But just this last year,' Markus said, 'she's gotten better at it. The thieving and the necromancy.'

'Anything bigger than a rabbit?'

'Well, yes. But it doesn't last. Anything bigger than a dog, she can only hold for a minute or two. Smaller things—her mice—those stick around. They only stop when she sleeps.'

Poppy tried to think of what else she should ask. But she didn't know much about kids, even less about magical necromancing ones.

She glanced around the room.

'Does she still shit herself?'

Because frankly, that might be the dealbreaker. She could raise an army of zombies for Poppy and Huk to practise sword drills on, but if she was still doing surprise shits? Well, that changed the game.

'She's basically toilet-trained,' said Markus.

'Define basically.'

'We all make mistakes now and then, don't we?'

'How often is now and then?'

'You know, most people focus on the necromancy part.'

Poppy shrugged. Markus smiled. Janey reached for another biscuit.

Her mostly skeletal mouse ran across the table toward Poppy. It climbed up her arm, heading for her neck.

She froze.

It was fine. It was *so* fine.

She wanted to say she wasn't afraid of mice—not even undead ones—but there was something about one climbing under your shirt that made you want to fling yourself through a window screaming.

It was Trevor-levels of discomfort.

She breathed deeply.

She would not run.

She would not panic.

'Janey,' she said, 'could you tell Mr Mouse to get off my shoulder?'

Janey giggled. 'He's just saying hi!'

Poppy took a steadying breath.

'Janey,' said Markus, more firmly.

But it was too late. The mouse scuttled under her collar, and all reason left her. It triggered something deep, something primal. That ancient part of the brain that said: you're being crawled on and you will die screaming unless you burn everything down and move to the sea.

Poppy screamed, tore off her shirt, and ran shrieking into the garden. She flailed wildly, hitting at her back, as if shouting at invisible demons.

Janey's laughter followed her, unstoppable and tear-inducing.

Poppy finally stopped by the hedgerow, panting. Markus jogged up behind her and handed her the shirt.

She tried, with great effort, to recover some dignity.

'Thank you.'

She slipped it on. Breathed.

'It's on backwards,' Markus said.

'I know *that*. I was hoping you wouldn't notice.'

She shoved her arm inside the collar, wriggling to fix it. She couldn't quite meet his eyes.

And still, despite everything—even the screaming, even the shirt—it didn't feel like failure. It felt like a start.

'I can only do Mondays, Wednesdays, and Sundays,' she muttered. 'Half a day on Sundays. Three hours on the others.'

'Wait—you'll do it? Even after... whatever just happened?'

'I work at Sunnywood House. You'll need to bring her there.'

'The old people's home?'

'Is that a problem?'

'No. Not at all.'

'I'll see you Sunday, then,' said Poppy.

AN UNSCHEDULED PROMOTION

Poppy fell onto her bed with an exhausted sigh. It had turned out to be one hell of a day, and she had the blisters to prove it. Ones the size of coins on her feet. She'd had to run back from the necromancer's house. The mice crawling under her shirt incident had chewed up more time than she'd allowed, and with what had happened to the cleaner, it felt like pushing her luck to be late to the dinner shift. The mailbox had even chased her up the driveway—in solidarity, she liked to imagine, for the rush she was in.

Her boots thudded to the floor. The room was small, clean, and most importantly, hers. One window cracked open to the evening breeze. A book on the nightstand she hadn't touched in days. A towel half-draped over the chair. A life she was still getting used to.

She rolled onto her back and looked up at the ceiling. Poppy groaned. She was trying very hard not to think about what had happened, and, as was usually the case, it became all she could think about. Her cheeks burned, and if she closed her eyes, she could see it pure as day: the way she'd run around that poor man's backyard, practically half-naked and shouting like a maniac. It was hard to believe that very morning she'd helped Hiro hide the body of a cleaner. It felt like an eternity had passed since then.

She closed her tired eyes and woke, it seemed, hours later to the faint but noticeable sound of ink being scratched across parchment. Poppy found her timetable was arranging itself: writing appearing, letter by letter. Her night off, it seemed, had changed.

There was a knock on Poppy's door.

She got up and opened it.

'Something has come up,' said Matron. She was dressed as if she were planning to walk for miles—or vanish entirely. Long cloak, raincoat, boots polished. The bag over her shoulder bulged like it had been packed for days.

It wasn't even raining.

She looked like she was leaving on a journey, or fleeing in the middle of the night — and it was impossible to tell which.

'I'm going to be indisposed, I'm afraid. I need you to do the rounds tonight.'

'Is everything alright, Matron?' Poppy frowned, her eyes still half-closed with sleep. 'You look worried.'

'That's just how I look. Now, everything's where it always is. You'll be okay, I trust?'

'Hang on, you're leaving me here alone... and in charge?'

'Certainly not. And unless all the residents have up and left—in which case, lucky you—but the last time I checked, they hadn't. So you won't be alone.'

Matron had already turned and was heading for the stairs.

Poppy chased after her. 'I meant alone with *them*.'

'You'll be fine. I've been watching you this past week, and you have what it takes. I'm sure of it.'

'I haven't even done the night shift before. I wouldn't know where to start.'

'There's no time to learn like the present, Poppy. I've left you instructions in your manual. They should finish scribbling across within the next ten minutes.'

Poppy took the small pocket-sized book from her back pocket. She flicked through it, and sure enough, a new page titled *Night-Shift Duties and Instructions* was being hastily scratched across it.

'Are you sure everything is alright?'

Matron was wrapping a scarf around her neck, and she suddenly had a briefcase in her hands along with her bag.

'Where are you going?'

'Don't forget to take Bernard with you. It's good for him to stretch his legs, and it won't hurt him to patrol the house with you. He is supposed to be guarding the place, after all.'

'You haven't answered my question.'

Matron grimaced at her. 'Good luck, Poppy. You'll do well, I think.'

'Well, now you're starting to scare me. You make it sound like you're not coming back.'

Matron smiled then—not at Poppy, but at something behind her. A wide grin of pure relief.

And then she was gone.

Suddenly. Viciously. In a magical kind of way. One moment she was there, and the next she was gone with a strange kind of snap.

Poppy had, of course, heard of people with the talent to do this. But she'd never seen it happen. And without any warning, it was a bizarre and discombobulating experience.

She looked at the spot where Matron had been and noticed there was a faint crack in the air, the kind you'd see if you threw a rock at a window. But it wasn't just visible—it felt wrong. The space around it pulsed faintly, as if it were holding its breath. Dust drifted upward instead of down. The floor beneath her feet felt ever so slightly... softer than it should.

Poppy ran her hand through it, and it felt warm and tingly.

'Matron?' she whispered. There was no answer.

She put her ear to the crack. It was slowly mending, snapping back together. She could hear Matron laughing through it, faintly.

Poppy sighed. She thought it was one hell of a time for Matron to develop some humour. Because that had to be it. There was no other explanation for it. She was making a joke, and she'd be back by morning.

That's what Poppy told herself, because the alternative was too absurd, too ridiculous and too downright terrifying to be true.

She turned to the staircase, to the yawning dark of the dining hall and the quiet kitchens beyond. The air felt different now. Thicker. Like the house had noticed Matron was gone, and was watching to see what happened next.

Poppy suddenly felt like a very small person in a very big house.

BEDTIME PROTOCOL

It was bitterly cold outside, the air sharp with the promise of snow. Frost glittered across the stone steps like crushed glass, and the air burned in her nose with that dry, metallic tang that meant snow was coming. Poppy hugged her arms to her chest.

'Go on,' she said, shivering. 'You've got to pee first, and then we can head back inside.'

Bernard whined. The dragon looked up at her imploringly, eyes as wide as tea saucers.

An owl hooted somewhere in the dark. A sudden gust stole her breath.

'Buggering hell,' she gasped.

She glanced at Bernard. He sat down, head between his paws, clearly having no intention of going.

'Oh, fine,' said Poppy. 'But if we go inside and you pee on the rug, so help me—'

The dragon turned and launched into a kind of half-sprint, half-flight—wings flapping, claws skittering, his back end outpacing the front. He bowled straight past her and disappeared through the front door like a furry cannonball.

The cold had followed them in, curling under doors and through window panes. She thought she ought to go about lighting the fires, but she didn't even know where to start with that.

Bernard circled her legs, and Poppy looked at her manual.

'First up, we've got to make sure Huk takes his medicine, apparently.'

Bernard bounded off up the stairs toward Huk's room. He knew the routine, it seemed.

She knocked, but there was no answer—fair enough, given the hour. It was so late, it was nearly early. Why had Matron left it so late? Poppy's stomach churned again.

Bernard scratched at the door to be let in. She opened it, and he squeezed through, bounding around Huk's room in search of him.

He wasn't asleep in bed, but rather in his armchair, head lolled back, greatsword across his lap, cleaning cloth dangling from his hand.

Poppy had never been in Huk's room before, and a small part of her enjoyed looking around.

The mantelpiece sagged slightly under the weight of odds and ends—a life distilled into trophies, trinkets, and things too strange to throw away. A clockwork beetle twitched once before playing dead. A broken compass lay beside it, its needle spinning aimlessly as if still trying to find the way home. Then there was a stick, ordinary but for the shock of bright green hair tied around it. All things Poppy intended to ask about someday—or maybe Kelzu would tell her on the radio, if he ever came back.

She turned down the bed and unfolded a blanket.

'How'd it go?' said Huk.

Poppy jumped with fright. 'I thought you were asleep.'

'I was, until this idiot licked my face. He's lucky I didn't kill him. Reflexes and all that.'

'Oh, I'm sure,' said Poppy. 'Get back, Bernard, or he'll have your head on a plaque.'

'He wouldn't mount well. Snout's too skinny. He'd look ridiculous. Help me up, won't you? My knees are sleepy.'

Poppy took Huk's greatsword and propped it in its sheath beside the laundry basket, next to an umbrella stand, a fishing rod, and what looked suspiciously like a narwhal tusk.

She helped him up from the chair and was surprised by the frail lightness of him.

'Well, go on then,' said Huk, easing himself into bed. 'How'd it go with the kid?'

'So you are interested, then?'

'I never said I wasn't. Just that it sounded an awful lot like babysitting.'

'Well, the babysitting starts in a few days. Markus—the dad—will bring her around on Sunday. Do you know she has an army of dead mice?'

'Of course she does. Be dead dogs next. You've got to work your way up. And then what do you know—you can say you once looked after the dreaded necromancer of Upper Susshingham.'

'I think you'll like her,' said Poppy. She sat down on the corner of the bed. Bernard jumped up beside her.

'Probably will, yes.' Huk gave her a side-eye. 'Why are you here anyway? Normally, it's the boss-lady tucking me in and yamming medicine down my throat.'

'She's gone,' said Poppy.

'What?'

'Yeah. It was strange. Honestly, I'm hoping she's just off on a date or something, and she'll be back by morning.'

'And I'm a two-hundred-year-old gnome,' said Huk. 'On a date. But no, really—where is she?'

'Gone,' Poppy repeated. 'Didn't say where to. She took a little briefcase and magicked herself out of here. Left a crack in the air that felt like pins and needles. I could hear her laughing through it. Socks on or off for bed?'

'Off, please. She took a briefcase, you say?'

'Mm. And a bag.' Poppy tried not to look directly at Huk's feet. They made her feel a little ill. It seemed his otherwise subtle half-orc features had all hidden themselves in his toes.

She threw the blankets over him and plumped the pillows.

'Does she go away often?'

'Never,' said Huk. He shrugged. 'Not once. Hardly even goes into town.'

The knot of dread pulled tighter inside Poppy's chest.

A silence settled. Even Bernard stopped sniffing Huk's slippers.

'She'll be back by morning, though,' said Poppy, firmly. As if saying it aloud might make it true.

'Now, I'm supposed to lock you in, apparently?'

Huk grinned proudly. 'She's not forgiven me for punching her favourite vase, I don't think.'

Poppy checked the manual. 'Doesn't say anything about a vase. What it does say—and I quote—is: "He'll murder you and everyone in this house in his sleep if you give him half the chance."'

Huk looked extremely pleased with himself. 'Did she just?'

'So if it's all the same to you,' said Poppy, 'I'm locking the door.'

'Probably for the best.' Huk yawned.

Poppy coaxed Bernard out and locked the door behind them. She noticed, for the first time, there were two deadbolts: one into the floor, one into the jamb.

Matron had gone to great lengths to make sure Huk stayed put. That knot in her stomach twisted tighter. She locked both. Just to be safe.

'You know,' Huk called through the door, 'if I really wanted to, I could just kick it all down.'

'Go to sleep.'

'Goodnight, Poppy.'

Poppy smiled to herself. 'Goodnight, Huk.'

THE SMALL PRINT

Granny Grack's door was painted lilac with little illustrations of flowers along the bottom. Bernard scratched at it impatiently.

'Come in, love,' said Granny.

Poppy pushed open the door, and Bernard burst in. His tail wagged furiously, and steam billowed from his nostrils in his excitement. Granny's room, unlike Huk's, could not have been further from what you'd expect of a retired adventurer. There were no souvenirs from epic battles past or knick-knacks from far-off distant lands; instead, there were family portraits and crystal-etched memory-stones. There were doilies and shelves lined with books—all of them, it seemed, romance. In fact, the only thing that might have looked remotely out of the ordinary was a brass clockwork badger, curled up on its very own table.

'What's with the badger?'

'It makes tea,' said Granny. She looked over her glasses at Poppy and closed her book. 'Would you like to see it in action?'

'No, not really.' Poppy sat down on the end of Granny's bed.

She kept replaying Matron disappearing on a loop. She couldn't stop that laugh from echoing in her head. 'Why not just make your own tea?'

'Why would I when I've got a badger to do it for me?'

'Yeah, fair point,' said Poppy, distantly.

Bernard jumped up onto the bed and nuzzled into Granny, who was still awake, sitting up and reading a book despite the hour.

'If only dragons were all like you, Bernie.' She scratched under his chin. 'Makes you feel a little guilty, really.'

'Guilty?'

'Mmm, all the dragon-slaying. The gold-robbing. The treasure-stealing.'

'How many dragons have you killed?'

'A few.'

'More or less than ten?'

Granny sighed. 'Look, my dear, if there was a dragon in a mountain, I was on it. They didn't stand a chance. I was relentless. For all the good it did me—can't even afford a fallen star now.' She looked at Bernard. 'But they were all big and greedy and vicious bastards. Not you. Nooo, not *youuuu*. You only keep buttons.'

Bernard made a kind of purring noise Poppy hadn't heard before and pushed his head into Granny's lap.

'It says here I'm supposed to rub some Pain-Away ointment into your elbows, knees and ankles. You don't really want me to do that, do you?'

'She's gone then?'

Poppy looked up from her manual. 'Matron?'

'She finally took off?'

'Well—yes. She teleported or something. Disappeared clean out of sight.'

'She never.'

'Yeah. Left a crack in the air and all,' said Poppy. 'How'd you know that? Did she say something to you?'

'No, she bloody did not. But something has been up with that woman ever since she employed the likes of you.'

'She'll be back, though,' said Poppy. 'Won't she?' She was hoping the more she said it out loud, the more she'd believe it, and the more true it would be. Because the alternative—of being left entirely alone in a big house with these only sometimes likeable psychos—was downright terrifying. 'Personally, I reckon she's off on a date.'

Granny got up and went to the windows. She drew aside her curtains. 'Teleported, you say?'

'I don't know if it's called that. But she was there one second and gone the next.'

Granny laughed, bitterly to herself. 'Someone's been rummaging around in my potions, I think.'

'What?'

'Off on a date, you reckon?'

Poppy shrugged. She'd gone back to reading her manual. It had stopped scribbling itself with directions now. 'Yeah. Huk doesn't think so, but I think Matron could be quite promiscuous, behind closed doors.'

'Oh, I bet,' said Granny.

Poppy held up the manual. 'She doesn't really expect me to read Alfred a bedtime story, does she? He's a full-grown man. More than that. He's a dead one. He's gone past full-grown and into overripe or something.'

'Poppy,' said Granny, 'come here and tell me if you think this is someone off on a date.'

Poppy got up and went to the window.

'There,' said Granny. 'Can you see her? Running off, just down there. The mailbox is chasing her.'

'Well then, what did she teleport off for?' said Poppy. It seemed an awful lot of work, to still have to run—and not to mention it was a waste of some good magic.

'What *is* she up to?' muttered Granny.

The mailbox had got her bag, and they watched as she engaged in a brutal game of tug-of-war. She kicked the mailbox in the head, snatched her bag, and ran off. She looked like she was still laughing. Poppy's stomach sank to her shoes.

'Oh, gods. She's not coming back, is she?'

Granny shook her head. She looked at Poppy over the top of her glasses.

Poppy realised, slowly and with a mounting sense of pure dread, that Granny was fully dressed, and her expression had shifted into one of anger.

'Do you normally go to bed in your clothes?' asked Poppy.

'No, dear, I do not.'

She left the window and headed for the hallway. 'Come on, we have some work to do.'

'I was doing my work,' Poppy muttered to herself.

'You can rub some ointment on my bunions and tell Alfred a bedtime story later.'

They were standing in front of Matron's office door. Granny had been twisting the doorknob and shoving her body against it with a surprising amount of gusto.

'This is ridiculous,' said Poppy.

Granny nodded. 'I know. If only Kelzu would hurry up and get back. He was always good at this kind of thing.' She rammed her shoulder into the door again. 'Curse that bloody gnome.'

Poppy turned and headed off, back down the hallway towards the stairs.

'Where are you going?' called Granny.

'To go and get Matron back. I'll spear tackle her if I have to. Beg her if that doesn't work.'

'Don't be daft, girl,' said Granny. 'She's not welcome back here, at any rate. And what's more, if we could get this bloody door open, I bet you'd find the reason she's sneaking off in the dead of night.'

Poppy thought the truth of the matter was this: Matron was just beyond fed up with dealing with them. You could only do a job like this for so long before it crushed your sanity or sent you on a granny-bashing frenzy.

'Get back here,' said Granny.

Poppy ignored her. She'd liked the idea of this job when someone else had shouldered all the responsibility. But to be left here alone with them all—whether they were legendary retired adventurers or not—it would be the end of her life as she knew it. It wasn't so bad, now. While they were still capable of showering and feeding themselves. But old people go full circle eventually, and then what do you know, you're wishing they'd worn a nappy so that you didn't have to wash the shit from their trousers. Like hell she was being left here alone with them. She'd run for the hills too, if it came to that.

'Don't you turn your back on me, young lady,' growled Granny.

Poppy took the stairs two at a time.

'Usually that works,' she heard Granny sigh. 'Fine, I'll teach you magic, just get back here.'

Poppy stopped. How the hell did she know she'd wanted magic lessons? She'd thought about asking, but hadn't worked up the courage yet.

'Hiro said you might ask. He told me not to laugh at you when you did. I'll teach you if you stay. We do need someone here, now that she's gone. I can't feed Trevor, give Huk his medicine and pay the bills. I didn't live my life the way I did to end it like that.'

Poppy walked back up the staircase and peered around the corner at Granny. 'You'll teach me?'

'That's what I said, wasn't it?'

'Not just useless illusions. I want to learn the good stuff. The shrinking spells. The teleportation potions. The indestructible skin charms. That kind of stuff. You'll teach me that stuff? Adventuring stuff?'

Granny sighed and banged her head against Matron's door. 'Fine. Yes. Whatever you want, just get back here and help me open this bloody door.'

Poppy couldn't believe she was negotiating for a magic tuition with someone who smelled faintly of sherry and mothballs. But gods, she wanted it. She passed Granny Grack the key Matron had given her. It was supposed to be a master key, so there was every chance it would open her office too.

Granny took it with a look of pure incredulity.

The door unlocked.

'You had this the entire time?'

Poppy nodded. 'Honestly, though. Why can't you be like Huk: I tucked him in and then locked his door, and that was it. Just a simple 'Goodnight, Poppy.''

'Huk's not in his room,' said Granny.

'Yes, he is. I locked him in there.'

Granny raised her eyebrows. 'I'm not saying you didn't. But he's not in there anymore. He's busy trying to kill Trevor on the third floor.'

'What? Why?'

'Trying to prove he's still got it, or some such rot. I don't know, and frankly, I don't care. I've babysat those fools for far too long.'

'He'll just get himself hurt—'

'Yes, and it'll serve him right. Now forget about him.' Granny went and sat behind Matron's desk. She started rummaging through papers. 'We've got enough of our own to be getting on with. Gods, she's got shit everywhere.'

Poppy watched Granny flick through envelope after envelope, some of them stamped with big red warnings.

'Well, don't just stand there, girl. Help.'

'I'm not sure what it is we're doing, exactly,' said Poppy. She felt, suddenly, like a child left alone with a crazy aunt. She wanted Matron back. Now.

'I told you, she was up to something. I'm sure of it.'

Poppy sighed. She flicked through some unopened letters. They were all overdue bills. There would have to be a hundred of them, at least. And these were just the ones on the desk.

'Granny?' Poppy swallowed. 'I think Sunnywood might be broke.'

Granny laughed. 'No, Poppy. It most certainly is not.'

'No, really.' Poppy held up a handful of unpaid, overdue bills. The interest alone was staggering. 'She's not been paying your bills.'

Granny snatched the letters from Poppy and looked them over. 'Well, I'll be. What the fuck is she doing?'

They began to look through the drawers. Stuffed so full with letters and papers that they were almost impossibly heavy to pull out.

'Oh,' said Granny. She held a folder open, frowning.

'What?' said Poppy.

'She saw you coming a mile off, my dear.'

'Me?'

Granny passed Poppy the folder. It was Poppy's employment contract.

'So what?'

'She's made you the owner,' said Granny, seriously.

Poppy felt her lungs forget how to breathe. Her tongue went dry.

'The owner?'

'You're doing that thing again, where you just repeat everything someone says to you. It's not very endearing. On the contrary, it's rather grating.'

Poppy pored over the contract again. But it was all troll-ish, and she could barely manage one language, let alone two. Truth be told, she barely remembered signing it. 'What does this mean?'

'It means you're the new owner and chief caretaker of Sunnywood House, and with that ownership, you've taken on any and all of its debt. In short, Poppy, dearest: you're a wee bit fucked.'

Poppy stared at the folder. Her name was right there, big as you like.

She wasn't sure when exactly it had happened, but somehow—somewhere between a tea break and an undead mouse—she'd become the new Matron and the old one was busy running away.

And this is around the point where Poppy will look back and think, I should've known better. And honestly? She should have. But that's the trouble with hope: it makes you run headfirst into things you'd avoid if you had any sense at all.

THE THIRD FLOOR

On the third floor, behind a door with a sign that said, DO NOT OPEN UNDER ANY CIRCUMSTANCES, a sword glowed in the dark.

Huk trod carefully.

His left knee kept clicking, and it sounded so bloody loud, alone and in the dark. He wished it would stop: he didn't want arthritis to be the reason a giant spider ate him.

The third floor was unrecognisable. Trevor had well and truly claimed it as his own. There were deep gouges in the floorboards and great sweeping webs where the walls ought to be.

There was a faint, terrifying clicking noise, and then eight eyes in the dark reflected Huk back at himself: great-sword in hand.

He thought to himself: I really ought to get some glasses.

'There you are, you big bastard.'

Huk swung the sword.

～

Granny was sitting back in Matron's chair, feet up on her desk, as she opened letter after letter. Poppy hadn't stopped staring at the contract. She didn't know where to start. It all looked like K's and S's that somehow swooped across and down on themselves. It was strange, she thought, to hold something that was as horribly life-changing as this contract, and to not be able to read a word of it.

'You're sure that's what it says?' repeated Poppy.

'I don't believe this,' said Granny. She sat up and held a piece of parchment to the rune-light. 'We're not just in debt. We're fucking broke! BROKE-broke. The old bitch has been running us dry.' She held the letter up for Poppy to see and then shoved it in her pocket angrily before she even got the chance to. 'I knew it, mark my words, Poppy. I knew it. From the moment she wouldn't get me that fallen star, I thought to myself, I did, that something is going on here.'

'We should have chased her,' said Poppy, dumbly. She sat down. 'I feel worse than the time I got kidnapped by a swarm of pixies.'

'It's no use,' said Granny. 'She'll have prepared for a chase, at any rate. And I wouldn't give her the satisfaction. And never, ever, under any circumstances, reveal to ANYONE that you were kidnapped by pixies, Poppy. You're the head caretaker and Matron of Sunnywood now, and I won't allow you to sully our name and your title with something like that getting out. Is that understood?'

Poppy started to cry.

'Don't,' said Granny, sternly. 'I won't have it.'

There was a loud, thunderous crash above them. The ceiling shook with the force of it, and dust spiralled down.

Granny and Poppy both looked at one another.

'Huk?' said Poppy.

They both scrambled out of Matron's office for the third floor.

~

But it wasn't Huk and his attempts to kill Trevor that had caused the noise. Kelzu had tried to park his wagon in his room again. But the problem was: he'd missed. Now his wagon was half in the hallway and half inside his room, where it ought to be.

K.S. lumbered out of the wagon into the hallway.

The automaton looked a little worse for wear than when he'd left Sunnywood: his metal plating no longer shiny, but instead etched and tarnished.

'It would appear,' said the automaton, sounding strangely exhausted, 'that you've parked in the middle of the wall and the hallway.'

Kelzu ducked his head out of the wagon. He looked a tad more unhinged than usual: his hair messier, his eyes wider, his grin chaotic and large. He made an oops face and ducked back inside the wagon. His voice, when he spoke, was strangely distant inside its stretched-out space. 'I'll try and reverse it in. K.S., tell me when to stop, won't you?'

'I do not think that's a good idea, master. You have an 8.27 percent chance of doing so successfully.'

But Kelzu did not listen, nor had he ever really listened—and especially not to K.S. The wagon began to shift, pulling into itself, its shape becoming a slow but somehow constant blur until it was no longer half inside the hallway but rather half outside of it.

The wagon became tangible again, and if you'd been standing outside in the garden, you would have seen a most peculiar sight. The outside of Sunnywood House looked like a wagon had somehow crashed into its second floor.

K.S. flinched. 'My prediction processes might need fine-tuning. 8.27 percent did not take into account the fact that you might drive in the complete opposite direction of which you had originally intended.'

Kelzu ducked his head out of the wagon's door once more. 'Oh, how fantastic,' he said. He did not sound as if he meant it.

~

Huk's greatsword missed Trevor altogether and lodged itself in the wall. Something he'd done on purpose; not that anyone would believe him, he was sure. Behind Trevor, there were yet more giant spiders. But they were young ones, though, so only as big as small dogs.

The hundred collective eyes were black and wide with fear.

They were scared, he realised.

And then it clicked.

Trevor was no Trevor at all. He was no male giant spider. He was a she. And she was a mother. And this mother was furious.

Huk held up his hands. 'Now, look here, Trevor,' he swallowed. 'Sorry, Trevor doesn't really work anymore, does it? Trevorina, perhaps?'

The giant spider took one thunderingly heavy step towards him.

It remained to be seen if this move was a warning or a precursor to violence.

'No?' breathed Huk. 'I agree. Terrible name. Trevonar? No, gods, alright. You can stop drooling venom at me; it's not a good look, Miss Trevor. Now look here, it's all just been a bit of a misunderstanding, yeah? You've had babies, beautiful little darlings, look at them. I didn't know you could do that without, you know, a daddy spider and well, I... if we'd known you were pregnant, we'd have thrown you a baby shower and—'

Huk turned and bolted—as fast as his arthritic knees would carry him. Miss Trevor launched after him, legs clicking loudly against the hardwood floors. Her children—young and quicker and more excitable—sprinted alongside Huk across the floor and the walls and the ceiling. Everywhere he looked, there was a spider with eight eyes looking back at him.

The thing was: if he'd known Trevor was a Miss Trevor—female giant spiders were infinitely more deadly when compared to the males—and a mother, no less, then he never would have snuck up there to chop off her head in the first place.

'Come on,' he shouted. 'Be reasonable.'

There was another loud crash then: this one shook the floor beneath him and knocked spiders from the ceiling and the walls. Giant bedsheet-sized cobwebs all dislodged, and a cloud of billowing dust swirled up around him.

Huk didn't know what was happening just yet, but he figured it had either saved his life or just ended it.

STUPID FUCKING STAIRS

Poppy was sprinting up the stairs when there was yet another crash that sent shockwaves through the house. She felt the floor beneath her feet tremble with its impact.

'Hold up, won't you? Does it look like I run?' Granny sighed, continuing to climb the stairs at her steady and slow pace. 'You shouldn't panic in an emergency, Poppy,' she shouted after her. 'Losing your head is a surefire way to lose your head.'

'Huk's probably already lost his,' Poppy shouted back. 'Bitten clean off by a giant spider. How the hell am I supposed to explain that to Matron?' She realised, as soon as she said it, that she probably would never have to explain anything to Matron ever again. Because apparently, *she* was Matron now. If she'd had the time, she would have vomited.

Alfred appeared through a wall, looking curious. 'Explain what to Matron?'

'OH, FUCK OFF, ALFRED!' shouted Poppy.

'Excuse her, love. She's a little stressed at the moment,' said Granny.

Kelzu walked around his wagon—the half that was still inside the hallway. He looked out the window and saw how the back of it was hanging in the air. 'Do you think if I just ducked in and went to bed, it would tip clean over?'

K.S. clambered toward Kelzu's side. They both tilted their heads together in contemplation, looking at the mess.

'You know, I'm unsure of how I would begin to calculate such risks, master. Without taking into account variables such as—'

Kelzu held up his hand and pinched his nose. He looked like he had a headache.

K.S. stopped speaking. 'This was one of your rhetorical questions?'

'Yeah. Sure. Why not?

'Perhaps alternative arrangements for bed should be made, just for tonight. We can reassess our options in the morning. I can compute alternative solutions while you sleep. Might I suggest asking Huk if he would share his bed?'

'No use,' muttered Kelzu. 'He'll still be mad at me.'

'Apologising has worked in the past.'

Kelzu sighed. 'Never tell a stubborn old half-orc he can't kill a giant spider, K.S.'

K.S. nodded. 'It is noted, master. I will not do so.'

Huk was running as fast as his knees would let him. He'd left his greatsword, Light-Bringer, twanging in the oak-panelled walls. Miss Trevor was behind him—and so were her dozen not-so-tiny babies.

Huk felt, for the first time in quite a long time, that he might die.

It didn't feel as thrilling as it once did. Maybe it was because he wasn't so sure he'd make it out of this alive. Of course, there were times, countless times, where that very thought had crossed his mind in the past. But this time felt different. He'd had himself to rely on back then—his strong and dependable body—and he'd had his friends. But this time he was alone. In front of him were stairs—so many stairs (and his knees! Gods, they were killing him!)—and behind him, well... he dared not look.

He stumbled down the first few stairs and wondered if it might be easier just to fall down the rest of them. 'Stupid fucking stairs.' His knees—gods, his knees—hurt so much. He had to take the steps one at a time. He didn't dare look behind himself. 'Stupid fucking knees. Stupid fucking spiders.'

He could hear Miss Trevor at the top of the stairs. She did what Huk now considered to be her roar—a strange kind of terrifying clicking noise.

'I'm bloody trying here,' he shouted. 'Who the shitting hell puts stairs in a nursing home anyway? Honestly, it's borderline psychotic—'

Huk was knocked over, thrown full onto his face, into the stairs beneath him as the giant spiders began to slip and slide and fall down the polished staircase. He landed with a cheek-sliding groan along the shiny hardwood floors.

He looked up and saw feet.

Human feet.

INITIATE SHOPLIFTER PROTOCOL

Poppy reached the top of the stairs just as Huk tumbled down, hitting the floor at her feet with a groan. Trevor loomed above them, looking about as pissed off as a giant spider possibly could. And then something behind him moved.

Then more of it.

Poppy stared, frozen. 'There's more than one Trevor,' she whispered. 'Why is there more than one Trevor?'

Huk groaned, 'It's *Miss* Trevor, and Miss Trevor has kids.' He tried to sit up but failed, then grabbed Poppy's ankle. 'Help me up, kid.'

Poppy didn't look away from the spiders. 'We should run. Right?'

'It's a bit hard to run when I can't even get up off the bloody ground.'

Kelzu and K.S. half-jogged, half-walked down the hallway towards them.

'What's going on?' shouted Kelzu.

'You're back?' said Huk. 'What are you doing back?'

'That's a lot of kids,' said Poppy, starting to whimper. 'Why's she got so many kids?'

'It's my home,' said Kelzu. 'I've got to come back at some point.'

'Home's where you park it, though. And you could park it anywhere.'

'Don't be like that, Huk.'

'No, but seriously, that's an absurd amount of spiders,' said Poppy.

Kelzu looked up the stairs. He didn't step back in fear, but moved forward with far too much purpose. 'BAD TREVOR,' he shouted. 'BAD! Get back to your floor, now! GO ON! GET!'

There was a beat where Kelzu and the giant spider looked at one another—a moment of appraisal and analysis, as if they were sizing each other up.

Kelzu looked at Huk and Poppy. 'See, a few stern words, that's all it takes. He... well, she, she remembers who her master is.'

Trevor, who up until this point hadn't moved from her spot at the top of the stairs, clicked her fangs indignantly. Her two front legs raised in a fury, and then, all at once, she launched forward, headed towards them with her children following close behind.

'Fucking hell,' said Poppy. 'You've just pissed her off even more.'

Kelzu reached down, grabbed Huk under his arms, and tried to drag him away. 'Yes, well, it could have gone one of two ways, really.'

Poppy reached down and helped him drag Huk, who was squirming and struggling to stand. One of the baby giant spiders scuttled alongside the wall near them. Poppy screamed, almost face-to-face with it.

Behind them, at the end of the hall, Granny had just finished climbing the stairs. She looked exhausted. 'Hold on, I'm coming.' There was a flash of light behind them as Granny sent a blast of eldritch energy crackling through the air. The spider nearest Poppy fell to the floor with a sickening and heavy thud, its legs beginning to curl inwards as it died. 'Has anyone else mentioned how stupid stairs are?'

'Covered it in great depth,' said Huk.

Granny paused to catch her breath, resting against the railing. She raised her hand and sent another blast of purplish lightning towards a spider that had almost knocked Kelzu to the ground.

The shock of it had caused Kelzu to turn invisible. Because that was something he was capable of, apparently, thought Poppy. He appeared again, this time nearest Trevor, looking panicky and just as confused about the turning invisible as the rest of them were.

Huk sighed. 'Not again.'

'Kelzu, love, you might want to move,' said Granny.

Kelzu turned to look at Trevor, towering above him. He disappeared from sight the moment the spider slammed its front legs down toward him.

Granny sent another blast, and another, but the spiders seemed to be multiplying. The anger of seeing their brothers and sisters curling up and dying fed their ferocity and their speed. Huk had finally gotten himself upright, but without his sword, he was useless.

He looked around for something to use as a weapon. 'Give me your sword, kid.'

'Me?' said Poppy.

'Yes, give me your weapon, now.'

'I don't have a sword.'

Huk looked disgusted. 'What? Why not?'

Poppy didn't know what to say to that. Or rather, she had too many things to say to that and not the slightest idea of where to begin. Firstly, she felt that working in a nursing home for old people was reason enough not to carry a sword at all times. It wasn't like she'd been given the job, handed a sword and wished good luck. Which, in hindsight, should have been exactly what happened, and really, it should have been exactly her kind of thing. On paper, she wanted to be a sword-wielding type.

Kelzu appeared beside her out of thin air. He'd gone deathly pale and looked like he wanted to vomit.

'I can't stop it,' he said. 'It's really set in this time, I think I—'

But he was gone again.

'May I render any assistance?' asked K.S.

Granny nodded. 'Be my guest. Any more magic from me and I'll be on the floor.'

'How might I help, exactly?'

'Fucking off the spiders would be a good start,' said Huk. He was currently holding one against the wall by its two front legs.

'I am afraid my protocols forbid me from harming a living thing.'

Granny and Huk looked at one another and then at K.S.

They both started to laugh.

'Yes, very good,' said Huk. 'I'll hold this one still, you punch a hole in its head.'

'I am not sure why you are both laughing. Given the current situation, it does not seem the appropriate response.' K.S. turned to look at Poppy. She was hiding behind a potted plant. He looked, she thought, to be judging her. 'Has the caregiver administered your medicine correctly?'

'Has Kelzu been mucking around with your programming again?' Huk shot back.

'I have not undergone a system upgrade in the last eighteen months.'

Another spider jumped at Huk from halfway down the staircase, launching itself at him. He punched it square in the face. It landed with a squeal and sprinted off.

'He just punched a fucking spider,' whispered Poppy. She started to tremble. She hated herself for it, but she felt itchy inside and out at the sight of them, and her body was revolting against it. He just punched a fucking spider.

'What's the deal then?' shouted Huk. 'Help us with these bastards, won't you?'

Kelzu appeared once more, this time atop the staircase, where he stood petrified and quite, quite surrounded. 'K.S., initiate shoplifter protocol,' he shouted. 'These spiders are thieves, and they must be stopped.'

K.S.'s normally friendly-looking blue eye rotated, turning a bright, angry red. The automaton launched forward with a sudden speed and fury that made the cleaners look like mice. Poppy watched in a mix of horror and awe as the automaton straight up ripped a spider in half. He produced a blade from who knows where and became a blur of polished steel and red light, sending the spiders retreating to the safety of the third floor.

LIKE OLD TIMES

Eventually, they got Miss Trevor and what remained of her children back behind closed doors. They all sat in a collapsed heap, backs leaning against the door.

'Oh bugger,' said Huk.

'What is it?' said Granny.

'My greatsword's still in there.'

'Serves you right, I should think.'

'What were you thinking, exactly?' asked Poppy.

Huk continued to stare off into the distance, chewing his lip.

She nudged him.

'Oh, I don't know. That we'd get our third floor back.'

Kelzu appeared just in front of them. 'What a bloody night.' He sounded and looked beyond exhausted. He disappeared again.

Poppy frowned. 'Why does he keep doing that?'

'He can't help it. Happens when he's stressed. It's like the hiccups, really. You never know how long it's going to last.'

Kelzu reappeared in the middle of a goopy, disembodied spider. He groaned.

'You were thinking you'd prove you were still able to deal with a giant spider on your own. That's what you were thinking, wasn't it, Huklin Eldaruk,' said Granny.

Huk shrugged.

'Well, I've got news for you. You were never able to deal with giant spiders on your own.'

Huk fired up almost instantly at that. 'Yes, I bloody was. In the Barren-Below, I felled a dozen of these bastards in the time it took you to brew a cup of tea.'

Granny smiled. Poppy couldn't help but notice it was a sad smile. 'They were time-slowed, Huk. Kelzu turned the air as thick as mud, remember? All of our battles, all of our adventures, we got through them because we worked together. And all the times we split the party, went wandering off on our own, those were the times when it all went wrong.' Granny squeezed Huk's shoulder. 'So what if you can't swing your sword as easily as you once did, and your knees won't let you jump quite like they used to? I can't hurl anywhere near as many spells as I used to be able to. I've done three tonight, and I feel like I could sleep for a week. Don't be so bloody hard on yourself, you stupid bastard.'

Poppy watched them talk and listened. A familiar ache began to blossom inside her chest. What a life they had lived—and lived together, how it must feel to have others like that, who you knew so deeply through some of the scariest, darkest parts of your life to the lightest, most hilarious.

'And anyway, our battle isn't with Trevor. We've got more important things to deal with.'

Kelzu appeared in Huk's lap. Huk grabbed him firmly around the waist. 'I got you, mate, just you try phasing out of this grip.'

Kelzu gasped, the air squeezed from his lungs. But he smiled.

Granny looked at them all, her face dead serious.

They watched her, because she was like that—she had that sort of presence. When she spoke, you listened.

'Sunnywood is in trouble. Matron has run it into the ground, and she's left the mess in this one's name.' She nodded at Poppy.

'What do you mean it's in trouble?' said Kelzu. He stuttered in and out of existence, but Huk held firm, anchoring him. 'We've paid for our rooms until death. In Alfred's case, he's still got another century.'

'I thought it was an employment contract I was signing,' said Poppy, by way of explanation. They looked at her, almost as if remembering she was there amongst them.

'How far into the ground has she run it, exactly?' asked Kelzu.

'We only opened a handful of letters,' said Granny.

'There were hundreds more,' said Poppy. 'Almost all of them were bills.' And all that debt, she thought, was in my name now.

Life moved on a knife's edge, she was beginning to realise. One minute, you were broke, homeless, and hungry. Next, you had a personal chef and a mansion to call home, and you were yet somehow worse than broke. You were, to be perfectly honest, not so subtly fucked.

'It looks like we've got a new job lined up, boys,' said Granny.

Huk nodded.

Kelzu phased in and out of his grip again, but the teleporting was slowly coming to an end.

They got up together and made their way down the hallway towards their rooms. Poppy stopped when she saw half of a wagon hanging out of the wall.

She sighed. 'I don't even want to know.'

'I buggered up my reverse parking,' said Kelzu.

'He went forwards instead of backwards,' said K.S.

'Where'd you go this time anyway?' said Huk.

'I'll tell you in the morning. I ahh, don't suppose you'd have enough room in your bed for me tonight?'

Huk grinned. 'I suppose. Just like old times, aye. Oh—I forgot.' He took something out of his pocket. It was a brass clockwork contraption—one of Kelzu's inventions, Poppy had seen him working on at the dining table in between meals.

'You didn't,' said Kelzu.

'I did.'

'The whole thing?'

'I turned it on the moment I left my room and headed for the third floor.'

'What is it?' said Granny.

'A recorder,' said Kelzu.

Huk nodded. 'The radio show must go on, me'lad.'

Granny groaned. 'You'd think after all these years I'd be used to you two.'

Poppy stood there, awkwardly. She felt suddenly like the odd one out. A stranger in a family's home. 'I guess I'll see you all in the morning then.'

'Goodnight, love. And don't worry, I haven't forgotten about our little arrangement.'

Poppy smiled.

But perhaps, she thought, they wouldn't feel like strangers for long.

'What arrangement?' said Huk.

Granny shrugged. 'Magic lessons, of course. It was total bribery, but I figure if she's going to stay with us, she'd best learn anyway.' Granny looked at Poppy. 'And you do want to stay, don't you, dear?'

They all looked at Poppy then.

It wasn't at all how she'd imagined this week should have gone. But despite it all, it felt like a step in the right direction. The first step in the right direction she'd taken in quite a while.

She nodded.

'Right, well that settles it,' said Granny.

'Well, hang on a minute,' said Huk. 'Sod that. If she's going to be our Matron, then she should know how to protect herself. We'll get you a sword.'

Poppy grinned. 'I'd like that a lot.'

'Good. We'll start in the morning.' Huk elbowed Kelzu. The gnome grumbled and rubbed at his side. Huk elbowed him again.

'Oh, what?' said Kelzu.

Huk looked at Poppy, then back at Kelzu, meaningfully.

'Ohh, fine. I'll teach you some enchanting. You'll never be broke if you can make an ordinary thing a magical one.' Kelzu looked up at Huk. 'Are you happy now?'

Huk shook his head, and then they headed off together towards his room. They started to talk about the radio show and that night's battle with Miss Trevor and her babies, and how they would intersect the live recordings with their in-studio commentary. It was as if they'd never fought at all.

Poppy watched them all wander off to their rooms, one by one, leaving behind a quiet so thick it buzzed in her ears. Eventually, she padded to her own, too tired to think and too wired not to.

But sleep didn't come.

She lay on her back, staring at the ceiling. The room was still, the air warm, the bedsheets soft—but her thoughts refused to be quiet. They ran wild, biting at the edges of her brain.

Matron had left.

Not just for the evening. Not for a date or an errand or a drunken moonlight stroll. She'd gone. And somehow, impossibly, stupidly—Poppy was now the one in charge.

She thought about the bills. The creaking floors. The ghost who drank six cups of coffee a day without once remembering to say thank you. The giant spider, who was, ridiculously, the mother of hundreds of smaller, yet still thoroughly giant, spiders. She thought of Huk's knees. Granny's spells. Hiro's temper. The broken cleaner in the pantry.

She wasn't ready for this. Gods, she wasn't even remotely qualified for this.

A floorboard creaked. Then another.

A small shape appeared in the doorway.

Bernard.

He padded into her room without invitation, steam puffing softly from his nostrils. He leapt up onto the bed, turned in a slow circle, and flopped down heavily beside her.

She didn't tell him off. Didn't tell him to move.

She just lay there, frozen.

After a long while, she turned onto her side and whispered, 'Do you think she's coming back?'

Bernard gave a low, questioning trill.

Poppy sighed. 'I was worried you'd say that. Me neither, I'm afraid.'

Silence returned. The sort that's full of suffocating weight.

What if she couldn't do it? What if Granny dropped dead, or Trevor escaped again, or Kelzu never came back, and she was stuck here forever, trying to manage a house full of ancient weirdos and misplaced enchantments with no plan and no magic and no clue?

Poppy rolled onto her stomach and groaned into her pillow.

After a moment, Bernard shuffled closer and flopped his head over her feet.

It helped. Not much—but just enough and eventually, somewhere between worry and warmth, between panic and the faint scent of lavender shampoo on the pillow, Poppy slept. It wasn't peaceful. It wasn't perfect. But it was enough for one night.

EPISODE 6

Excerpt from the transcript of
The Sunnywood Signal.

Episode 6: *"Mother of the Year"*
Transcribed by KS-01.
Broadcast on The Upper Susshingham Radio 102.3EM

HUK

In the spirit of last week's episode, we've decided that instead of telling you all about past adventures, we might flash-forward and talk about what's been happening here and now. Today's headline: Trevor has given birth.

KELZU

To what can only be described as a medium-sized army. Now, listener, you might be wondering how, after all these years, we hadn't known that Trevor was a mother, or indeed even female, and to that I say, fair point, but you try getting a close enough look at a Giant

Spider to identify their sex. It's not so bloody easy, is it? And anyway, Giant Spiders aren't like your normal garden variety arachnid. They don't lay eggs in a silk sack or carry them round on their back. No. They have what we call a brooding chamber, which is a warm kind of pouch inside her abdomen, where she incubates the eggs.

HUK

I don't think anyone actually cares about this, Zu.

KELZU

'Course they do. And so, even if we had known Miss Trevor was pregnant, we had no way of knowing the due date. Giant Spiders live centuries, you see. So, twenty to thirty years is just a regular pregnancy term by comparison.

HUK

Had I known this before I stumbled into the third floor, sword in hand? No. No, I hadn't.

KELZU

Few things are more violent than a giant spider trying to protect her wee babies.

HUK

Well, perhaps Granny, if she ever gets her hands on Matron again.

KELZU

Yes, that's right. So, listeners, to get you up to speed: our dearly fearsome leader has decided—somewhat unilaterally—to vacate the premises. In the dead of night. Without telling anyone. Leaving behind one magical contract and one very confused twenty-something-year-old wannabe adventurer.

KELZU

Welcome to Sunnywood House, Poppy.

HUK

Do you think she knew what she was signing?

KELZU

Not a chance in the nine cursed hells.

HUK

And yet, she's still here. First week on the job, she gets chased by a spider the size of a tavern, survives a Trevor-induced remodel of the dining room, and somehow manages not to scream bloody murder at any of us.

KELZU

It's a low bar.

HUK

Sure. But you remember the last three hires?

KELZU

They all left after half an hour. You can hardly call them hires.

HUK

So, compared to that...

KELZU

She's not doing too bad.

[Pause. Sound of glasses clinking. Possibly tea, possibly something harder]

HUK

You think she'll last?

KELZU

No idea. Buddy, old pal. Not the foggiest. You think we should bring her down here? Put her in the chair and ask her some questions?

HUK

Not yet. We'll let her sleep. The poor kid has earned it.

BABYSITTING A
NECROMANCER

Poppy was snoring quite terrifically the following morning. She was dreaming, and in this dream she stood on a cliff's edge, looking out over a dark ocean. The wind tore at her travelling cloak. To her left and right stood her friends, her family. Her very own party. They'd just saved a town from a ravaging band of undead, and now they were off—off on their next adventure. There was a big, beautiful boat down in the sea, far beneath them.

It was, Poppy knew, their boat.

One of the cloaked figures removed their hood.

It was Huk.

Even in the dream, Poppy felt that this wasn't quite right.

'Wake up, kid,' said Huk.

'But we set sail at first light?' said Poppy.

'Your creepy baby and her dad are here.'

Another cloaked figure removed their hood.

It was Granny.

'And the father, hooo-eeee, let me tell you this, if I were forty years younger, I'd be climbing him like a tree.'

Poppy sat up in her bed. Granny and Huk were in her room, sitting on either side of her. She'd slept in. Shit. *Shit*. She'd slept in.

'What's the time?'

Granny checked her pocket watch. 'Just gone past eleven, love.'

'Fuck!' Poppy jumped out of bed. 'Why didn't anyone wake me?' She ran around her room in a mad dash, grabbing her clothes and hopping on one foot to put on a sock whilst trying to squeeze into a sweater.

'Well, you were having such a lovely lie-in, and after last night we thought you deserved it.'

'And it's not our job to wake you,' said Huk.

'It's quite the other way round, I'm afraid,' agreed Granny. 'You're not really going to wear that sweater with those trousers, are you?'

Poppy, who'd been hurriedly doing up her shoelaces, looked at Granny in horror. 'What's wrong with them?'

'Oh, nothing, love. You look great.'

Granny left the room and headed towards the staircase. Poppy followed at a run, dodging past Huk, who had taken to looking around Poppy's room in an altogether overtly nosey kind of way.

'I don't suppose Matron changed her mind and came back?'

Poppy looked down the hallway expecting to see it absolutely trashed as it had been the night before, but the cleaners had done a marvellous job. There was not a stain on the rug. Kelzu's wagon wasn't even crashed through the wall anymore.

'No, I don't suppose she is. But trust me, Poppy, if she ever comes back here, it'll be the last thing she does. I swear it before you and all the gods.'

Poppy sighed. 'You know, I was thinking, it could all just be a bit of a misunderstanding. Maybe she is coming back. And maybe—'

'Don't be daft, Poppy,' cut in Granny. 'A bit of a misunderstanding is Hiro decapitating a cleaner. A bit of a misunderstanding is me making slime crawl out of your toilet and rummage through your things because I thought you were a spy. This is not a bit of a misunderstanding, mark my words.'

Poppy had a sinking feeling: there was a grim determination to Granny's voice. One she hadn't heard before, and it terrified her.

'You do have a sword!' shouted Huk. She looked back to see him holding an old rusty longsword she'd paid far too much for, back when she thought adventuring would be as easy as buying the supplies and setting off into the field with everything strapped to your backpack.

Poppy ignored him and looked back at Granny. 'The slime was you?'

'I've already informed Hiro and Clay about Matron,' said Granny, ignoring her. 'They weren't too happy. Well, I say that, they didn't really seem to give a sod, but...' She shrugged. 'What is it you plan to do with the necromancer and her father, anyway? It wouldn't be sporting to kill a child. Best wait until the girl's proper evil before you try anything, I think.'

'Gods,' hissed Poppy, 'I'm not going to kill her.' She felt like pushing Granny into a wall.

'No? What are you going to do then?'

'Baby-sit her,' said Poppy. 'The father's well hopeless and in over his head. And I don't think he's had much luck getting anyone else to do it.'

Granny frowned. 'Baby-sitting is a bit beneath you, isn't it?'

'I babysit you lot all the time.'

'If anyone asks, tell them you're teaching her to control her magic. Sounds much more grand, far less embarrassing and banal.'

'Embarrassing for who?'

'For me,' said Granny, scandalised. 'I don't want people thinking our matron is some common variety carer.'

The front door opened, and Markus peered in. 'Is this a bad time?' he asked.

Gods. Fucking hell. Yes. It was a terrifically bad time.

NOT VERY ORGAMISED

The farmer and his daughter stood awkwardly at the front door. They were surrounded by Kelzu, K.S., Alfred—who was floating above them—and Bernard, who was jumping on them. They looked so dreadfully out of place here, amongst the rest of Sunnywood's residents. Janey was giggling, though, and trying hopelessly to fend off Bernard's face-licking.

'He's a bad dragon,' said Janey.

'And you're certain she's a necromancer?' asked Alfred.

'Yes. We're fairly sure,' said Markus. He looked, thought Poppy, to be utterly terrified of the ghost.

'She doesn't look like a necromancer,' said Alfred.

'But what's a necromancer supposed to look like, though?' asked Kelzu.

Granny shrugged. 'Lots of black. Skulls everywhere.'

'She does have lots of skulls everywhere, but as for her favourite colour—'

'It's green,' sighed Janey, as if this were a question she was tired of answering.

'That's a lovely colour, Janey,' said Poppy.

'I know.' Janey nodded, matter-of-factly.

'But how can you be sure?' said Alfred. 'What if he's the necromancer, and in typical evil necromancer fashion, he's using his daughter as cover? Blaming it all on the child. It wouldn't be unheard of.'

'Now there's a thought,' said Kelzu.

They all looked at the ghost. Then at Markus.

Markus instantly reddened. 'I—ahh, well, that's just absurd. When would I even have time to—'

Poppy sighed. 'Alfred, piss off, won't you? And Kelzu—seriously, man? Really?'

'You can't talk to me like that,' said Alfred.

'I can do whatever the bloody hell I want, apparently,' said Poppy. 'Seeing as your old Matron saw fit to fuck me over ten ways to next Sunday.'

Alfred bristled. Ghostly steam rose around him. He shot Poppy a look with daggers in it, then vanished through the wall.

'I'm sorry I swore, Janey,' said Poppy.

'It's fine. Dad says swear words all the time.'

'It's true, I'm afraid,' said Markus. He swallowed. 'I just want to check I'm not going mental—but, sorry... that was a ghost, yeah?'

Poppy nodded. 'He's a terrible nosy bore.'

'But as for if you're going mental or not, that we cannot answer,' said Kelzu. 'For what constitutes madness, anyway?'

'Madness is a psychological state defined by a severe loss of touch with reality, but is not reserved just—'

'—I was trying to be philosophical, K.S. Do you know what that means, you daft bastard?'

'Yes, master. To be philosophical is to—'

Kelzu and K.S. wandered off into the dining hall, arguing and shouting and listening and talking, as they always did and probably always would. Poppy found herself hoping she wouldn't have to put up with it for the rest of her natural life.

'Well, I should be off too,' said Granny. 'There's a particular bedroom I must rummage through.'

Poppy was left, finally, with Markus and Janey. They stared at one another awkwardly for a moment.

'Your hair is a mess, and you have sleepy eyes,' said Janey.

Poppy rubbed the sleep from her eyes. It was true. They were positively caked with it.

'Yes, I might have slept in. On accident,' said Poppy.

'You're not very orgamised,' she said, matter-of-fact.

Markus squeezed her shoulder. 'It's *organised*. And that's not very polite, Janey.'

'Neither's being unorgamised,' said Janey. 'You say it's plain bad manners and that's why half the village don't like us, cos we're not very orgamised. You said we couldn't orgamise a—'

'Yeah, that's enough, kid,' Markus cut her off, hand over her mouth. He looked at Poppy. 'Sorry.'

Poppy shrugged. In comparison to Alfred, Janey was a delight. 'Don't be,' she said. 'It's cute.'

'It stops being cute very quickly, trust me.'

Janey bit her dad's hand.

'Ow! Janey!'

'I couldn't breathe. You were strangling me.'

'Where are your mice, anyway?' said Poppy.

Janey sighed. 'At home. They're not 'llowed out. I wanted to go back and get 'em to show the see-through man and prove to him I am a nekkeramancer, but Dad won't let me.'

'I'm sure we can find you a pet for when you're here.'

'What kind of skellingtons do you have here? I can't turn anyfing bigger than a rabbit, but I could try.'

'I meant something alive. Like Bernard.'

Janey looked disgusted. 'Bernard?' she said, doubtfully.

Poppy knelt beside the dragon, who was sitting with his tail wagging, watching them all with great interest. 'I believe you've already met.'

'He's not dead though.'

'No, he's not. He's very much alive.'

'Look,' said Janey. 'I'll fink about it. All right? I've already got lots and lots of pets.'

Markus nudged Janey, knocking into her shoulder.

She sighed and looked at Poppy.

'Fank you, Poppy,' she said, voice dripping with far too much sarcasm.

'That's alright. Should we go and see Hiro in the kitchen, see if he has any biscuits?'

And so began Poppy's first day with Janey and Markus. It wasn't exactly the first big adventure she'd had in mind when she imagined dealing with a necromancer, but it was, she was sure, a much more fun time. Poppy had never met a five-year-old so sarcastic and so intelligent. She understood the bags under Markus's eyes and the weary but loving smile he seemed to wear almost perpetually.

The day, as days spent with five-year-olds only can, went by in a chaotic blur. They went out into the garden to meet Clay, and Janey was no sooner running off with Bernard in tow. Both of them came back covered in mud. She screamed with joy and laughed like... well...

Poppy looked at Markus. 'Her laugh, it's...'

'I know,' he sighed. 'I know... I try not to think about it.'

'No, but truly, I think it's the most evil laugh I have ever heard.'

He nodded. 'It worried me at first, too. You know, she's already a necromancer, why does she have to laugh like a madman, too? It's a laugh a villain could really grow into.'

'Villains could learn a thing or two about laughing like that, I think,' said Poppy. 'But I also don't think villains are usually so obvious, so I'm not sure you need to worry about it.'

Janey emerged from behind the hedgerows with a pitchfork. She took to jabbing it dangerously into the earth, but it was almost too heavy, so she looked at risk of impaling herself. They both sprinted after her.

Later that day, over lunch, Janey was seated with Huk and Kelzu while Poppy set about ferrying the food from the kitchen to the tables. Granny Grack had stolen Markus away, having found out he studied law before throwing it all away to become a farmer and a father.

He'd taken some convincing, but she got there in the end. 'Oh, don't be silly, my love. She'll be just fine with Huk and Kelzu.'

Markus had looked at the half-orc and gnome, then at Granny. 'I'm not sure it's them I'm worried about.'

Kelzu had produced one of his magical little contraptions. It looked like a brass spin-top, but it was made from clockwork and glowed a warm golden colour the faster it spun. Janey was laughing her most evil villain laugh.

Markus had looked back at Granny. 'It's Huk and Kelzu I fear for.'

'We fought a horde of giant spiders last night—I'm sure they can keep a child out of trouble for ten minutes.' Granny took him by the arm.

'I've dealt with my fair share of necromancers, son. Don't you worry, none. She'll be right as rain. And if things turn south—' Huk made a throat-cutting gesture with his thumb and winked. Janey clapped and laughed and copied Huk: throat-cutting gesture, wink and all.

'He's joking,' said Markus. 'You're joking, right? I need to know that you're joking.'

'Lighten up, man. If you wind yourself up any tighter, you'll shit a cog,' said Kelzu.

And so, with Janey taken care of, Granny convinced Markus to look through the paperwork in Matron's office.

'It's the troll contract I'm most concerned about,' she said, whisking him away.

BUCKY HORSES

Poppy returned from the kitchen to see Huk and Kelzu digging into a cream cake and talking excitedly about their radio show. Janey, though, was nowhere to be seen.

Poppy passed Alfred his second plate of beans on toast. They slopped over the sides.

He groaned.

'Shut up,' she said severely. 'Or you'll be getting nothing for dinner. Huk, where's Janey?'

'Where is who?' said Huk.

Poppy frowned. 'The kid. Janey?'

Huk shrugged. Whipped cream smeared across his lips. 'Don't know what you're on about.'

Kelzu sighed. 'She said she needed to potty. I asked her if she was equipped to deal with that on her own, and she assured me she was more than capable.'

Poppy looked from Kelzu back to Huk. 'Do you seriously not remember Janey?

'Course I do. Tall girl. Had funny ears. Saved her and her stupid family from the dark elves, didn't I?' said Huk. 'Not that she was too grateful about it.'

'You did give him his medicine this morning, didn't you?' whispered Kelzu.

Poppy was about to say that no, she had not given Huk his medicine—because up until a few hours ago, she'd still been in sodding bed—but then she heard a crash and a scream.

It was coming from upstairs.

Kelzu went back to eating his cake. 'You know, I thought it strange when she went upstairs when she said she needed the loo. But I said to myself, "Children these days, Kelzu, keep your opinions to yourself."'

'She's five. What could you possibly mean by that?' Poppy groaned. 'You know what? Never mind!'

Poppy sprinted upstairs—and when she got there, the door to the cleaning room was open, and it was chaos. Pure, unbelievable chaos. A cloud of dust so thick that the occasional light from the cleaners' single crystal eye illuminated it in terrifying blood-red flashes.

Janey was screaming.

Yes.

But it was screams of pure joy.

She was somehow sitting on the shoulders of a cleaner, like she might on her father's—but this cleaner was not her father, and it did not like having someone perched on its shoulders. It smashed its way around the room, knocking into things left and right. This then had the other cleaners leave their charging posts to get to work fixing the mess. And then it became some kind of ramming game, where they all knocked into one another and got increasingly mad about it.

'The golden 'orseys go bloody fast, Poppy!' screamed Janey. Her face was one of pure glee. 'Look at me go!'

Poppy didn't know what to do or say.

She wanted to scream, but that didn't feel helpful—and more

than that, she didn't want Janey's father to hear anything and come running.

Janey giggled as the cleaner beneath her tried slamming itself against the wall to throw her off. 'They love it,' she yelled. 'We're playing bucky horses now!'

Poppy found herself completely unsure of how you were even supposed to talk to children. She felt, suddenly, very stupid. She'd only given thought to the necromancer bit and never paid any attention to the fact that she was a child first.

She cleared her throat. 'Could we perhaps stop playing bucky horses, do you think?'

'No,' said Janey. 'I don't fink so.'

'Please? Before you get hurt,' Poppy pleaded.

The cleaner swung around viciously, trying with all its might to get rid of her. It passed beneath the low rafters, narrowly missing the top of Janey's head.

Poppy tried to catch her, but the bastard cleaner shot off to her left. 'You can't bring yourself back from the dead, you know!'

Poppy chased them both around, frantically. The cleaner increased its speed to an almost dizzying blur. Meanwhile, the other cleaners buzzed in their wake to tidy the mess. It all became rather savage, and Poppy began to understand Hiro's fear of them.

She closed her eyes as two went whirling past her, dangerously close to knocking her clean over.

'Careful, Poppy!' shouted Janey. 'You'll get hurt!'

'Right,' said Poppy. 'You!' She pointed at a cleaner.

It froze in the face of her sudden anger.

'Return to base. Now.'

The cleaner looked longingly at the mess surrounding them. Their usually spotless cleaning cupboard was now covered in debris and dust from things knocked off shelves and smashed out of storage boxes.

'I SAID NOW,' shouted Poppy.

The cleaner bowed its head like a dog who'd been told off, and it rolled itself slowly and reluctantly to its base.

Poppy turned to see Janey nearly halfway up the wall, clinging to the cleaner as it rolled itself—defying gravity—up towards the low ceiling. Poppy stood beneath them and, when Janey hung upside down above her, she reached for her dangling hands.

'Let go,' she said sternly. 'Now, Janey.'

Janey giggled. She did not let go.

'I'll let you raise whatever skeletons we find in the woods,' said Poppy.

'Bigger than a rabbit?'

'Fine. But not people. We draw the line at people.'

Janey unclenched her knees from around the cleaner and fell into Poppy's hands. They crashed to the ground.

Janey looked down at Poppy, smiling. 'Shake on it,' she said, suddenly businesslike. 'You have to shake on it otherwise s'not a proper deal.'

Poppy sat up, lifting Janey off her chest. 'It will have to be our secret. I don't think your dad would like it if he knew I was letting you raise more things from the dead. I'm kinda supposed to be doing the opposite with you, you know?'

Janey zipped her lips. 'Our secret. Shake on it.'

Poppy couldn't help but smile. She put out her hand.

Janey reached forward to grab it.

Poppy pulled hers away before Janey could grasp it. 'But we have to promise to listen to one another, okay?'

Janey nodded, and they shook on it.

'Our secret,' said Poppy.

'Ours,' nodded Janey.

And Poppy thought then that maybe talking to kids wasn't so hard. Maybe you just spoke to them like they were people. It felt like a small win after a long line of losses.

A REASON TO STAY

It was nearly dinner time when Markus and Janey left Sunnywood. They'd tried convincing them to stay for tea, but Markus wasn't having it.

'He looks like he could do with a nice hearty meal though,' said Granny.

Markus smiled, pretending not to hear. He had a bag full of paperwork he'd promised Granny he'd look over.

'Well, it's true, love. You get any skinnier and Miss Janey here'll be using your skeleton like a puppet in a play.'

Janey smiled. Too tired to laugh. Her head was leaning against her father's leg.

'So you'll return next week then?' asked Poppy.

Markus nodded. 'If it's alright with you.'

'I meant just Janey,' said Poppy. 'You can drop her off and pick her up.'

Markus looked down at Janey, unsure.

'That's what the job was, right? You needed some help.'

'Yes, but—'

Granny cut in. 'You'll need the free time to read over those papers.'

'And tidy your house,' added Poppy. 'I mean, honestly, man. It was like a bomb went off.'

'We haven't been apart since... well, it's been a while.'

'All the more reason then,' said Granny. 'You both could do with a break from one another. So it's settled then. We'll see you next week.'

Poppy and Granny watched them leave. The sun had just started to set, and the garden was full of shadows and golden light.

'What lovely people,' said Granny.

'Mm.' Poppy nodded.

'What happened to her mother?'

'She died,' said Poppy.

'How?'

'I dunno. Felt wrong to ask.'

'And her grandparents?' said Granny.

'Not in the picture, apparently.'

Granny nodded. 'Well, the kid got her talents from somewhere. It's clearly not the dad, so it must have been the mother. Makes sense, I suppose, that her grandparents should want to stay away. Least they teach her any bad habits.'

'Bad habits?'

'It's a small leap from an army of mice to an army of undead, my dear.'

'Right.' Poppy sighed. 'What did Markus think about the paperwork?'

'We've been colossally fucked,' said Granny.

'He said that?'

'Well, not in those exact words.'

'She's *really* not coming back, is she?'

Granny shook her head.

They stood in silence for a while. Janey and Markus had disappeared from sight by the time Granny broke it.

'The more paperwork we found, the worse it looked. There've been transfers out of Sunnywood's account. Big ones. Ones that leave it empty. Ones that mean you won't be getting paid anytime soon, I'm afraid. Neither will Hiro or Clay, for that matter.'

'And what if I did a runner?' said Poppy.

Granny chuckled. 'You'd want to run bloody fast, my dear. No—you're stuck here with us, I'm afraid. Your name's on the contract now. Troll-ink and all.'

'I can't run a nursing home on my own,' said Poppy.

Granny Grack slapped Poppy's arm. Not lightly, either. 'It's hardly a nursing home. You're not helping us wipe our arses, are you?'

'But how long before that starts? I forget one day of Huk's medicine and he's already forgetting things. I wouldn't be surprised if he asks who I am before the night is out.'

Granny sighed. 'Well, whatever happens, you won't be doing it on your own, love. And anyway, you can't leave—you've got your lessons, after all.'

She waved her hand.

There was a shimmer of heat—like stepping too close to a forge —and Poppy's hair lifted in the breeze of it.

Her scalp tingled. Something shifted.

'What the fu—'

She caught her reflection in the glass.

White hair.

Wrinkled eyes.

Spotted, crooked hands.

'What have you done?' she hissed.

Granny grinned up at her from the bottom of the stairs. 'Your first lesson, dear. Curses 101. If you want to be an adventurer, you've got to learn how to undo a few things first.'

Poppy stared at her reflection, horrified. 'You *cursed* me?'

'Oh, don't be so dramatic.'

'Granny—!'

'Consider it extra motivation not to bugger off like the last one.'

Poppy said nothing. Her hands shook. They weren't her hands anymore. They were old and trembling and traitorous.

'You cursed me so I wouldn't run?' she said, quietly.

Granny paused at the top of the stairs. 'No, I gave you a reason to stay.'

'It's the same fucking thing,' she shouted.

There was a beat. Granny didn't turn around.

'Matron was tricked into staying too, wasn't she?' Poppy said. 'You lot fucked her over with that many tricksy spells and duties and godsdamn guilt until she couldn't breathe. And then, when she robbed you lot blind and ran, you acted surprised.'

Granny didn't reply.

'Now it's me. One punching bag to the next.' Poppy looked at her reflection. The old face looking back was unfamiliar, but the rage in her eyes—that was hers. 'If someone turned up at that door tomorrow and looked even vaguely competent, I'd be gone before they finished introducing themselves.'

Granny shrugged. 'Well, then I'd curse them too. I suppose.'

She disappeared down the hallway.

Poppy stood at the window, her hand pressed to the glass. She watched the sun dip lower, watched the light bend over the hedgerows and melt away.

Her knees ached.

Her back twinged.

She stayed there for a long time, until her breathing evened out and her hands stopped trembling. Then she whispered: 'You old bastards really don't know how to ask someone to stay, do you?'

EIGHTY SUITS YOU

Poppy's back was throbbing, and there was a constant droning ache in her joints. She'd been reading about curses in an old spell-book she'd found in Sunnywood's small library. But her eyesight was no good, and the rune-lights weren't nearly bright enough to make out the words anymore. She sighed and threw the book into the room behind her. She was sitting out in the cool breeze on her bedroom balcony.

She closed her eyes.

What in the world was she doing here?

She wasn't even getting paid anymore.

And while she knew that Granny would eventually turn her back to normal, she couldn't help feeling terrified at seeing herself as this old woman she barely recognised; it made her want to run away—from herself and from everything. She looked in the mirror and saw her future, and she didn't like it. Not one bit. Had the Poppy who looked like this lived? Truly lived? Had she done anything worthwhile? Seen anything worthwhile?

She sighed. It didn't end well when all you did was ask yourself what the point was. But still, she felt the nihilism creeping into her old bones. To her left, she heard a door open, and Kelzu strolled out onto his balcony. He was wearing a dressing gown and smoking a cigarette.

Poppy froze, feeling like she ought to move as slowly as possible back into her room before he spotted her. She wasn't in the mood to talk.

'Well, eighty suits you,' said Kelzu. He blew out a stream of smoke. It curled into the air.

'She's seventy, Zu. Honestly, how dare you,' said Granny. She was leaning out of her window, looking at both Poppy and Kelzu.

Poppy groaned.

'Who's seventy?' said Huk. He opened his bedroom door and leaned against his balcony, looking up at them both from the floor below.

'Can I not have even a single moment to myself?' said Poppy.

Huk looked at Poppy. He smiled at her in a way she didn't recognise. 'Hello there. I don't believe we've met. I'm Huk.'

Kelzu coughed out a laugh. 'Steady on there, old boy. You'll make me jealous.'

'It's Poppy,' said Granny. 'I've just cursed her.'

'Tell me,' said Kelzu. 'Why did you curse her?'

Poppy was straining so fiercely to hear what was being said that she dared not say a single thing for fear of missing it.

Granny shrugged. 'She wanted magic lessons. No other way to learn than to face it head on, I reckon.'

Poppy narrowed her eyes. Maybe that was true. But what it sounded like—what it really felt like—was: *she wanted to make sure I stayed. This was her way of tying me down. Her completely deranged, utterly backwards way of saying: please don't leave.*

'Well, turn her back to normal,' said Huk, annoyed. 'How's she supposed to learn to fight with a sword when she's got arthritis?'

'You seem to manage it,' said Granny.

'But what are you teaching her exactly?' said Kelzu. 'By making her old?'

'Oh, lots of things I should think. How to remove a curse would be top of the list.'

Kelzu chuckled to himself and stamped out his cigarette. 'You're bloody mad.'

'Who?' said Granny.

'The both of you. You, for cursing her. And you, Poppy, for wanting to live here with us.'

'Well, I was getting paid up until this week,' said Poppy. She turned to look at Granny. 'And if you don't turn me back, I'll find someone who can. And so help me, when this mess gets sorted out, I'll sell the sodding place right from out underneath you. Don't think for a minute I won't.'

Granny chuckled. It wasn't a kind laugh, not at all. 'Yes, well, good luck with that, deary.'

'And stop calling me fucking deary,' shouted Poppy. She got up and slammed her door shut. She'd about had enough of them. All of them. And she was in half a mind to pack her things and leave, just as Matron had.

Maybe Matron hadn't been cruel or careless. Maybe she'd just run out of ways to say "please help me."

Sunnywood's debts and the stupid contract could up and bite her on the arse for all she cared.

Who wanted to look after these old bastards when they treated you like they did?

Nothing but giant spiders and magical wagons crashing through walls and metal cleaners that attacked you, given half the chance.

No, a comfy bed and a hot bath and a room to call her own: it wasn't quite enough to make up for it. Poppy angrily pulled her hair into a bun. She'd been muttering to herself, out loud, she realised. She sounded old, now. Gods knows she felt it. Or maybe that's how she always felt, and now her outside just matched her inside.

Poppy climbed into her bed. 'Bitter old thing,' she cursed.

And she wasn't even sure she was talking about Granny, not really.

She felt rather as if she were talking about herself. But she wasn't packing her bags. Not yet.

She wasn't ready to give them the satisfaction of seeing her quit. Not while she still had knees to curse and curses to break.

GROUND RULES

The following morning, it took Poppy ten minutes to descend the stairs. She thought if they had the nerve to trip her, she would just lie there and die rather than go through all the effort of standing back up. It was still dark out, and although Poppy had fully intended to lie in, she found she simply couldn't. Perhaps she wasn't wired for it anymore. Or maybe it was just part of the curse: early mornings and brittle knees included.

'I don't know if you know this,' said Hiro. He stormed out of the kitchen towards her, tea-towel slung over his shoulder. 'But to cook food, I need ingredients, and to have ingredients, you need to buy them and...' Hiro's voice trailed off. He frowned. 'What the fuck happened to you?'

'This job is killing me. That's what's happening to me, Hiro.'

'You look about eighty-five.'

'Yes,' said Poppy, angrily. 'And good morning to you too.'

Hiro crossed the kitchen and placed his floury hands on Poppy's cheeks. He looked at her closely, far too closely. Poppy could smell his morning coffee on his breath.

She slapped his hands away. 'The hell do you think you're doing?'

'I was seeing if it was an enchantment or a curse.'

'It's a curse,' said Poppy, sighing.

'Grack's back at it again?' said Hiro. He laughed.

'She's done this before?'

'I mean, yeah, she's fond of a curse. Her grandmother was a hag, after all. Had one of them houses with chicken legs, apparently. Would wander around Upper Susshingham cursing anyone who got in their way. The Gracks are all domestic terrorists, really.'

'Domestic terrorists?'

Hiro nodded, matter-of-fact. 'You know the big plague in Westdown? Grack's great-aunt started it for a bet. Or so the story goes. And her great-aunt was rumoured to have kicked off a war by bewitching the wrong ambassador's trousers.'

Poppy groaned. It would have been interesting if you weren't so bloody involved in it— a bit like only being able to enjoy gossip when you remained about five steps removed from it.

She poured herself a cup of coffee and sat down at the table whilst Hiro expertly folded a ball of dough into a loaf tin. 'So has she cursed you, too, then?' It wouldn't be so bad, thought Poppy, if she wasn't the only one to suffer. It would feel less personal, for a start.

Hiro laughed. 'Gods, no. Not me. She loves me. And anyway, you never curse the hand that feeds you, or however the saying goes.'

Poppy mimicked him, bitterly. Maybe it was because she suddenly had a great deal more skin, but it felt as if everyone was getting under it.

'You're even muttering like an angry old lady now,' said Hiro.

'Oh, piss off.'

There were going to have to be some ground rules, she decided. If she was going to live here amongst these eccentric bastards, then she was going to have to put her foot down.

But first of all, she needed to figure out how to remove this sodding curse. She couldn't take it anymore. Every part of her ached, and walking down the stairs seemed to knock the wind right out of her sails. I mean, really, thought Poppy, what sadistic bastard had put stairs in a nursing home? She would have to do something about that, too. Sooner or later, someone was bound not to be able to walk up them anymore. And what if Huk got up to his night wanderings and had a fall? So, that was three things. Or was it two?

She needed to make a list.

'I need a pen and some paper.'

Hiro looked up from his sticky flour mess. 'And?'

'Be a dear and fetch some for me?'

'Be a dear?' repeated Hiro. 'Now, Poppy, I think it's you who can piss off.'

Poppy groaned and got up from her stool. 'You've no respect for your elders.'

'You've seen the lot we live with.'

He had a point. Poppy found Hiro's grocery list and a pencil. She sat back down with another fresh cup of coffee.

First, she thought, ground rules. No cursing was chief among them. Trevor needed to sod off too, she thought. She couldn't live with a giant spider terrorising the place anymore. And anyway, it wasn't right to trap that poor thing and her babies inside. They belonged out in the wild. And then... what else had she been thinking? Remove the curse and fix the stairs.

Hiro looked over her shoulder at the list. 'And groceries. We need food. There's only so much I can do with bread.'

Poppy chewed the end of the pencil.

'You know Matron is gone, right?'

Hiro nodded. 'They were in my kitchen last night gossiping about it.'

'Who was?'

'Who do you think? The troublesome trio.'

'And you heard about the money situation?'

'Look, as long as I have food to cook with and a bed to sleep in, I don't care about much else if I'm being honest.'

Poppy grunted. It was all right for him to say that. But what about her? She... well. She was in charge of the place now, she supposed, and... what about her adventures? What about saving up and sodding off to fight whole hordes of undead and slinking away from dragons with bags full of gold? She'd had dreams of a life out there living, and this wasn't at all how she'd imagined it.

'I'm surprised she lasted this long. I thought she would have sodded off after your second day. She lasted the week,' Hiro pulled a face. 'It's a week longer than I thought.'

'Hang on, what do you mean you're surprised? You knew? You knew she was going to leave?'

He shrugged. 'I had an inkling.'

'Why didn't you say anything?'

'What? To you?'

'To anyone you spell-soaked muppet.'

'And what would I have said? Hey, I think the lady who pays all our wages and looks after everyone here has probably had more than enough and is due, any moment now, to either run for the bloody hills screaming 'I can't do this shit anymore' or to implode and begin stabbing every ungrateful bastard with whom she crosses paths with?'

Poppy nodded. 'Well, yeah. That. Exactly that. That would have been brilliant. It would have saved my arse, for one.'

Hiro returned to his baking. 'Well, I didn't.'

Poppy sighed. She looked at her list and sipped her coffee.

Today was going to be a long day.

'And for Hearth's sake, don't forget Huk's medicine. He put me in a headlock last night. Said my skin was too pale, and it reminded him of someone from The Barren Below. I thought he was going to rip my head clean off.'

'I'd hardly forget something like that,' said Poppy, dismissively.

Though when Hiro was no longer looking, she made sure to write 'Huk - medicine' at the very top of her to-do list.

Then, with a scowl of determination, she got up, fetched the dusty old spellbook from the library (she ducked the books that punched you with practised ease), and returned to her coffee with a plan. If Granny could curse her, then she could bloody well un-curse herself.

She turned a few pages, muttered some words under her breath, and jabbed a finger in the direction of her own forehead. The kitchen lights flickered. Hiro ducked instinctively.

There was a soft pop and the smell of burnt hair.

Poppy blinked. Her fringe was smoking.

Hiro watched her for a long moment, then turned back to his dough. 'Please don't explode in here. I've just cleaned the stove.'

YOU PEOPLE ARE ANIMALS

An hour later, Poppy was standing on a step-stool in the foyer, painting on the wall with thick red paint. She stuck out her tongue with concentrated effort.

'What on earth are you doing?' said Granny, coming down the stairs.

'I'm setting some ground rules,' said Poppy. She was rather impressed with herself. She was no sign-writer, that was for sure. But it looked good, and most importantly: it got the sodding point across. She stepped off the stool carefully—her knees were quite achy —and stood beside Granny to admire it.

Granny looked from the wall with its thick, bold letters to Poppy. 'And, why?'

'Because,' said Poppy, picking up the step-stool. 'You people are animals.'

Granny nodded. She looked, Poppy thought, to be impressed.

Another hour later, Kelzu, Huk, and Alfred were standing at the bottom of the stairs, looking at the graffiti-covered wall. Huk pulled his trouser leg out from his left shoe, and Kelzu wrapped his dressing gown a little tighter around his waist.

The gnome frowned.

Huk looked a little more vacant than usual.

Alfred flew closer to get a better look.

'What is this?' said Huk.

'Rules,' said Kelzu, hesitantly. 'Lots of them.'

'I know, I can still read,' said Huk.

Kelzu shrugged, distractedly. 'You asked.'

'I meant, why's there a heap of rules on the wall all of a sudden. And I'm taking umbrage with number three, especially.'

'No animals larger than a dog inside the house?' said Alfred. 'Except Bernard?'

Huk nodded. 'What if I wanted to get a pet?'

Kelzu was astounded. 'You hate pets. You've always said they're useless—'

'—Liabilities for the mentally weak who need to fill a void. And I stand by it.'

'Then why do you give a sod about rule number three?'

'It's the principle of the thing. What if I woke up one day and decided I wanted a pet... oh, I don't know, a Ragnortuk, perhaps?'

Alfred floated upward. 'What is a Ragnortuk, exactly?'

'Big-horned thing,' said Kelzu. 'Has molten blood. What the fuck would you do with a Ragnortuk?'

Huk shrugged. 'Teach it to play fetch, I suppose.'

'Have you had your meds yet?' said Kelzu.

'They're not crazy pills,' said Huk, defensively.

'Well, maybe they ought to be.'

Alfred rolled his eyes. 'You two should save this for your radio show.'

Huk and Kelzu looked at one another.

They were deep in thought.

'How would that even work?' said Huk.

'We change up the format? Like a kind of in-the-moment commentary on what is happening in our lives now? Instead of us reminiscing on the adventures we had, we talk about the realities of living in a home full of retired adventurers.'

'That could work,' said Huk.

Alfred sighed. 'I was being sarcastic.'

They ignored him.

Poppy walked out of the kitchen into the lobby. Her purposeful footsteps slowed as she noticed Huk and Kelzu reading the wall of rules she'd painted earlier that morning.

'I need to talk to you two,' she said.

Huk ignored her completely. 'We could interview the residents. Talk about how Sunnywood has been abandoned and left in the care of an absolute tyrant.'

'What?' said Poppy.

'Kind of like a situational comedy. We'll talk about the absurdities of it all.' Kelzu looked at Poppy. 'We're not getting rid of Miss Trevor, by the way. So you can cross that one off your stupid bloody rules list.'

'But you said it was a good idea.'

'I changed my mind. It's Miss Trevor's home. She's been here a lot longer than you.'

Huk crossed his arms. 'And I want a pet Ragnortuk.'

'Have you taken your meds yet, Huk?' asked Poppy.

'THEY ARE NOT CRAZY PILLS!'

'So you admit it's mental to want a pet Ragnortuk, then?' said Alfred.

'I'll get the transmitter and the notepads,' said Kelzu.

'I'll get the microphones and the energy stones,' said Huk.

And then they burst off in opposite directions, Kelzu muttering the whole way about its simple genius. The absurdity of it being the thing that makes it. The heroes of the realm are now left to be babysat by a young girl who can't even remove an ageing curse.

Poppy watched them go in a kind of dumbfounded shock. She looked up at Alfred.

'What just happened, exactly?'

Alfred shrugged. 'Now, rule number ten—when you say all ghosts are hereby restrained to using hallways and staircases; strictly no flying through bedrooms and bathrooms—do you mean me?'

'Are there any other ghosts who live at Sunnywood, Alfred?'

'Well, no, not yet, anyway.'

Poppy walked off. 'Then I think it's safe to assume I meant you.'

Alfred flew after her. 'Can I ask why?'

'Because I'd rather like to use the toilet and bath without living in fear you're about to come flying up the drainpipe.'

EPISODE 7

Excerpt from the transcript of
The Sunnywood Signal.

Episode 7: *"The End of Days?"*
Transcribed by KS-01.
Broadcast on The Upper Susshingham Radio 102.3EM

HUK

Friends, things have taken a turn.

KELZU

A sharp turn. Like a wheel coming off a runaway cart.

HUK

And so we can't talk to you, as if it were business as usual.

KELZU

Because it's not business as usual. Something terrible has happened. Something life-altering awful.

[A tense and dramatic pause]

HUK

The house is broke.

KELZU

We mean properly broke. Interest-accruing, organs-as-collateral broke.

HUK

And who's in charge of fixing it all?

KELZU

A clueless numpty in the shape of a wannabe adventurer that's been cursed into a prune. Yes, that's right. Our dear Poppy has gone from twenty-something to seventy-something.

HUK

Courtesy of our very own curse-maker, the Grack-o-meister. So we've had a thought. A crazy idea, probably. But then all the best ones are.

KELZU

We're going to stop looking back quite as much as we have been. And instead, we thought, why not take you along for the ride? Our day-to-day, as it were.

HUK

Which is a lot less lying around and eating of late.

KELZU

And a lot more giant spiders, bank foreclosures, all-powerful necromancing toddlers, and you guessed it: hopeless idiot caregivers.

HUK

Join us, dear listeners, as we document the inevitable collapse of a long-standing institution, a shining beacon of hope at the end of the road for all adventurers. And remember—

KELZU

This isn't fiction.

HUK & KELZU *(together)*
It's Sunnywood.

[THEME MUSIC: sounds suspiciously like someone strangling a
kazoo]

AND CUT!

Half an hour later, the dining room was alive with activity. There was a crackling energy in the air that hadn't been there at breakfast—or not that Poppy had ever noticed. There was gossip and laughter and snide remarks. But the moment Poppy walked in—well, hobbled in —the laughter and gossip stopped dead.

There was an almost pin-drop silence in the room, broken only by Kelzu and Huk hurriedly trying to set up their recording equipment.

Poppy had long since dismissed their so-called "radio show" as just another retirement home eccentricity—like morning tai chi in full battle armour or scrapbooking adventures past, cursed artefacts and all. Occasionally, she'd hear them muttering in the basement about 'segments' and 'listener numbers', and occasionally they'd force Granny or Alfred to join.

'Quickly,' whispered Kelzu. 'I want this properly recorded. We will all be turning on her, I'm sure of it.'

'I'm bloody trying, the stupid mic won't—'

There was a loud, ear-splitting ringing noise that stopped almost as soon as it had begun.

Poppy ignored it and instead took a seat behind an empty table. Ever since Huk had recorded his battle with Miss Trevor, though, they seemed to be talking a lot less about the past and a lot more about what was happening now. It was beyond infuriating. The microphones shoved in your face. The live commentary about you, as if you weren't standing right there.

She poured herself a cup of tea and flicked through the morning paper. She found, ever since having to turn the pages for Alfred, that she rather enjoyed them. There was another article on the TrollBank expansion. New branches were opening across the south. "Flexible interest terms," it read.

Across the walls of the dining room, her new house rules were slowly drying in a particularly angry red:

SUNNYWOOD HOUSE: HOUSE RULES

No unsolicited visits to the third floor.
(We've sealed it for a reason. That reason has many legs.)
No curses. Full stop.
We're in this together. Try acting like it.
No pets bigger than Bernard allowed.
(And they can't be deadly. Or venomous. Or from another plane of existence.)
No flying through walls.
USE DOORS, ALFRED.
IF IT'S SHUT, IT'S SHUT FOR A FUCKING REASON.
If it seems like a terrible idea, it probably is.
Let's just start using this as our rule of thumb, shall we?
Kelzu and Huk must get recording consent.

'You look pleased with yourself,' said Granny, appearing beside her with a suspiciously full teacup.

Poppy shrugged.

'They're right, you know,' Granny nodded at Huk and Kelzu. 'You can't tell an adventurer what to do. It just rubs us the wrong way. I remember an alchemist told me not to touch a flower once, and so I picked it.'

Granny lifted her sleeve to show Poppy a long, vicious scar that trailed from the palm of her hand to the crook of her elbow.

'You'd think you'd learn your lesson and listen to what other people have to say, then, wouldn't you?' said Poppy. She turned the page. There was another article about the new troll bank that had opened in town.

'Oh, this is going to be good,' whispered Kelzu. 'Are you getting this?'

Granny shot Huk and Kelzu a glare. 'That wasn't my point. The point is, we're stubborn, dear. And we don't like being told what to do, even when we know it's the right thing to do.'

Poppy gulped the rest of her tea and placed the cup back on its saucer. She felt like she'd entered a sparring match with a lion. She looked at Granny Grack and tried to quell her nerves.

'*Retired* adventurer, don't you mean? Retired being the keyword.'

'What?' said Granny.

'That's why you're here, right? Because you're retired. You're not an adventurer anymore. You're a... a...'

'A what?'

Huk stretched his hand out a little more, the microphone now nearly between Poppy and Granny.

'Go on. Say it.'

'A granny,' said Poppy.

There was an audible gasp. Everyone in the room stopped pretending they weren't listening and turned to look openly, mouths agape.

Poppy's cheeks flushed red.

Granny Grack smiled. There was no humour or light in it. It was the kind of smile you expected to see just before she ran you over with a horse-drawn cart.

'Rich, coming from an old bag like you.'

Huk laughed.

Kelzu made an 'ooof' noise.

'Poppy,' said Kelzu, 'could you tell us how that feels?'

Huk pointed the mic toward her face. 'Embarrassing, I'd imagine.'

Poppy stood up from behind the table. Her knees hurt more than she'd like to admit, and she couldn't help but wince a little. She looked them all dead in the eye.

'It's no wonder Matron robbed you lot blind and left. It's a miracle she didn't kill you.'

'A quick refresher for the listeners at home wondering just who this Matron is,' said Huk, 'our previous head of caregiving emptied the bank and ran. Now we're left with a—'

'Sorely underprepared and woefully inexperienced teenager with the body of an eighty-year-old,' finished Kelzu.

Poppy looked down at the microphone pointed toward her mouth. 'What are you two doing?'

Granny smacked the microphone away from her face. 'Apart from being irritating little shits?'

Kelzu looked at Huk with a cheeky grin. He chuckled and leaned into his mic. 'And that's where we'll end today's episode. Find out next week if...'

There was a moment of silence as Kelzu thought through what he wanted to say next.

Huk took the mic. 'Tempers continue to flare between the hag-blooded sorcerer Grack and our very own cursed head caregiver?'

'Will the new ground rules, still freshly painted on the walls, be followed or broken with careless abandon?'

'Only time will tell. And Kelzu?'

Kelzu cleared his throat and tried on his best radio voice. 'Yes, Huk?'

'I believe we need to start thinking of names,' said Huk.

'Names for what?'

'Oh, didn't you know? Sunnywood is soon to be home to a pet Ragnortuk.'

'AND CUT!' shouted Kelzu. He was beaming. 'Brilliant. Just brilliant.'

He frantically began picking up their equipment, coiling wires and piling microphones into K.S.'s open and waiting arms.

'I think we'll still do some edits. Nothing major. It feels fresh and personable like this.'

Kelzu looked at Granny and Poppy, who were both standing there, shocked and at a loss for words.

'You two were brilliant. Just brilliant. Maybe next time, though, one of you could really play it up. Really spit your dummy, you know?'

'Grack, maybe another spell?' said Huk. 'Doesn't have to be a curse. But something to really ramp up the stakes.'

'You know, fill it with drama,' added Kelzu.

'I'll give you bloody drama,' muttered Granny, bitterly.

'Uh-huh,' said Huk, wagging a finger at her. 'Just you save that for next week's episode. And speaking of next week's episode.' He turned to look at Poppy.

'What?' she said. 'Why are you looking at me like that?'

YOU CAN'T STAY HERE

Markus and Janey had just been about to knock on the front door of Sunnywood House when it swung open, and Hiro looked out at them, meat cleaver in hand.

'You're not groceries,' he said, matter-of-fact.

Markus took a step back—on account of the cleaver—and pushed Janey behind his legs.

'No, we're not... sorry?'

Hiro sighed. Behind him, in the foyer, Bernard slinked lazily out of a room—only to realise it was Janey. He whined (as only a book-wyrm pretending to be a dog could) and launched himself at them both.

'Hello Bernard,' said Janey.

The dragon licked her face and pressed his disproportionately large head into her chest.

'You'd think he was a golden retriever in costume, the way he acts,' said Hiro.

Markus scratched the dragon behind the ears. He noticed Hiro was still holding the cleaver a little too naturally.

'We're still not food, I'm afraid.'

Hiro tucked the knife into the back of his apron. He looked at the small bag they'd brought.

'I hope you've packed snacks for the little one,' said Hiro. 'Pretty soon, this lot'll be resorting to cannibalism, and I'll be powerless to stop it. There's only so much you can do with cabbage and flour, and we're nearly out of cabbage, so.'

Markus managed a laugh—awkward and a little delayed.

He still had all of Sunnywood's paperwork to return to Granny: a mess of troll contracts, binding runes, and debt summaries written in half a dozen magical dialects. He was heading to Upper Susshingham that evening to meet his old law professor—one of the few people he knew who'd survived a troll-backed foreclosure. With luck, they might finally decipher what exactly a "contingent tithe clause" entailed, and whether it really did mean someone owed the bank their second-born.

He'd spent the last three nights trying to make sense of one clause alone. It mentioned "ancestral debt obligations," the "souls of signatories," and—possibly—bodily fluids.

'I wasn't joking,' said Hiro flatly.

Markus blinked. 'What?'

'About the cannibalism. Not with this lot.'

Markus frowned. 'See, I still can't tell if you're joking.' But Markus never got his answer, because at that moment, Poppy came tottering down the stairs. She smiled at him—much to Markus's shock, because she was, unmistakably, Poppy... only sixty years older than she had been last week.

He took a step back, tripping over Bernard, and landed in the flowerbeds, knocking over a terracotta pot loaded with colourful blooms.

Poppy stumbled forward on creaky legs, frowning far too wrinkly a frown. She leaned down and offered him a hand. Markus looked at it like she was contagious.

'What'd you go and do that for?' she said. 'Are you alright?'

'He's just a little scared 'cos you're a lot older now than when we last saw you,' said Janey helpfully.

Poppy's face fell. She hadn't thought about it. Not really. She'd been cursed for nearly a week now, and though she refused to get used to it, she wasn't surprised by her reflection anymore. Just… resigned.

'Granny Grack cursed me, I'm afraid. It's fine, don't worry. It's supposed to be a lesson, but honestly, I think she's just being a vindictive old bag.'

Hiro muttered something and disappeared back into the kitchen.

Poppy watched him go, then turned back to Janey and Markus.

'So, are you ready for your sleepover then, Janey?'

Janey nodded enthusiastically.

'Dad let me bring just one pet mouse as an 'motional support animal.'

She held up her hands, and a small mouse skeleton sprinted up her arm. It was wearing a bright blue dinner jacket.

'I like his coat,' said Poppy.

'It has buttons,' said Janey. 'See?'

The mouse now stood proudly atop her somewhat chaotic plaited hair. If it still had whiskers, Poppy was sure they'd be curled like a gentleman's moustache.

'He's very dapper indeed.'

In the distance, Clay waved. He was picking flowers for the house, his basket overflowing to the point he'd begun stuffing blooms into his overall pockets and trusty gumboots. He looked like a man mid-blossom.

Janey took off towards him with Bernard on her heels, leaving Poppy and Markus alone.

'Are you sure this is a good idea?' said Markus. 'I mean, gods, are you even alright?'

He peered past her into the foyer.

'Do you need help? Are they trapping you here against your will?

Should I call someone? The town guard are all useless, but—they'd help you if you asked.'

Poppy smiled. Then laughed. It started as a chuckle, but seeing Markus's genuine concernfor her—for some reason, it was the funniest thing in the world. She laughed so hard her ribs hurt.

Markus stared at her as if she'd finally cracked. He grabbed her arm.

'Come on,' he whispered. 'I'm getting you out of here. Quickly! Before they notice you've gone. Janey! Get back here!'

Poppy laughed harder.

'Stop. You're going to make me piss myself.'

Markus paused.

'Why are you laughing? This isn't funny. Last week you were what—twenty? Now look at you. You're at least eighty-five.'

'I look no older than sixty, thank you very much.'

'This isn't right. It's not safe for you to be here. And there's no way I'm leaving Janey.'

He looked back to where Janey was now helping Clay pick flowers. Bernard was stalking through the tall grass like a lion cub, pouncing and vanishing and returning again.

'Janey!' Markus shouted. 'Come here, now! We're leaving.'

He turned back to Poppy. 'Come on, hurry up.'

But Poppy pulled her arm free.

'Markus. Stop.'

He didn't.

'I said STOP!'

Markus froze at the sudden sharpness in her voice.

'You can't stay here. They're insane. Clinically, probably.'

'Yeah, I know. Almost definitely.'

'Well then—'

'But they'd never hurt me,' said Poppy. 'Not really. And they'd never hurt Janey. Not in a million years.'

Markus shook his head. 'I'm not leaving her here. I'm not coming back to find my daughter is suddenly an adult.'

'Could I be grown-up when you come back?' said Janey, sounding excited.

ARE YOU FEELING STRONG?

In the dining room, crouched beneath the open window, Granny Grack and Huk were hiding. They weren't spying or listening in. At least, not at first. But then they'd heard Poppy shout 'stop', and it all sounded rather interesting.

Huk looked at Granny and frowned. He kicked her foot.

'This is your fault, you realise.'

'My fault?'

'You cursed her!'

Granny folded her arms and frowned—quite spectacularly.

'It wasn't a curse, not really. I was just winding her up. It will start to fade shortly. Honestly, I'm amazed it's lasted this long.'

Huk grunted.

'What?'

He shook his head.

'No, go on. Say it.'

'Well, now he thinks we're insane, he won't let the kid come back. And if you keep pushing the girl, she's just as likely to leave.'

Granny looked at Huk, frowning. She'd been about to say that they weren't insane—they'd fought against insane before, fought against it more times than she could count, and they didn't come close—but she stopped herself, because something interesting was happening here.

'What's it matter if the kid won't come back, Huk?'

He folded his arms. His lower jaw jutted out just slightly. He looked far more orcish than human when he was in a huff.

'I like having them here,' he said quietly.

'It's always been just us, and we've been perfectly fine. Haven't we?'

Huk looked at her. His eyes softened. 'We can do better than *just* fine, Grack. Now help me get up, my knees have started to ache.'

Granny shhh'ed him and waved him back down. But Huk pushed himself up without her help and flung open the window fully, so that he was looking out at Markus, who was somehow now trapped in a headlock by Poppy.

'Gods, Poppy,' shouted Huk, proudly. 'That's good form, that is. Though you want to hold his neck a little higher so that you stop him from slipping out.'

Poppy looked up at them and stopped what she was doing. She dropped Markus in the process, who fell to the ground for the second time that afternoon.

'What are you two doing?' said Poppy, suspiciously.

'What are *we* doing?' said Granny. 'What, my dear, are you *two* doing?'

Poppy flattened her shirt and looked at Markus. She offered him her hand, but he got up without taking it.

'You're all mental,' he said, angrily.

He looked out at Janey, who was running around the field of wildflowers with Clay. They were being chased by the half-rotten skeleton of a rabbit. Clay didn't look to be having half as much fun as Janey.

Markus sighed.

Granny leaned against the window frame, head in her hands. She smiled fondly at the girl.

'We're as mad as your lovely daughter, which is to say we're not mad at all, just grossly misunderstood. And a little overdrawn, I suppose.'

Poppy smiled, despite her still-livid fury at Granny. She looked at Markus and said, quietly: 'Please don't take her away. She can be herself here. And you... you can have some time to yourself for once.'

Markus started to interrupt her, but Poppy cut him off.

'You need the alone time. You need to do normal adult things, even if that means just cleaning your house and sleeping in. Or getting drunk. Or doing whatever the fuck it is you want to do. But you need to do these things—not just for you, but for Janey too. She deserves to have a father who isn't on the brink of a mental break.'

Markus held her gaze for a long time.

Finally, he relented.

'I'm not going to Upper Susshingham for alone time or to get *drunk*, Poppy.' He looked down at the briefcase in his hand. 'I'm going to meet with my old professor. This contract Sunnywood is involved with, it's... it's really quite terrifically bad.'

'I know.'

'No, like it's really, *really* bad.'

'I *know*. Granny says one clause legally entitles the bank to our skeletons upon insolvency. I'm not even sure she's joking.'

'She's not... and I am not on the brink of a mental break, by the way.'

'The fact you have to say you're not, probably means you are, lad,' said Huk. 'No, we'll take good care of the girl, don't you worry. You go and sort this mess out.'

Markus sighed. He pinched his nose and scrunched up his tired eyes. He looked at Janey—the rotten rabbit carcass had turned into three rotten rabbit carcasses.

'JANEY!' he shouted. 'What did I say about reanimating rotten corpses!'

Janey stopped laughing and running around in circles with Clay. 'Nothing bigger than a mouse and nothing with flesh still on it—the stains don't come out of the carpet.'

Markus grinned a little at that. Just the corner of his mouth, but it was a smile nonetheless.

'If I come back and she's anything more than a day older, I swear to gods I'll—'

'Yes, yes. We get it. You'll kill us all in our sleep or something similar,' said Granny. 'We're all terrified, I'm sure.'

Huk elbowed her.

'The kid is safe here, though,' repeated Huk. 'You don't have to worry.'

'It's impossible not to worry. If anything happens—and I mean anything at all—send word to The Roving Rambler. I'll be gone for a couple of nights. Assuming the professor doesn't burst into flames trying to interpret Clause 19b. It really is the *most* ridiculous contract I've ever seen. Honestly, if he can't find a loophole, you lot will be needing a miracle—or a bank robbery.'

'Stop,' said Poppy. 'You'll give me a stress rash.'

'Where am I staying?' said Markus.

'The Rambling Rover in Upper Susshingham,' said Poppy.

'I said The *Roving Rambler.*'

'No, you didn't.'

'Yes, I did.'

'I'm not sure you did, lad,' said Huk.

Markus sighed. 'Look, I'll write it down.'

In the end, Markus did leave Janey. He went with a worried look and an incredibly slow walk, but he did leave. That was progress in Poppy's eyes. That was trust.

She looked at Granny and Huk, both still leaning out the window and watching her.

'What are you two looking at?'

'Seems to me your hair isn't as grey as it was yesterday,' said Huk.

Poppy hurriedly undid her messy bun from its tie and examined the ends. They were darker and almost red. There were still greys, yes, but not nearly as many as there had been the night before.

'Does that mean I've done it then?' said Poppy.

Granny frowned. 'Done what?'

'Broken your bloody curse?'

Granny chuckled. 'Don't be ridiculous.'

And with that, she left the window.

Huk rolled his eyes and smiled at Poppy.

Poppy smiled back. It was an awkward smile, and it lasted for far too long.

'No, really, Huk. What are you looking at? You're starting to freak me out.'

'Are you feeling strong, Poppy?'

'Why? Are we going to fight?'

Huk laughed.

'Yes. Yes, I think we are.'

EVEN IF YOUR ARMS ACHE

The early afternoon light was golden and hazy amongst the hedgerows and lavender. Clay ducked up from between the perfectly manicured bushes to wince and shout his be-carefuls. Not because Poppy was clashing very sharp, surprisingly heavy swords with Huk, but a 'be careful of my garden'. They'd already been warned that if they squashed so much as a flower, he'd set the bees on them. And no one doubted that for a minute. Though Janey had said, rather vocally, that she'd quite like to see them all attacked by bees.

'Stop running away,' shouted Huk.

'You're trying to kill me,' said Poppy, indignantly. 'Running away seems the smart thing to do.'

'It's sword-fighting, Poppy,' said Janey. 'Not a game of chase-ies.'

Kelzu shoved a microphone in front of Janey's face. 'Would you mind repeating that? For next week's episode?'

Janey looked at Kelzu as if he'd grown another head, then reached for the recording machine.

'You're very silly,' she said, deadly serious.

Poppy jumped back from Huk—who swung at her wildly—and tripped, accidentally letting go of her sword, which spun through the air. Kelzu ducked it with a practised ease that could only come from a lifetime of finding whatever it was he was doing more interesting— even when surrounded by things like sword-fights.

He looked at Janey, seriously.

'I might be silly, yes. But silliness is a vital, vital trait. Do you understand?'

Janey shook her head.

'Quite. Now, do you have anything on topic to say for next week's episode, or would you like to give me back my recorder?'

Janey giggled. 'Do you want to see me make zombies?'

'Well, no, I-ah. Well, actually, now that you mention it, it could make for interesting subject matter.'

Poppy hopped past Janey and Kelzu on their picnic blanket and retrieved her sword from where it had landed, wobbling and lodged in the grass.

'No zombies,' she said. 'We made a deal, remember?'

Janey nodded solemnly. She looked at Kelzu. 'I hate deals.'

'Now square up,' said Huk. 'Shoulders back, hold the sword up straight.'

Poppy lifted the sword, her arms shaking under its weight. It felt like her shoulders were going to pop out of joint at any moment. She grunted and dropped the sword again, unable to hold it.

'I'm too old for this shit.'

Huk groaned. 'You're getting younger by the minute, you idiot!'

'It doesn't seem fair to me. Here I am, slathering on swamp mud from Faeland for the last decade,' said Kelzu. 'And do you think I can get my wrinkles to disappear that quickly?'

'Maybe I ought to try a shortsword. Or a scimitar or something. I don't think greatswords are for me, Huk.'

'Useless,' grumbled Huk. 'Bloody useless.'

'Oh, alright. It's my first lesson. Go easy on me.'

'Do you think a roving band of zombies will go easy on you? Or a vampire in the mists? Or a dire-beast, woken from hibernation? If

you want to learn to fight, Poppy—if you want to be an adventurer
—then you have to damn well swing your sword, even if your arms
ache and you feel like you can't. Because the alternative is *death*.'

Poppy's cheeks burned.

She said nothing, but the heat in her face swelled. She feared,
more and more lately, that she really wasn't cut out for adventuring.
As if up until this point, she'd just been playing pretend.

'Oh, dammit,' said Kelzu.

Both Poppy and Huk looked at him.

'What?' said Poppy.

'I wasn't recording.'

Poppy groaned.

'It was wise... and mildly touching! It's exactly the kind of thing
we need in our show—the battles, the laughter and the wisdom,' said
Kelzu.

They continued clanging swords and—to Clay's disgust—
trampling flowers until the sun had set and the fireflies swam through
the fields around them. Janey and Kelzu had both fallen asleep on the
picnic blanket. It almost felt a shame to wake them.

'Dinner's ready!' shouted Hiro. 'And I'm a world-class chef, not a
fucking service maid!'

'God, he's got a temper on him,' said Huk.

They headed back through Clay's wildflower fields. Janey rode
atop Huk's shoulders, despite clearly being too heavy for the
stubborn half-orc. The fireflies danced around them, hiding in
blossoms so the field looked like fairy lights on an All Hallows' Eve. It
was, thought Poppy, the most magical thing she'd ever seen. She
trailed a little behind, listening to their voices, their laughter echoing
in the dusk. Somewhere between the lavender and the fireflies, she
felt something tighten in her chest. Like a thread being tugged.
Perhaps I'm not chasing glory, she thought—but something softer.
Something that feels like home.

Kelzu rambled on about his plans for their new recording studio in the basement, but Poppy wasn't really listening. Her ears were tuned elsewhere.

Janey leaned forward, her chin resting atop Huk's head.

'Why do you have so many scratches on you, Mr Huk?'

Huk feigned ignorance. 'Where?' he said, quickly glancing about. 'Where do I have scratches, Miss Janey?'

Janey laughed her usual laugh.

'You have one here. And here. And one all the way across your face.'

'I don't,' said Huk. 'I can't!'

'You do!'

'No, no, no. My perfect, beautiful, amazing face. What will I do?'

Janey giggled. 'How did you get dem?'

Huk pointed to the scar on his cheek—the deep one, the one that ran from his left eye all the way down his jaw.

'Where do you think I got this one?'

'You got it... umm. You were ice-skating! Yes! You were ice-skating, doing one of them spinning round tricks, and you slipped and went flying across the ice. Cos ice is sharp when you're flying cross it, you cut yourself, and there was prolly blood everywhere, and everyone was prolly screaming "Oh no, Huk! You're bleeding everywhere, you're going to die!" but you knew better. Cos you're strong, and smart, and dead clever at ice skating.'

Huk laughed—uproariously loud. The kind of laugh that would send birds scattering from trees.

'Ice skating, you reckon?'

'Mmm.'

'And dead clever, you say?'

'Oh yeah. Defininietly.'

Huk's chest puffed out.

'Defininietly indeed.' He looked up at Janey and grinned widely, showing his filed-down tusks.

'Well, what about this one?'

He pointed to a deep, burn-like scar across his arm. The skin was shiny and calloused, catching the dark with a faint glow—as if it still might have been burning even now.

'Your turn,' said Janey. 'You tell me how that one happened.'

Huk's smile faltered. He seemed, thought Poppy, to be weighing something up—and decided to tell her anyway.

'It was a dragon. Ten, twenty times the size of Bernard.'

Out of the corner of her eye, Poppy saw Kelzu's hand shoot up, recorder raised.

'But why would a dragon burn you? They're too clever for that. They're misundermestood,' said Janey, matter-of-factly.

Poppy grinned. Where in the realm had she picked that one up from? Was her father some sort of magical creature activist, then? She'd have to ask. At the very least, it sounded interesting.

'Yes, but this was a particularly nasty, chronically misunderstood dragon.'

'Oh, Mr Huk,' said Janey, knowingly. 'You weren't trying to steal its treasure, were you?'

'Of course I was. It had mountains of gold! It shouldn't have noticed a small bag going missing. What's it need all that for, anyway? Plain greedy, if you ask me.'

Janey tutted.

Poppy watched Kelzu lean toward his mic.

'Hoarding wealth is bad for the economy, after all. A dragon's influence has ruined many a village and city.'

'You didn't hurt it, did you?' asked Janey.

'I'm the one with the great big bloody scar,' said Huk. He looked up at her, seeing the seriousness on her face. He sighed.

'But, no. I didn't hurt it.' And then he muttered, 'Not for lack of trying, either.'

Janey pointed at another scar and leaned forward—losing her balance and falling off Huk's shoulders. But he caught Janey easily, tickling her until she giggled that terrifying little giggle of hers.

'I can't imagine you hurting anyone anyway, Mr Huk.'

Huk smiled—a smile that didn't quite reach the eyes.

Poppy felt that smile like a stone in her gut. What stories had he left untold? Was this what growing old as an adventurer looked like —laughing at dragons by day, haunted by them at night? They walked in silence for a moment. Janey's words hung in the air like smoke. Poppy could have been imagining it, but it seemed to her that Huk looked... well, sad.

Because he had hurt people, hadn't he?

Killed them, more than likely.

That was the life of an adventurer in these parts. Monsters, yes— terrifying creatures up to all sorts. But still: it was murder. And everyone thought they were the good guys. Who was Huk to judge? No—it was murder, all right. And Poppy wasn't sure she was capable of it.

And she wasn't sure that was a bad thing.

'You're too old anyway,' said Janey, dismissively. 'You couldn't hurt anyone if you wanted to. They'd just run off, and you'd never catch them.'

They all laughed at that.

Huk set Janey down, then chased her toward Sunnywood House —proving that even if he was old, he could still catch her.

PLEASE SCREAM IF YOU
REQUIRE ASSISTANCE

The sleepover, under Janey's strict instructions, was to take place in the library. Everyone was invited, and non-attendance was not an option. If leading an undead army was, thought Poppy, indeed in Janey's future: then gods help us all. The child's knack for leadership was unparalleled; where leadership failed, she went in for overt dictatorship. If it wasn't so cute, it would have been terrifying.

The library, up until that point, had been a storage room of sorts. So they'd had to move old desks and battle dummies and decades worth of just general crap to the side. Once the floor was cleaned and covered with blankets and pillows, a fort was to be built.

Poppy grimaced, watching Janey chide Kelzu for his lack of enthusiasm. 'Well, if you want us to listen to your silly show tonight,' she said, adamantly, 'you'll stick your finger out your bum and help.'

They'd turned off the Ether-lights, upon Janey's insistence ('it's not cosy enough!'), and Granny had cast a small spell that filled the room with soft and slowly moving globules of warmth. They bounced from wall to floor to ceiling like balloons.

K.S. had taken to attaching ropes to the upper shelves and gallery bannisters with his mechanical precision, whilst Kelzu sat atop his shoulders like a small child directing him. Janey had been allowed to reanimate a dead swallow as her dedicated 'Sunnywood pet'—much to Bernard's disgust. He, in protest, had taken to sulking atop a blanket pile in the corner.

Clay had been convinced to join them, albeit begrudgingly. The gardener preferred to stick to his small cottage and the grounds surrounding it. Poppy barely recognised the man out of his overalls and mud-stained boots.

He was dressed instead in jeans and a t-shirt.

It shocked her. He looked so painfully normal amongst the rest of them.

He smiled, looking across the mess and chaos of the dining room. He had a bunch of flowers in his hand, which seemed to be his custom. It was impossible to leave the man's presence with empty hands. You were getting something green whether you wanted it or not.

'CLAY!' shouted Janey. 'Come meet my dead bird. He actually flies, *unlike* Bernard.'

Bernard growled in his sleep and rolled over.

Poppy grinned. 'You're just in time for the grand reveal.'

'The grand reveal?'

Kelzu leapt down from K.S's shoulders with practised ease.

'Huk and I are treating you lot to an early premiere—our latest episode, and a bold new direction for the show. *Sunnywood House.* The adventures, past and present, of those who'd very much like to be remembered as the world's *greatest* adventurers.'

Clay looked confused.

'Look,' said Huk. 'We're still working on the title.'

'What happened to The Sunnywood Signal? I liked that.'

'It was too reductive,' said Kelzu. 'Too naive. I felt we needed a rebrand. Thought it might help with listener numbers.'

'And we thought, instead of talking about the past all the time,' said Huk, 'we might talk more about what's happening here, and now, you know?'

Clay nodded, though he looked like he didn't really get it at all.

Just then, as K.S was engineering an ambitious crossbeam of pillow-anchoring ropes across the upper shelves, a magical scroll exploded into the room.

It zipped over their heads in a sizzling spiral, did a loop-the-loop around one of Granny's floating light globes, and smacked Poppy square in the forehead.

'Ow—what the fu—'

The scroll unfurled mid-air and, in a booming, far-too-cheerful voice, began to speak:

'FINAL NOTICE! Your quarterly payment for The Twice-Remortgaged Mortgage is now ONE MONTH OVERDUE. Your property may be subject to magical repossession. A representative of The United Troll Bank Association will be calling upon you shortly. Thank you for choosing TROLLBANK™. Please scream if you require assistance.'

Everyone froze.

Even Janey.

The scroll burst into glittering confetti and vanished.

Granny looked suddenly like she wanted to punch a wall. 'Those bastards dare to send enchanted mail into *my* home?'

Poppy sighed. 'It's probably because your mailbox eats all the sodding letters.'

'Good,' said Huk, savagely. 'As it bloody should.'

'Have we killed any trolls before?' said Kelzu.

Granny shook her head. 'Gods, no. What would be the point?'

'We're not killing a bunch of trolls,' said Poppy. 'We're not—we're not killing anything.' She looked at Janey, who, if anything, seemed to be enjoying this line of discussion. 'It's not how civilised people deal with things.'

'I wipe my arse with civilised,' said Huk.

'No, you don't. You use three-ply toilet paper and get angry when it's not the lavender-scented stuff. Now shut up. Let's just enjoy tonight, yeah? We can talk about this when the little one is gone?'

The fire behind Huk's eyes dimmed a little. He nodded. And the sudden silence was awkward.

Clay cleared his throat. 'It's very, ahh...'

'Cosy. Yes,' said Janey. 'Sit here. This bit's extra EXTRA comfy.' She patted the spot beside her aggressively.

It took a while, but soon the anger and the silence was replaced by conversation again.

'You spend as many years camping out under the stars as we have,' said Granny. 'And you learn a few tricks along the way to make things more comfortable.'

Clay nodded and sat cross-legged atop a pillow at Janey's insistence.

K.S was muttering to himself now, more than usual. Occasionally, he'd freeze mid-knot, blink twice, then continue as though nothing had happened.

'What is K.S doing, exactly?' said Poppy.

K.S spun his head a full rotation, like an owl, to look at her. 'I am preparing the pillow fort. Structural integrity must be maintained throughout for optimal lounging and comfort. It will all make sense shortly, Matron.'

Poppy felt like she'd been punched. 'I am *not* Matron.'

K.S tied off the final piece of rope to a lamp sconce at the end of the library. 'I apologise. I meant no offence. If you would like me to refer to you in some other way, please be sure to let me know.'

'Just Poppy. Just Poppy is fine.'

'My logs have been updated, Just Poppy. Now, if you'll excuse me, this is taking rather a lot more processing power than I anticipated.'

Huk laughed.

Kelzu looked concerned and began writing in his notebook, which he carried with him everywhere.

Granny's illusioned ceiling was now blooming with magical bunting. K.S tied off the final rope, then yanked a single thread—triggering a great cascade. A circus-tent of bedsheets unfurled from above them, rippling down in waves.

Janey giggled in her terrifyingly evil-sounding way.

Granny sighed. 'I thought I'd be happy if I'd never seen the inside of another tent as long as I live. But you know... I think I've rather missed it.'

She raised her hands again and with a flick of her fingers, colour bloomed across the ceiling like ink in water—swirling auroras of green and blue and violet, curling amongst illusionary stars.

'Now all we need is food,' said Granny.

'I hope we get cake. I like cake. Cake with cream and icing. Or if Hiro can't do cake, I'll have just the cream and icing,' said Janey.

'You don't ask for much, do you?' Poppy smiled. 'It'll be cabbage cake, more likely, I'm afraid.'

'Cabbage cake?' Janey looked horrified.

The sad part was: Poppy wasn't even joking. Hiro hadn't had a grocery order delivered in a week. They had no money left. Not even for food. She'd tried not thinking about it. She still rather hoped that the problem would solve itself.

But in the back of her mind, that officious scroll was still shouting.

And she wasn't sure how long the fort would hold.

BOOTS THAT FINALLY FIT

'There must be something we can do,' said Poppy, no more than ten minutes later. The scroll was consuming her, and if she didn't talk about it, she felt liable to explode.

'I thought we weren't talking about it when I'm here,' said Janey, pointedly.

Granny pulled Janey into her lap and rested her chin atop the girl's head. 'You know I really thought this mess would have sorted itself out by now.'

'Do messes usually sort themselves out?' asked Poppy. 'Or did Matron just tidy everything up for you?'

'Now, there's no need to be snarky,' said Granny.

'Well, I'm sorry, but I don't think this is going to just sort itself out.'

'Dad'll figure it out,' said Janey, matter-of-factly. 'He's dead clever.'

Even with Markus in Upper Susshingham trying to sort out the contract, Poppy wasn't so sure it'd work. He'd left sounding less than confident about the whole thing.

'I mean, really,' said Clay, 'the whole thing should be null and void anyway. It was a set-up. It should be Matron footing these sodding bills. Not us.'

Everyone was quiet.

They nodded in agreement.

It was bizarre, thought Poppy. But she didn't blame Matron for this. Not really. This felt like a problem of their own making. If they hadn't tripped her down the stairs twice a day and antagonised her like it was their most favourite thing in the world to do, then perhaps none of this would have happened. But then, thought Poppy, indeed *none* of this would have happened. She wouldn't be the head caregiver of the world's most famous retirement home for the world's most famous adventurers. And suddenly the boots to fill didn't feel so damned big; on the contrary, she rather liked the fit. It was a mess, don't get her wrong. But it was a particularly satisfying and thrilling kind of mess all the same.

No, Poppy found that even if all of it did make her want to tear her hair out, she was beginning to feel quite at home. And it was bloody typical, she thought, that the moment that should happen, it was to be ripped out from underneath her.

You spend your whole life not having a home, and then just when a place begins to feel like it, what do you know, great big fucking trolls in suits probably.

It was ridiculous.

'We could evict the giant spider from the top floor,' said Clay. 'Clean out the rooms and take in more residents?'

They all looked at him as if he'd gone mad.

'And what, live with strangers?' said Kelzu.

'I was a stranger once,' said Poppy.

'What's your point?'

'Well, people stop being strangers after a while. They become your friends, don't they?'

Kelzu had started to say something, but stopped himself.

He looked, thought Poppy, briefly flustered.

'I'm not sure I like the idea either,' said Granny. 'Imagine the place full of old people. Ugh.' She made a disgusted face.

Janey leaned into Granny. 'But aren't you old people?'

'No, we're just pretending,' said Granny. 'We don't sit around and knit and hobble about with walking frames. We have dignity. No, we're not old people: we're retired adventurers. There's a difference.'

Janey mulled this over quietly. 'But you do knit. I've seen it. It's quite good.'

'Well, I...' Granny looked stumped. 'Thank you. I've been having horrible trouble weaving hexes into my cross-stitch, but what can you do?'

'Although, honestly,' said Huk, 'sometimes I think a chair lift up those stairs wouldn't be a bad idea.'

'And a walking frame is basically a portable seat,' said Kelzu. 'I'm not sure I'd say no to always having a chair to sit on.'

'There must be others like you out there,' said Poppy. 'Adventurers who've had enough but aren't quite done yet.'

They thought this over for a moment.

'Maybe we should have gone after Matron,' said Granny.

'I bloody told you,' said Poppy.

'Oh, I know, but chasing after people is so beneath us, dear. Don't you think?'

Huk sighed.

The silence stretched out.

'So they'll be sending someone round, then.'

'A represen-ment-ta-tive,' said Janey.

Poppy nodded. She looked over the scroll again for what felt like the hundredth time. 'They'll be here before the end of the week,' she said.

'And we're sure we don't want to...' Huk mimed slicing his throat with his thumb.

'We're sure,' said Poppy, solemnly. 'We'll figure it out.'

'You won't,' said Alfred.

The ghost had flown up through the floor and was sitting in the fireplace, amongst the burning hot coals and sparking logs, looking out at them.

'What do you mean by that?'

'Well, you're all perfectly hopeless for a start. And if anyone listened to me when I mentioned the troll bank—at great length, might I add—you'd know perfectly well just how buggered you all are.' The ghost sighed. 'No, what you've done is rob me of a good home. One I've paid for centuries in advance, and *poof*, all lost to some predatory contract just like that. And for what? Gods only know what they'll do with the place afterwards. A hotel, probably. Actually, it would make quite a profit as a bed and breakfast.' Alfred drifted out of the fireplace. When he was thinking hard, he had a tendency to float. Like it was sheer willpower and concentration alone that kept him on the ground. 'You know, I might bring that up to them. Living in a bed and breakfast would be interesting, at least.'

Granny sighed and waved her hand through the air. Magic burst out, and Alfred was sent flying out through the library. He hit Hiro and lost his shape, exploding into a ghostly mist with a shout.

Hiro flinched and nearly dropped his tray. 'Oh fuck off, Alfred.' He looked flustered and furious. 'How many times must I say it: I'm a chef. Not a waiter. If you want your food next time, you bloody well come and get it.'

He slammed the tray of still-steaming, glistening bread rolls down hard. 'Enjoy your cabbage loaves. I hope you all choke on them.'

Everyone watched the ill-tempered chef storm back down the hall.

Janey raised her eyebrows. 'Well, he needs a nap.'

Kelzu sniffed the bread.

Poppy sighed. 'Should I go after him?'

Clay stood up. 'No, it's fine. I'll go.'

'Ask him if there's any dessert, please, Mr Clay?'

'I think he'd murder me on the spot for mentioning dessert.'

'Well, I can bring you back to life,' said Janey, shrugging. 'So ask. Please.'

THE TALE OF NO
ONE LIKE YOU

Once they'd all settled amongst the cushions and blankets, Kelzu began opening up K.S.'s chest panel, revealing a labyrinth of cogs, glass vials, and runic wires. He pushed and prodded and pulled.

Poppy watched, entranced. 'What are you doing to him?'

'Trying to find out where he put our blasted radio show,' said Kelzu. He flung a cog over his shoulder, followed by several chocolate wrappers. 'It should be in his memory logs down here, but—Poppy, come here for a second.'

Poppy knelt beside him and peered into K.S. He really was all clockwork and glowing spells. It made her eyes water just to look at it.

'Hold this.' Kelzu grabbed her hands and pushed them against the inside of K.S.'s main rotor. 'It's not heavy, it just needs the support while I dig around.'

She took the weight of the cog. It stopped spinning. K.S.'s head dipped slightly.

'Where are his memory logs exactly?' she asked.

'Just past the cogitation disks. There—did you see?'

Poppy had to shut her eyes. 'It hurts to look at. It's like cutting onions.'

'Who's got onions?' said Hiro.

Poppy hit her head on K.S.'s chest. Clay had dragged Hiro back into the tent. He still looked royally pissed, but the mention of onions had perked him up.

'No one,' she said. 'Kelzu's trying to find his radio show.'

'What's it doing in there?' said Janey.

'He hasn't lost it, has he? Really?' said Huk.

Kelzu gasped, and the cog in Poppy's hands began to turn against her. She yanked her hands away before she lost any fingers.

'Bastard,' muttered Kelzu. He slammed K.S.'s chest shut and tapped him on the head, hard. 'Wake up, you big oaf. Now listen: play the new episode of Sunnywood, please.'

There was a hum inside K.S., followed by a pause. 'I'm sorry, master. It appears the file was... CORRUPTED.'

'So I don't have to stay then?' said Hiro, hopefully. 'I'm free to go?'

'No,' said Janey. 'You're staying for the sleepover.'

'I am afraid there will be no premiere tonight,' said K.S. 'With your permission, master, I will enter a state of hibernation and begin recovery processes.'

'Yeah, recover away, you big idiot,' groaned Huk. 'We worked bloody hard on that, you know.'

Granny frowned at him.

'What? We did. I was quite looking forward to kicking back and talking about how clever we are.'

Poppy snorted. 'Oh, I bet you were.'

'Can we still have a story?' said Janey. 'I do fink it is story time, if I'm being honest.'

They all looked at Janey. She was standing with her arms crossed, serious as a magistrate.

'A story?' said Poppy.

'Yes. We've had dinner. Now it's story time.' She said this as matter-of-factly as one might declare the sky blue or fire hot. 'Do you know any stories about nekkermancers? Ones like me?'

The room grew quiet and tense.

Poppy looked at Huk and shook her head slightly. The girl didn't need to hear that, whatever that was. Huk opened his mouth, then closed it again.

Kelzu busied himself scribbling in his notebook.

Granny shifted, then tapped her lap for Janey to sit on. 'There are no necromancers like you, Janey.'

'Yes, there are. There's oodles. There was one in Lower Westfax only last week. He terrorised an entire street with a dozen dead pirates. It was wicked.' Janey glanced at Poppy. 'I don't mean the good kind of wicked. I mean the bad kind.'

'What I meant, Janey,' said Granny, 'was that there are no necromancers like you—just like there are no warriors like Huk, no witches quite like me, no chefs as good as Hiro, no gardeners like Clay, and no Poppys as good at being Poppy as our Poppy.'

Poppy rolled her eyes.

'So yes, we know stories about necromancers. We've even fought a few. But telling you those stories wouldn't be fair because they have nothing in common with you. Not a thing. Because no one is you, and no one is as good at being you as you are.'

Janey grinned. 'Fanks. I still want to hear about them, though. Did they fight you with dead pirates like the man in Lower Westfax?'

They all seemed to relax a little then. Maybe the kid, like most kids, was far cleverer and more resilient than adults gave her credit for.

Kelzu looked up from his notes as Granny settled in to tell the story. Poppy noticed a small clockwork beetle had crawled out of Kelzu's pocket. It scuttled towards Granny, abdomen ticking, its tiny recording antenna glowing.

Maybe she'd just grown used to it—or perhaps she no longer minded—but there was something oddly endearing about it now.

He wanted so desperately to share their story.

To record it.

To have it remembered.

And so she made a quiet vow to roll her eyes a lot less about it. She joined Janey on her blanket mound, curling into the pillows as Granny, Huk, and Kelzu argued about what actually happened all those years ago. They laughed, listened, interrupted, and questioned. They debated the legitimacy of Huk's backflip off a church spire into a zombie-filled town square.

'What were you even doing on top of a church?' asked Poppy.

'And then—huh? Oh, I don't know. I don't remember. That's not important. What's important is that I looked very impressive doing it,' said Huk.

Granny leaned into Poppy and Janey. 'It was less a backflip and more of a clumsy fall, if I remember.'

'It was not!'

'And it wasn't a church spire, it was a tavern. A small one.'

'How dare you?' said Huk. He looked scandalised.

'And it wasn't a town square full of zombies at all,' said Kelzu. 'It was a fenced paddock. With quite possibly the fattest zombie I've ever seen.'

Janey laughed and laughed at that. So much so that Huk's indignation melted into sly humour. It was impossible to stay sour when that strange, evil laugh came bursting out of a toddler.

'And then what happened?' asked Poppy. She was thrilled to learn that even accomplished adventurers still exaggerated and fell off tavern roofs.

'I slipped and hit my head on a fence post,' said Huk, flatly. 'Knocked me out cold.'

And so the night went on like that. Kelzu recording, K.S. occasionally asked to verify the facts—though the automaton revealed nothing, blaming either his hibernation or corrupted memory logs.

Poppy didn't believe that for a second, though. Regardless of their still growling stomachs (the cabbage bread had barely touched their sides) or the cold of the room without a fire crackling, the residents of Sunnywood laughed more than they had laughed in a long time. Quite possibly ever.

FISHING FOR STARS

They'd all fallen asleep on whole mounds of blankets and pillows. Bernard had curled up beside Poppy in such a way that keeping any of her blanket was going to be an ongoing battle. The book-wyrm was a gigantic bed-hog, and with the entire library-sized pillow fort free, he'd seen fit to sleep squashed between Poppy's back and Huk's feet.

It had been awfully cosy and warm and comfortable at first. Poppy had dozed off. And then someone had started snoring. Maybe it had been her?

No, it couldn't have been—they were still snoring.

She'd managed to drift off again when Bernard kicked her in the back. She groaned and turned over to look at the dragon. He was sitting bolt upright, like a German shepherd on high alert.

Beside him sat Janey, cross-legged and wide awake. They were both peeking out through the pillow fort's bedsheet walls.

Poppy sat up.

'What are you two looking at?'

Janey ducked her head back inside the tent. Her hair was knotted from sleep, but her eyes were wide.

'There are shooting stars, Poppy. A whole entire sky of 'em. Bernie woke me up to show me.'

Poppy frowned. Shooting stars?

She crawled out of bed and pulled Janey into her lap, yawning. But she stopped mid-yawn. The kid was right—the sky was full of shooting stars.

Bernard growled: a long, low rumble that turned into a kind of howl.

She'd never seen anything like it. For some reason, it terrified and amazed her in equal parts. The night sky, she thought, looked to be falling around them.

Bernard cried out—in his doggish way—and then launched forward, sprinting off towards the tall arched windows that lined the walls of the library.

Behind Poppy, she heard Granny Grack roll over and mutter something.

'I said what's that giant lizard barking at!'

Poppy was too stunned to answer. She watched, mesmerised, as the sky streaked with light.

'I said shut him up,' shouted Granny.

Poppy jumped in shock.

Janey turned to look at Granny. 'He's only telling you to get up and look. He doesn't want you to miss out.'

'Miss out on what?'

'Come and look. It's bootiful.'

Granny pulled the blanket over her head. 'No, thank you. I've seen enough beautiful things in my life. I'd rather sleep.'

Huk continued to snore like a freight train.

'Will you—' Kelzu kicked him. 'Stop snoring—' He kicked him again. 'You intolerable, sodding bastard.'

Huk choked on a snore and sat bolt upright. He had his fists raised, as if ready for a fight.

'What is it?' he said. 'I'll kill 'em.'

Granny groaned and sat up. 'I forgot what it was like to sleep in a tent with you two.' She got out of bed, flinging the blankets aside. 'Alright, what is it? What's so bloody important you'd rather be looking at it than rugged up and asleep, hmm?'

Janey turned briefly to look at her.

'The stars are falling out of the sky. All of 'em.'

'Stars don't fall together, love. They prefer to do it one at a time —unless they're grumpy or protesting something, and then they—' She stopped. 'Mother of gods.'

Granny's jaw dropped. The strobing flash of star after star streaking through the sky reflected in her eyes. She almost ran towards the windows alongside Bernard.

'It's—I've never seen—but it's not the season for it—fishing!'

Poppy tore her eyes away from the sky and turned to look at Granny. 'Did you just say fishing?'

Granny ran back toward the tent. 'Get up, you two! We're going fishing!'

Kelzu sat up. 'You don't mean—?'

Granny was already halfway down the hall. 'I do mean! And there are hundreds to catch! I've never seen conditions like it.'

Huk rolled over with a sigh. He sat up and stretched, looking as well-rested as all heavy snorers looked. 'Was I dreaming, or did she say fishing? As in, like, the fishing we used to do?'

Kelzu was running around the pillow fort, looking for his shoes and dressing gown. He ducked his head out to look at the sky and swore with pure joy. 'Better than old times. Look for yourself, old boy.'

Huk rolled out of bed and, upon seeing the sky, laughed.

He sprinted off straight after Granny.

'The fishing rods are in the garden shed! I saw them there last week!'

Poppy and Janey watched all this with a kind of stupefied disbelief.

'It's the middle of the night,' said Janey. 'Why are they going fishing? I don't even like fish.'

'Something tells me they don't mean to catch fish, Janey,' said Poppy. She rummaged through the blankets for the kid's slippers. She had a beanie in here somewhere, too.

'But that's what fishing means,' said Janey, confused.

Huk sprinted back into the hallway. 'Well, come on, you two! HURRY UP—WE'VE GOT STARS TO CATCH!'

Poppy and Janey looked at one another.

Bernard sprinted after Huk.

Kelzu, still rummaging, frantically tapped K.S on the head. 'WHERE ARE THEY? SLIPPERS, K.S. I NEED MY SLIPPERS.'

K.S powered up, his eyes glowing faintly in the tent's darkness. 'I have not seen your slippers, master. Have you considered looking where you last left them?'

'Where did I last leave them?'

'Research has shown that an exercised mind is less vulnerable to memory loss and degradation. Trying to remember where you last left your slippers is an example of one such exercise you can do to delay the onset of—'

Kelzu screamed. 'FUCK THE SLIPPERS THEN!'

And with that, he sprinted off. Poppy quite agreed.

'Fuck the slippers,' she muttered, hoisting Janey into a piggyback. And they sprinted off after him.

ARCHIVED RECORDING

Status: **UNAIRED**

Recording Date: **UNKNOWN**

Transcribed by **KS-01**

Note: This recording was not approved for broadcast.

HUK

Right. It's just gone past midnight, and the sky is AFLUSHHHH with stars. You've never seen so many.

[Distant: excited cackling from Granny Grack]

HUK

I don't have much time to talk, because Grack will be going fucking mental soon. She's been after a fallen star for years—literally years—for some longevity spell she's been cooking up. Says it'll keep us all ticking a bit longer. You know. Delay the rot. Pause the prune, if you will. Add some bend back in the old knees. Stop me pissing twenty-five times a day, hopefully.

[A loud splash]

HUK *(continued)*
In saying that, Grack will probably get messy either way: star or no star. But at least with the star, it's the fun kind of messy. Yelling and victory drinks—
POPPY *(off-mic)*
Huk, what are you doing?
HUK
Some narration. I thought the fallen stars and Granny's spell could use context for the listeners.
POPPY
Bugger the listeners, *I* could use some context. Tell *me*.
HUK *(sighing)*
At least let me mic you up properly.

[Muffled static]

HUK
Right. So you know that spell Granny has been brewing for the last five years.
POPPY
It's not some fancy kind of whiskey at all, is it?
HUK *(laughing)*
No. We banned her from brewing spirits in the house a decade ago. It's a vitality tether. Which is a fancy way of saying it adds a little pep back in your step and a few more years on, if you know what I mean.
POPPY
It'll make you younger?

HUK

No. I *wish*—but no. It's just something to help us fight fit for a while longer yet.

POPPY

Right. And why a shooting star?

HUK

Temporal manipulation, I think that's what she called it. Something about folding time: I don't know. It sounded like bollocks, but it felt very, *very* important.

GRANNY GRACK

HUKLIN ELDARUK, WHERE ARE THE FUCKING FISHING RODS!

HUK

Right. Yep. That's our cue. Wish us luck.

JAM JARS AND MAYHEM

Granny Grack had turned the garden shed over. Her floating lights had been cast into existence and swarmed around her like sparks from a wayward wand.

'I can't find the bloody fishing rods!'

'They were next to the skis,' said Huk.

'Where are the skis?'

Huk shrugged. 'I don't know. Haven't seen 'em in years.'

Granny groaned and continued throwing things.

'Can we help?' said Poppy. Janey was still on her back.

'Go and get some jam jars off Hiro, then,' said Granny. 'As many as you can carry.'

Poppy was still breathless from all the running, and despite now looking the ripe age of forty—and getting younger by the day—she still had a sore arse and a stiff neck from sleeping on the floor.

'What do you need jam jars for?'

Janey slid off her back and was already running toward the kitchen. 'It's for trapping stars in, stupid.'

Granny grinned. 'That's my girl.' There was a massive crash

inside the shed as one of the many teetering piles of junk toppled over.

Granny shouted triumphantly. 'Found you, you bastards!' And she threw the fishing rods out at Huk and Kelzu, who caught them easily.

Poppy and Janey sprinted into the kitchens with little else on their minds than the shooting stars. And so it was a great shock and surprise when they ran into Hiro and Clay, whom they hadn't noticed missing from the pillow fort earlier that night.

Hiro had started on his late-night bread-making, as was his routine. But the flour was on his nose—and on Clay's, for that matter— and their lips were locked, and their hands were on each other's hips...

Well. Poppy didn't know if that was part of the routine or not.

She covered her own eyes—then realised it was Janey's that needed covering.

'Oh gods.'

Both Hiro and Clay sprang apart like they'd been scalded.

Hiro looked horrified. 'Poppy. We were just—Clay had some flour on his nose, so I was—'

'He was helping me... me...' Clay's voice trailed off. His face burned with embarrassment.

'You were just helping him clean it off,' said Poppy. 'Of course.'

Janey sighed. 'We don't have time for this. You two were smooching, and we caught you at it, fair and square. Big old smoochers. Smooching away like you wouldn't believe.' She made exaggerated kissing noises and passionately kissed the air. 'Good for you. Now—where are the bloody jam jars?'

Poppy tried not to smirk at their mortified expressions. She nudged Janey's back.

'Language. Don't go saying "bloody jam jars"—it's bad manners.'

'But we're probably missing all the shooting stars, Poppy.'

Janey groaned and grabbed one of Hiro's favourite stock pots off the bench. She nearly dropped it—it was almost as tall as she was.

'What do you think you're doing?' said Hiro.

Janey grunted as she ran out of the kitchen with the pot. 'I'm going fishing. Go back to your kissing, lover boys.'

Poppy turned back to Hiro and Clay. They were the colour of beetroot.

Clay avoided her stare. 'We weren't kissing.'

Poppy took an awkward step back—and turned to run after Janey.

Hiro shouted after them: 'IF YOU DARE TELL THE RESIDENTS, I'LL—I'LL—'

'You'll what?' said Poppy. 'Burn the cabbage bread? Don't worry. I think it's brilliant.'

Janey ducked her head back into the hallway. 'QUICK, POPPY! BEFORE THEY'RE ALL GONE!'

Poppy ran after her and took the stockpot out of her hands. They sprinted out into the cold dewy grass and across the field of wildflowers, down toward the river's edge.

They could see Granny's floating lights bobbing around—and the silhouettes of them all standing at the riverbank, fishing rods in hand.

Poppy's feet had already started to go numb from the cold, but she found she didn't care. Not in the slightest. Janey was sprinting beside her, her face serious and determined.

'You look like you again,' said Janey.

Poppy didn't need to feel her face or look at her hands to know that she'd returned to her normal age. She'd felt it happen—a kind of warm shiver that ran over her.

'I feel like me again,' she said, smiling.

'What kept you two?' shouted Granny. 'I had to trap one under my sweater.'

She shivered.

'This kind of cold gets into your bones, you know.'

'We could only get this pot,' said Janey. She pointed at the large stockpot Poppy was holding. 'Hiro and Clay were too busy kissing each other's faces off to help us find the jam jars.'

Kelzu looked at Janey in surprise. 'Kissing? Hiro and Clay?'

'Well, it's hardly a surprise, is it?' said Huk.

Granny scoffed. 'It's a miracle they're only just getting caught now.'

'You knew?' said Poppy.

Huk and Granny nodded.

Kelzu shook his head.

'Have to be blind not to see it,' said Granny.

'Why do I never know anything?' muttered Kelzu.

Huk's fishing rod jerked in his hands, pulling him forward and nearly off-balance. 'I've got one—A BIG ONE!'

The stillness of the lake rippled where the line sat submerged. Further off, the babbling of the creek and a lone toad filled the sudden hush.

Poppy looked up at the sky—still streaked with light from the shooting stars. 'I don't get it,' she said. 'If you're trying to catch a star, why are you fishing in a lake?'

Granny rolled her eyes. She was busy trying to shift the star she'd already caught from under her sweater and into the stockpot. Janey sat hunched in front of her, holding the lid, ready to slam it shut.

'Well, what do you expect us to do?' said Kelzu. 'Cast our lines into the sky? Don't be daft. The stars exist up there as they exist down here.'

'In the reflection?' said Poppy, doubtfully.

Granny held her wriggling sweater to her chest. 'Stop trying to understand things, love. Just let them be as they are. We don't have to know why, and how, and what all the time. It's healthy just to let things be, sometimes. Now, Janey, dear, on the count of three I'm going to throw my sweater over the pot and remove it—and you're going to slam the lid down, alright?'

Janey nodded, face set and determined. 'One, two, and free.'

'Exactly,' said Granny. 'One... two... three—now!'

Granny unleashed her sweater inside the pot and pulled it back out. Her face lit up by the bright, shining star. It was so bright, in fact, that Poppy's first instinct was to look away for fear of blinding herself.

Janey slammed down the lid of the pot, her eyes scrunched up tight against the starlight. She managed to catch almost every single one of Granny's fingers in the process.

Granny screamed and fell backwards with a wail. She knocked Kelzu from his spot and straight into the lake. He landed with a splash at almost the exact moment the trapped star inside the stockpot shot upwards. It paused somewhere high above the lake, as if getting a closer look at its kidnappers, before darting off into the sky.

Meanwhile, the star Huk had been in the process of catching, was putting up an almighty fight. It bent the fishing rod in its struggle to get away.

Huk's feet sank deeper into the earth as he braced himself.

Kelzu's small head ducked back above the lake surface, gasping and shouting and screaming.

Granny lay on the ground, nursing her fingers and groaning.

Janey looked at Poppy, and Poppy looked back at her.

Huk's fishing rod snapped. He fell backwards, landing flat on his arse in the damp earth.

'Well, that all turned to shit rather quickly, didn't it?' he said.

The stars in the sky above no longer looked to be falling. The meteor shower—or whatever it was—was quickly coming to an end.

Poppy glanced out at the gnome, treading water and splashing about frantically.

'Kelzu can swim, can't he?'

Huk sighed. 'Yes. He's just being dramatic.'

'I'm sorry, Granny. I didn't mean to get your fingers,' said Janey. 'I just didn't want the star to get away.'

Granny looked up at her. Her eyes were glassy with tears.

'Oh, it's quite alright, dear. It's hardly your fault.'

'It is my fault, though,' said Janey.

'I know it is. I was being sarcastic,' said Granny.

Poppy shot her a glare.

'What? It is. I didn't jam my own fingers in there, did I?' Granny looked at Janey, sighed, and pulled her onto her lap. 'It's all good, though. My fingers needed a decent squashing. They've had it too easy for far too long. It'll keep them on their toes.'

Janey squirmed as Granny began to tickle her with her good hand—until, finally, there it was: that evil little laugh. The one that came with expectations, and none of them good.

Poppy helped Huk to his feet—and noticed that Kelzu was nowhere to be seen.

The lake's surface was perfectly still.

'Kelzu. Where is he? KELZU!' shouted Poppy.

She jumped into the lake.

It was so cold that it knocked the air from her lungs. She gasped —and accidentally swallowed a mouthful of water.

At the lake's edge stood K.S., walking toward them at a steady pace, holding—ever so carefully in his large metal hands—a pair of Kelzu's slippers.

'I found Mr Luckyhand's slippers,' said K.S. proudly. 'Where is Mr Luckyhand?'

Behind Poppy, there was a splash, followed by a splutter and several choice swear words. Kelzu was now standing in the middle of the lake, arms stretched above his head, clutching a rather large star. It was holding him aloft in the water and trying—quite violently—to get free.

'Mr Luckyhand?' said K.S., confused.

Kelzu shouted something like: I've got the bastard and caught him myself! — though it was muddled with: Hurry up and get me out of this fucking lake, you daft hunk of metal!

And it was all said with such furious, manic joy that it took everyone—including K.S.—several seconds to decipher what he'd said.

But when they got the message, K.S. launched into the water, pushing past Poppy and nearly trampling her in the process.

Everyone else on the bank burst into shouts of triumph and glee.

'WE CAUGHT A STAR!' Janey clapped.

'Whatever you do, Kelzu,' shouted Huk. 'Don't you let it go!'

The star, now aware of K.S. storming toward it, tried even harder to flee Kelzu's grasp. It lifted him further from the water so that only the very tips of his toes remained submerged.

Poppy swam to the bank—clearly not needing to rescue anyone anymore—and pulled herself out of the lake, panting and trembling on the cold mud.

'No, it's f-f-fine. I'll j-j-just help myself up,' she shivered.

No one heard her. Or at least, they pretended not to. They were all too busy watching Kelzu, now hovering above the lake, gripping the star as tightly as he could.

K.S. reached up and plucked Kelzu from the air like a balloon.

Kelzu curled into his arms, the star hugged tightly to his chest.

Poppy couldn't help but notice he looked like a child wrapped safely in his father's arms, and despite the cold and her indignation, she smiled.

WE SHOULD NAME IT

They all sat around the table, looking at the star through the walls of a large, upturned glass bowl. It floated there, softly pulsing. Occasionally, it would push against the bowl's sides, trying to escape.

Poppy poured steaming tea for everyone, and Hiro—with his uncanny ability to make something out of nothing—had somehow managed to serve up scones with wild gooseberry jam and clotted cream.

'Just don't ask where I got the cream from,' he said.

Granny stopped mid-chew, the corners of her mouth flecked with cream.

'It's not from some weird animal, is it? I'm not eating Dire-Beast cream or something.'

Hiro shook his head, sheepishly proud.

'The neighbour has cows. I might've jumped the farm gate and borrowed some.'

Poppy looked at him in shock. 'You stole it?'

Hiro shrugged. 'It's hardly stealing. And I had to bloody work for it. That cow didn't give it up easily—kicked me in the back twice.'

Huk chuckled, nearly snorting his tea.

Janey's entire face was, somehow, covered in cream.

'You ever fink about why it's not weird to drink cow's milk? Why are cows so good anyway? All they do is moo. Why don't we drink mouse milk or cat milk? I'd like to try cat milk.'

Poppy glanced at Janey, then at the others. No one had an answer for that, so they all ate their jam-and-cream-laden scones in contemplative silence.

'You wouldn't get much milk out of a mouse, though, would you?' said Huk.

'But it's probably delit-cious,' said Janey.

They turned their attention back to the star. It was pushing against the bowl again. Still trying to escape.

It had no real features. And it seemed to Poppy you couldn't even see where the star started or ended. It was just light—gaseous, bright, and warm-looking.

'It's beautiful, really, isn't it?' she said.

Granny smiled. 'Oh yes. There's nothing quite like starlight. Stare at it long enough, and you'll find all your worries are gone, and you're just left with this full feeling of warmth.'

'Like I'm all bubbly inside,' said Janey. 'But they're slow bubbles that float around all lazy and soft. Like a rabbit's tummy—but before it starts to go rotten.'

Kelzu frowned. He looked at Poppy and mouthed: *What?*

Poppy shrugged. 'So what will you do with it now, exactly?'

The star made a faint plink against the bowl.

It wanted out. And it wanted out *now*.

Granny reached for the bowl. 'I'll shock it in ice-cold water, before boiling it for ten minutes. That should lock enough light into its skin. And then when that's done, I'll crack it open like an egg and pour it into the cauldron upstairs.'

Everyone looked at her as if she'd gone mad.

'You can't do that,' said Janey.

'No, she bloody can't,' said Kelzu. 'I caught it. Who's to say *I* don't want it?'

'And what would you do with it?' spat Granny.

It felt like they'd captured something divine, godly, and by shoving it into a stockpot, then into an overturned bowl, they were desecrating something pure. 'I think we ought to set the poor thing free, if I'm being honest,' whispered Poppy.

Janey, Granny, and Kelzu all shouted at once—a chorus of shock and disbelief.

'And what, just get rid of it?' said Kelzu indignantly. 'Are you daft, Poppy? Are you the daftest daft numpty to ever have daft-numptied?'

'You have to admit, it feels wrong. It's like we've stolen a wondrous pup or cub from its mother, just to keep it as a pet.'

Poppy had seen this before. She remembered going to the market in Upper Susshingham on an outing with the orphanage. They'd all flocked towards the stalls of wondrous pets. The creatures were fantastic, yes—but they had been miserable. Poached from their homes, separated from their families. This felt a lot like that.

'Yes, but you forget that it was falling,' said Granny, trying her very level-best to remain calm given the circumstances. 'Do you know what happens to a falling star?'

Poppy thought this was an unfair question.

Who the bloody hell knew what happened to falling stars, other than that they fell?

'They die, my dear. A slow death. Far from home. This one would've landed two villages over in a paddock somewhere,' said Granny. 'Its light would've stuttered out as the sun rose and the cold, frosty mud leached away the last of its warmth.'

'It'd be nothing more than a rock if it weren't for us,' said Kelzu. 'We saved it.'

The star stopped pressing against the glass. It seemed to be listening.

'And I haven't looked after a spell for five years to piss it up the wall, either,' said Granny, viciously.

'We should name it,' said Janey.

'Name it?' said Kelzu, in disbelief. 'Name it? What would we name it for?'

'It's our pet. It lives here now,' said Janey, matter-of-factly. 'It needs a name so we can call it. And tell it off when it does bad things. And say "good job for piddling outside"—that was very good behaviour.'

'It is *not* our pet.' Kelzu half-groaned, half-cried. 'I was going to use it to power an arcane capacitor for my wagon.'

'Oh FUCK OFF, Luckyhand. That star is mine, through and through,' shouted Granny.

'I caught it!' said Kelzu. He reached out for the bowl and the star.

Huk choked on his fifth or sixth scone. 'The only reason you managed to grab it was because I'd spent ten minutes reeling it in.'

He looked at Granny and Kelzu, serious.

'It's the kid's. She wants it. She can have it.'

Janey jumped up and down with joy.

Granny and Kelzu looked like they wanted to strangle her—and then each other.

'Huk, need I remind you, that spell bubbling upstairs isn't *just* for me,' said Granny.

Huk shrugged. 'Whoopie doo, mate. We're old. So what. Let the kid have her star.'

'If your dad says you can keep it, that is,' said Poppy.

Janey instantly stopped celebrating.

'But Poppy, he won't let me. He reckons I've got too many pets as it is now.'

Which, to be fair, Poppy thought was entirely reasonable—what with Janey having a literal army of dead mice and the occasional dead cat or rabbit.

She shrugged.

'It's not up to me. I'm not your parent.'

Janey's face crumpled. 'I wish you were.'

'Wish I was what?'

'My parent,' Janey gasped—and burst into tears. Great, heaving, stomach-twisting sobs.

Poppy looked to Granny and Huk for help, but they both froze.

Giant spiders and werewolves? Fine.

A crying child? No, not a chance.

Hiro rolled his eyes. He looked at them all and said, 'Must I do everything?'

He picked Janey up and hugged her. She sobbed into his shoulder—tears and snot all down his back.

'How many hours of sleep has she had?' he asked.

'Don't look at me,' said Huk. 'I'm not her babysitter.'

'Oh, now you speak up,' said Poppy. 'A minute ago, it was all "let the kid have the star".'

Kelzu had produced a recording device from his pocket and was holding it up.

Granny swatted his hand. 'Not now, Kelzu. Come on, man.'

'She's been up with the rest of us,' said Poppy. 'Since the stars started to fall.'

'So she's just tired, then.' Hiro rocked her gently.

The sobs softened. In no time, Janey was asleep in his arms.

They all stared at him, stunned.

'How'd you do that?' said Granny.

'It's basic kid law. If they're upset, they're either tired, hungry, or in desperate need of a laugh. They're just like adults—but worse at pretending they're fine.'

Granny tilted her head.

She sighed bitterly.

'Never cared for kids, if I'm honest. Smelly, grotty things. But if she's not allowed the star, I'd best just—'

She reached for it.

Before her fingers could touch the bowl, Huk smacked her hand away.

'It's still hers. If she has to keep it here, then so be it. I'll look after it when she's not around. But the star is hers, alright?'

Granny rolled her eyes. 'What's gotten into you lately?'

Poppy wanted to say a heart—a heart had gotten into the old half-orc—but she knew when to keep her mouth shut.

'We've got enough pets,' muttered Kelzu. 'We've got Miss Trevor. And Bernard.'

Poppy took a bite of scone—buttery, sweet, and crumbly all at once.

'Speaking of which,' said Poppy. 'We're getting rid of that spider this week.'

She grabbed another scone and started walking out of the kitchen.

'And once it's gone, we're cleaning the third floor top to bottom.'

Granny, Huk, and Kelzu all started to protest at once.

Hiro tried—and failed—to remind Poppy that Janey was her responsibility, and what exactly was he supposed to do with a sleeping child now?

But Poppy had already gone.

She had a to-do list painted on a wall somewhere.

And today, she was going to tick something off it.

TROLL STANDARD TIME

There was a man in a waistcoat, briefcase in one hand, pocket watch in the other, standing at Sunnywood's front door. He sighed, stowed the watch, and rang the bell again.

Poppy watched through a crack in the curtains. She knew she'd seen him before, though from where she couldn't say. Something about him—his sharp nose with quick little twitches, perhaps—made her think of a weasel trying on human clothes. The effect was almost undignified.

And perhaps, Sunnywood had warped her over time, because she felt a sudden urge to hit him with a broom.

He rang the bell again. Somewhere in the house, Kelzu shouted about trying to record a fucking interview, as was to be expected.

This weasel man had to be from the bank. But which bank? Could be the original mortgage lot—Bank of Lower Westfax—or the United Troll Bank of Central Totswolds, who'd funded the first bank's debt, then redrawn it twice.

Poppy sighed.

She was going to have to open the door, she knew that.

If only hiding from your problems made them go away—the world would be a simpler place.

Alfred flew into the room. 'There's a man who looks like a rat out on the doorstep.'

'I know,' said Poppy.

'Aren't you going to see what he wants?'

'I think I know what he wants.'

'Big bags of money or the house and the grounds?' said Alfred.

Poppy nodded.

Alfred floated there awkwardly. 'I could possess him? Try and scare him away, you know. Get him to run off screaming.'

'Do you even know how?'

'No, but I could figure it out, I'm sure.'

Before Poppy could respond, the man was suddenly in front of the window, staring right at her. Alfred yelped and vanished.

The man pressed a sheet of paper to the glass. "We need to talk. Things have been set into motion that cannot be undone."

She cracked the window. "You're standing on the flowers."

'Yes, well, the front door was proving inefficient.'

'Right.' Poppy swallowed. It was starting to bother her. She had seen this man before; she just couldn't for the life of her remember where. She'd been about to ask when he handed her an envelope.

'You received our letter last night, I trust?'

'You could hardly call it a letter.'

'You were made aware I would be calling 'round, then?'

'I've seen you somewhere. Do we know each other?'

The weasel man frowned. He ignored her, nose upturned as if she smelled. 'I have come to explain how final notices work. If you are unable to pay the amount owing today, as of this moment, then the final grace period in which you are expected to vacate the premises—the premises being Sunnywood House, property of United Troll Bank of Central Totswolds—will begin effective immediately. Do you understand?'

Poppy opened her mouth to reply, but nothing came out.

They didn't have the money, of course. If they had the money, then they wouldn't be in this mess.

'Do you, in fact, have the required amount to settle?'

'Remind me again, how much is it we owe?'

The weasel man pointed to the piece of paper he'd held against the window.

It was, Poppy realised, a page full—almost exclusively—with just numbers. And it was nearly four times the amount she'd seen owing on the last bill. And the previous bill had already been beyond absurd. This was just—

'You're joking.'

'I do not joke.'

No, thought Poppy. You don't, do you?

'So,' said the weasel man. 'No payment? No settlement?'

'I—'

'Right. This is how it will unfold. On this very day next week, at midnight Troll Standard Time, repossession will begin. All unclaimed personal effects will be sold, consumed, or absorbed into the ground. Please note: any item over the monetary value of five gold pieces is now property of the United Troll Bank. Theft of troll property will be met with suitable punishment—up to and including death. You have been warned. We recommend that you promptly begin your exit from Troll Bank property; if a late check-out is observed, we cannot guarantee you will make it out alive. Do you understand?'

Poppy swallowed. It made an audible noise.

'Good. Brilliant,' said the weasel man.

He passed her an envelope.

'Inside you will find transcribed records of the meeting we have just held. I would like to thank you personally for your business. It is unfortunate that things have escalated and unfolded as they have, but alas, this is business. I bid you a good day, and once again, I do strongly suggest you begin packing.'

'Packing,' repeated Poppy, dumbly.

'That's right. But nothing over the value of five gold, remember.' The weasel man turned to leave.

'The sweet shop,' said Poppy.

It had hit her.

The man stopped and turned. 'I beg your pardon?'

'That's where I recognise you from. You were in the sweet shop.'

The weasel man smiled. His teeth, thought Poppy, did not look like the teeth of someone who bought out the entire stock of a sweet shop. 'I'd start packing now, if I were you,' he repeated. 'The trolls will be here shortly.'

NEAR PERFECT ORDER

Half an hour later, Poppy had found K.S recharging in the sun on the front porch. He'd gone into his strange hibernation mode, where his clockwork no longer made his chest move. She knew that logically, his chest didn't need to move. It wasn't like he needed to even breathe, for that matter. But it still made her feel uneasy to see him sit there like a brass statue. There were even swallows trying to build a nest on his head.

She prodded him on the shoulder, lightly.

Nothing.

She had an eviction notice in her pocket and a list of things to do before the trolls arrived—and absolutely no time for a statue impression.

'Ahh, K.S?' Poppy touched his forehead this time.

The automaton's eyes began to glow, and his chest moved as the barely perceptible ticking and whirring inside of him kicked into gear again.

'It is a truly splendid day, is it not?' He looked from Poppy to the sky.

'Yes, I suppose.'

'I suppose so too, Just Poppy.'

Poppy didn't know why, but the automaton was weirding her out. He seemed down. Depressed, almost. K.S was sighing in his own gear-grinding kind of way.

'Is everything alright, K.S?'

'Oh yes. I am running with everything in near perfect order, thank you.'

'Near perfect order?'

K.S's smile faltered. A rigidity to his movements settled over him. 'Near perfect indeed.'

Poppy sighed. She was going to ask him for the speaker phone and get on with it—they had things to organise, and fast—but he was looking at the swallows like they'd just told him bad news.

'Of course,' whispered K.S. 'There is the small matter of my memory logs failing me.' He seemed to her to look far more human in that moment than his normal self.

'Well, can't they just be fixed? Just get Kelzu onto it,' said Poppy, a little impatiently. They needed to be getting a move on, and quick, if they were going to stand a chance.

K.S shook his head. 'Mr Luckyhand seems to think they are replaceable, but I fear that without them, my programming will be compromised. Furthermore, I wonder, without my memories, will I be who I am? Or will I be someone different?'

Poppy blew out a long, exhausted breath. This, she thought, was going to take a while. She sat down beside the automaton. They watched the birds flit from tree to tree, sometimes swooping up into the air in a great dance together.

'So everything isn't okay then?' she said, eventually. 'Not really?'

'I'm diverting energy from my arcane capacitor to keep them going, but I fear that at this rate, my memory logs will fail by the end of the month. I'm trying to conserve energy where I can, and recharge when time permits. In this way, I am managing for now.'

Poppy frowned. 'And does Kelzu know it's this bad?'

'No. My core programming forbids me from keeping secrets from him, but I've found he has not noticed. Or if he has, he has not said anything. And keeping secrets and avoiding the truth are a tightrope I am becoming rather adept at traversing.'

Poppy rubbed at her tired eyes. Why was everything turning to shit? She leaned her head against the automaton's shoulder.

'If it is any consolation, Just Poppy, I prefer it this way. It would not be right to outlive my maker. My entire reason for being, the very essence of my programming, is to protect him and his store. I cannot protect him from old age. I cannot stop him from dying. And without him, I... I would have no purpose. I would be... obsolete.' The automaton tilted his head up towards the sky. The fine wire filaments across his metal face glowed with the energy they collected from the sun. 'No, I think, this is best.'

'Couldn't you just change your programming? If we got you new memory logs and edited your... your purpose, couldn't you... just... I don't know... live for yourself?'

K.S smiled. Or rather, it was what Poppy knew to be his smile, which was to squint his eyes, causing the lenses to zoom in and out. To become unfocused and hazy with happiness. 'No. No, I could not. Nor would I want to.'

Poppy nodded.

They sat there in silence for the next ten minutes or so. The warm breeze spoke of spring, and Clay's flowers were doing things no normal flowers would do. They were budding and opening, right before them.

'Just Poppy?'

'Mmm?'

'How may I be of assistance?'

'You have a voice amplifier I could use, don't you?'

ONE WEEK TO FIGHT

K.S opened a panel in his chest, and a strange kind of speaker moved towards the front of his internal workings. He held up his palm towards Poppy.

'I just speak into your hand?' she said.

K.S nodded. 'It will carry your words clearly,' he said. 'And I will remain here, should you need me for more than that.'

'Right.' She felt stupid all of a sudden. Like she ought to just go and round them up one by one and sit them down, tell them how it was going to be.

K.S cleared his throat. A completely unnecessary gesture, of course. The automaton had no need for throat clearing. But he was trying to encourage her.

Poppy gave him the smallest nod—a silent thank you.

'Okay, so…' Her voice echoed loudly through the hallway and walls. She could have sworn that if anyone out in the garden, and possibly those further out in the village, would have heard her. 'Everyone to the foyer, now. Kelzu, I don't care if you're recording an interview—this is more important. Hiro, step away from the stove. Granny, spell off the burner. And has anyone seen Huk and Janey?'

It took them ten minutes or so before they'd all walked into the foyer. It was, Poppy felt, time they couldn't afford to waste. She caught K.S.'s eye, and he inclined his head—a quiet reminder to lean towards courage.

'Forgive me, Poppy,' said Kelzu, descending the stairs. 'But I'm not sure I recall saying you could use K.S as a loudspeaker whenever you're in the mood to feel authoritarian.'

'Thankfully, I don't need to ask you. K.S is his own person. He offered. Where's Huk and Janey?'

Granny shrugged. 'Is this going to take long? Past experience has taught me, if you leave a fertiliser spell unattended, you're no longer cooking a potion, you're making a bomb.'

Hiro stormed out of his kitchen towards them. 'What. Do. You. Want?'

Clay smacked him in the chest. A warning to be nicer.

'No, seriously,' said Poppy. 'Where are Huk and Janey?'

'Probably napping in a hammock somewhere,' said Kelzu. 'Who cares. Get on with it!'

Poppy sighed. It wasn't that she didn't trust Huk to be left alone with Janey. It was... no, it was that. When those two got together, they both became nothing more than misbehaved toddlers, and she worried what kind of terrorism they might be plotting.

But she'd find them later.

Right now, she needed to focus. She straightened her shoulders, the echo of her conversation with K.S. still in her chest, and fixed her gaze on them all.

'Well, as you're all aware. Sunnywood House is going broke. And I mean broke-broke.'

'We're aware of that, Poppy,' said Kelzu.

'If it's the food you're worried about,' said Granny, impatiently. 'I'm working on a fertiliser spell for the veggie patch right now. And let me tell you, it would be done a hell of a lot quicker if this wasn't happening. Whatever this is.'

'And speaking of food,' added Hiro. 'I can't afford to burn what little of it we have left. So unless you want to scrape charcoal off of your dinner tonight, I suggest you—'

'We're going to lose the manor,' Poppy burst out. 'And the grounds it stands on. They're taking it.'

'That's generally what repossession means, love,' said Granny.

'You don't understand,' said Poppy. She held up the letter the weasel man had given her. 'They're not just threatening repossession, they're starting it. We have one week to be out of here. The trolls will start to arrive shortly.'

There was a shocked silence. It lasted for several heavy heartbeats, and then there was shouting. Everyone and all at once.

Poppy squinted. She was getting a stress headache, and it was a thumper. 'I don't understand it. But what I do understand is this: we're fucked. Completely and utterly.'

'But Sunnywood is owned by its residents?' said Clay.

'No,' said Poppy. 'It's not. It was. But then Matron had to re-mortgage to keep up with fees, upkeep, wages, and food. Sunnywood has been barely keeping its head above water for quite a long time, I think.' And now, she thought, it was about to well and truly drown.

'Well, how much can we possibly need?' said Kelzu.

Poppy chewed her lip. She showed them the letter properly. Most of the page was taken up with numbers for the amount owed. 'And that's not including interest. The interest owed is on the back page.'

Clay shifted uncomfortably. 'Well, what can we do, then?'

'I'll sell everything in my shop if I have to,' said Kelzu. 'Hell, I'll sell my wagon if it comes to that.'

'Don't be ridiculous, Kelzu, you're not selling your wagon.' Granny shook her head angrily. 'That's your home.'

Kelzu shrugged. 'Sunnywood's my home. The wagon's just a comfortable bedroom.'

'I'll take a second job,' said Hiro. 'The inn-keeper is always at me to quit Sunnywood to work there instead. I can cook enough food there to cover my duties here and make the extra cash.'

'You can't work two jobs,' said Clay. 'You barely have enough time in your day with the one.'

'I'll make it work. I'll make anything work if it means we get to stay here.'

Poppy noticed his hand had curled around the small of Clay's back. It was clear that he wasn't just doing this for the residents of Sunnywood, but he was doing it for them. For himself and for Clay. She couldn't help but smile at that.

'And the third floor,' said Poppy.

Kelzu sighed. 'Don't say it, please.'

'We need more residents. We can't afford to lose an entire floor of rooms because a giant spider and her babies have claimed it.'

'She's not just any giant spider. She's Trevor. Miss Trevor.'

'And I think Miss Trevor deserves more than just a couple of rooms and a hallway, don't you think?' said Granny. 'There's a whole entire neck of woods out there she could be roaming, Zu.'

'But she's been with us since...' Kelzu let his voice trail off.

Granny nodded knowingly.

She hugged the gnome to her side.

He barely came up to her hips.

'I know. I know. But she's not going to leave us. She'll just be out there. Room to spread her legs, and pretty soon her wee babies won't be so wee anymore.'

Kelzu nodded.

Poppy was shocked to see the gnome's eyes were wet with tears. She thought Miss Trevor was just a pet that had gotten seriously out of hand, but now, she wasn't so sure.

She looked at the envelope. The letter still held tightly in her hands from the moment she opened them. 'We have one week,' she repeated.

Everyone nodded. The silence grew heavy, and then it was gone, shaken off like an old musty blanket.

Poppy knew it wouldn't be enough. Not by a long stretch. But there was a stubborn kind of grace in the way they were already scattering to fight a battle they'd almost certainly lose.

'I'll head into the village now,' said Hiro. 'If I'm not back by 8:30 at the latest, come to the inn, and I'll have your food ready there. I'll make sure it's free of charge.' Hiro was practically shouting this as he ran off in a rush towards the kitchens to grab his apron and knives.

'I'll do up some bouquets and a flower stand in the centre of the village,' said Clay. 'It's not much, but it's something.'

Poppy nodded.

'Clay,' said Granny. 'Before you go, I'll need a shovel.'

'I'll leave my potting shed open.'

'What do you need a shovel for?' said Poppy.

'You'll see. Come on.'

She looped her arms through Poppy's and led her up to her room. Kelzu stood there, nervously pacing backwards and forwards.

He looked at K.S. 'What do you say, old boy. Should we take the wagon on one last whirlwind tour of the world?'

'Like old times?' said K.S.

Kelzu grinned. He strung his fingers up and down the elastic of his overalls. 'Not quite like the old days, I hope.' He laughed, and together they ran off to his room and the magical wagon parked inside of it.

It wouldn't save Sunnywood—the numbers were too big, the week too short—but she couldn't bring herself to tell them to stop.

Sometimes you only fought because giving up wasn't an option.

APPLES ON MOSSY LOGS

Huk and Janey sat atop an old mossy log, sharing an apple—one bite each, back and forth.

'Do you fink he's scared?' Janey asked.

Huk didn't answer. He was staring off into the distance, lost somewhere in the far reaches of his own mind. There was a distinct itch in him—the sense that he'd forgotten something important. Something dangerous. Like a candle burning where it shouldn't be left unattended. Lately, that feeling came more often. It left him foggy, blunt-edged. He hated it. And the worst part was, the feeling had been growing stronger since Sunnywood's trouble began—as though whatever was coming wasn't just about the land or banks, but something older that had been sleeping for too long.

'Mr Huk!' Janey tugged on the half-orc's arm.

He blinked down at her, snapping back. 'What is it?'

'I said, do you fink he's scared?'

For a moment, Huk wasn't sure who she meant. In fact, for the briefest instant, he wasn't entirely sure who she was—only that they were in the woods together, sharing an apple. But he was used to this by now. Used to pretending he knew exactly what was going on, and to whom, even when he hadn't the faintest idea.

'No. I don't think so. I think he's brave. Quite brave.'

Janey beamed. Beside them, a glass jar rested on the moss, glowing with the light of a fallen star.

'You hear that?' she told it. 'We fink you're brave. Quite brave.'

The jar brightened, just a fraction. And Huk remembered. This time, the memories stayed—caught and held before they could slip away.

Janey. The fallen star. He sighed in relief. 'My turn with the apple, kid. You're being a greedy gobble-gannet.'

'I am not!'

Huk swiped the apple and took two monstrous bites, leaving barely anything behind.

Janey collapsed into giggles. She laughed so hard, Huk briefly worried she might wet herself. After that, they settled into a comfortable, companionable silence.

When he looked down, Janey was staring up at him with a smile.

'What are you looking at?' he asked.

'I'm looking at you.'

'Well, stop that!'

She giggled. 'Did you really know other nekkermancers, Mr Huk?'

He nodded.

'Will you tell me about dem? Please? No one will—they fink it'll scare me, or make me evil. But I fink I'm not going to be evil just because I'm a necromancer. I fink I'm just... me. Janey.'

Huk smiled, pulled her into his side, and rested his head atop hers. 'All right, then. What would you like to know?'

'Did they have an army of dead mice, too?'

'No. One of them had an army, but it was all long-dead warriors, risen from their tombs in the Mistling Mountains.'

'Did he make them dance and skip about?'

'No... well, yes, in a way. But mostly he used them to gain power. Hard to fight someone whose army couldn't die—being dead already and all. You'd knock their head clean off, and they'd just get up and chase you. Felt like cheating, if you ask me.'

'He sounds clever,' Janey breathed.

'He was. In his own way.'

'Mr Huk, if I made a graveyard come back to life, I'd take dem all dancing. We'd pick flowers, have picnics. And den, when they'd had a jolly good day, I'd tuck 'em back into their coffins so they were nice and comfy. And den I—'

Huk realised this was heading far from the battlefield stories he'd been hoping to tell—about the time he'd downed fifteen zombies in under a minute with nothing but a rusty old shield and Granny's broomstick.

Janey was still talking, now about playing chasies with an entire graveyard, and whether she could raise enough zombies for a good game or just a mediocre one.

'You and Granny would need a head start, though, 'cause your knees look like they'd ache.'

'Yeah, yeah, I get the picture,' said Huk. 'It sounds lovely.'

'It does sound lovely.'

But Huk wasn't listening anymore. He was back in the thick of it —battles where death was close enough to taste, and that strange aliveness it brought. His stomach clenched at how far away those days felt, and what he'd give to feel them again.

It had never been about the gold, or even the treasure. It was the adventure. The camaraderie. Gods, how he missed it.

These memories were sharp, not blunt. Close your eyes, and they might have happened yesterday. And perhaps that was the trouble— thirty years ago felt like yesterday, and yesterday felt like thirty years ago. And if Sunnywood fell, there'd be no one left who remembered those stories—except maybe Poppy and Janey.

'Do you fink, Mr Huk, you'd let me wake up just a few people in the graveyard—to go dancing and play chasies wiff?'

'Oh, yeahhh,' Huk sighed.

Janey squealed and hopped off the moss-covered log.

The movement jolted him back. What had she just said? More importantly, what had he just agreed to?

Then she flung her arms round him, hugging so tightly he was—for a fleeting moment—impressed by her strength.

He rather liked it. Even if he had no idea what he'd done to earn it. But as she held on, he felt that itch of unease again—the one that whispered the fights ahead wouldn't be like the old ones. And this time, he wasn't sure he'd survive them.

ACT OF WAR

Granny was rummaging through her alchemy supplies while Poppy stood behind her, arms loaded to the brim with a random assortment of things. Granny flung a scarf over her shoulder, and it landed squarely on Poppy's head.

'I take it, we're not looking for a big bag of cash, then?' Poppy said.

'No,' said Granny. 'I'm afraid not. Not that it would make any difference if I did, would it?'

Poppy shook her head. 'It's too much money. More than we can raise in a week.'

'So, we have to prepare for alternate arrangements, don't we? If Kelzu can sell it all, we'll come close—he's got more value in that wagon than a dragon's hoard. But there's a very high chance he won't get done what needs doing in time. And when time runs out, Poppy, it won't be a knock at the door—it'll be boots on the path.

So listen here, duck. Things are going to get messy, I'm sure of it. We will fight the bank if it comes to it. And I don't mean with letters from lawyers like our young Markus intends. I mean with weapons. With magic. Do you understand? Taking Sunnywood from us would be an act of war. And you don't respond to an act of war with a letter. You show force. You meet force *with* force. No one threatens Sunnywood. And I mean no one. Not while I'm breathing. Are you keeping up, Poppy?'

Poppy sat down on the edge of Granny's bed. Her stress headache was turning into a migraine.

'You said it yourself, Granny. Fighting them would be pointless. We might deal with the trolls that try and take Sunnywood, but more will just come—and they'll bring the town guard with them next.'

There was a fire behind Granny's eyes, the likes of which Poppy had never seen. But under it, there was something else—the faint urgency of someone who knows she's running out of time, and that this might be her last big fight.

'Do you know what I've realised, Poppy? That I've been brewing a spell for five years in the hope it would change something inside me. Something no magic—not even a fallen star—could touch. And I realised... that strong, stubborn old bitch who once burned down an entire city just to watch it burn hasn't gone anywhere. She's still right here.' She thumped her chest, above her heart. 'So I think you're in danger of underestimating us, Poppy. And indeed, yourself.'

'No,' said Poppy bluntly. 'I'm just being realistic.'

'Oh, fuck realistic,' said Granny. 'When has anything of real consequence ever been accomplished with realism? No—it takes foolhardy, stupid, naïve bravery nine times out of ten. The kind that makes sensible folk step aside and leaves us to get the job done. And mark my words, Poppy, we will. We will start as we mean to go on. We will fight, and we will not stop until Sunnywood is ours, or we are dead.'

'Fuck me,' said Poppy.

'Yes,' said Granny. 'Fuck you, indeed. Find a thing worth dying for, and it won't sound so wrong.' She turned back to her alchemy supplies. 'Now, what we're after is a small golden acorn. Dwarfish made. Problem is, I can't for the life of me remember where I put the blasted thing.'

'What do we need a golden acorn for?'

'Protection. You'll see.'

Granny opened one of her trunks, ignoring the question. A faint, barely perceptible whoosh echoed through the air. She knelt before it with an impressive economy of groans—only two—and leaned inside, rummaging.

'Take hold of my ankles, won't you?'

'What?' said Poppy.

'Grab my ankles. I don't want to fall in.'

Granny leaned farther, and somehow more of her fit inside than should have been possible.

'Is this like Kelzu's wagon, then?'

'Mmm. He practised stretching dimensions on luggage before moving onto his wagon,' said Granny, her voice echoing from below. 'Used to sell them. Called them Luckyhand's Ludicrous Luggage.'

Poppy smiled, picturing a younger Kelzu working on suitcases and backpacks, climbing in and out of them with tall ladders like some sort of street magician.

'He was a terrifically clever little bastard,' grunted Granny.

'Was?'

'Well, he doesn't invent anymore, does he? Just records things for that ridiculous radio show. But he's still got fight in him, I'm sure of it. If he remembers to use it.'

There came a sound like a cutlery cupboard collapsing into a box of fine china. The noise seemed to echo far longer than it should have, as if it were tumbling down a stairwell that had no bottom. Granny swore.

'Is this going to take much longer?' Poppy peered into the trunk. Shelves and cupboards stretched down as far as the eye could see. Somewhere in that impossible space, a faint golden light winked—or perhaps it was just her eyes playing tricks. 'It's just that... you're quite heavy.'

'You can pull me back up now, love,' said Granny.

Poppy struggled to haul her out, and when Granny emerged, she was holding a small golden acorn, no bigger than a thumb.

'The Warden's Seed,' she said. 'Bought it years ago, when we graduated from fighting one big monster to whole armies. Never used it, though—didn't want to waste it. Turns out I was just saving it for this moment.'

She passed the seed to Poppy. It was surprisingly—almost impossibly—heavy, and it thrummed with a faint magnetic, static-laced pulse. Holding it made the hairs on Poppy's arms rise, as though the thing were quietly deciding whether she was a friend or a foe.

'So what do we do with this, then?'

'Plant it, of course.'

'And what—it just *protects* us?'

'You'll see,' said Granny. 'Now come on. You've got a hole to dig.'

THE MUSEUM OF US

Kelzu opened his bedroom door in Sunnywood—which opened into his wagon—which opened into his shop. The lights hummed to life, the ether crackling in the glass tubes along the walls and ceiling with warmth and magic. The familiar sound was comforting, but tonight it felt a little like the first creak of a theatre curtain before the final act.

K.S. followed him inside, shutting the door behind him.

They both looked over Luckyhand's Lootland—a labyrinth of aisles and alleys crammed with everything from shelves of arcane and non-fiction and fiction alike, to endless rows of glass vials brimming with spells, to racks of enchanted cloaks, be-spelled boots, and magical armour.

It was strange to Kelzu, in that moment, to look at it all and see not just a shop, but a past... and a future. Just one he wasn't entirely sure he'd be around to see.

He passed an umbrella stand that, if you touched it just so, would turn into a monster that would have you near dead within minutes. He, Huk, and Granny had come across it decades ago inside an old mansion on the Meravian Moors. Vampires had been behind it. Misty old mansion on a moor, thought Kelzu—hardly a shock. The real shock would've been if there weren't any vampires.

The shop was full of such things, each with memories attached. Normally, Kelzu felt protective of that. Granny always said he didn't run a shop—he ran a museum—because he never bloody sold anything. And maybe she was right.

But now, looking at it all, he felt it was time.

Kelzu breathed a sigh of relief. He'd been living in the past, he realised. For quite a while. And now it was time to think about the future.

If he could get there.

'You know, it's strange, K.S.,' he whispered, 'but I don't think I'll be sad to see it all go.'

'Yes, you will, Master,' said K.S. 'You'll be devastated.'

'But a good kind of devastated, I think.'

'The end of a chapter,' said K.S., 'the beginning of another. And so the stories of our lives are written.'

Kelzu grinned. 'Have you been reading poetry again?'

'Reading is good for your memory,' said K.S., almost defensively.

Kelzu's grin faltered. He knew about the automaton's failing memory logs—how could he not? He ran diagnostics and repairs on him almost nightly when K.S. recharged. The automaton wouldn't know this, because technically, he was "off" while Kelzu worked. He'd already done everything he could for him; short of replacing the memory logs—which would mean erasing the very core of what made K.S., K.S.—there was nothing else he could do.

He also knew there would come a night when the repairs no longer held, and K.S. would wake not knowing his own name. Or Kelzu's.

Kelzu looked up at him. His eyes were moist, but no tears fell.

'Well, you read all the books you damn well please, K.S. Read and read and read until you feel so full of words you might burst with them.'

K.S. tilted his head, confused. 'You're acting strange. Are you feeling alright, Master?'

Kelzu turned and wandered down the aisles toward the part of the shop that became the wagon. He needed to warm the engine. They had quite a ways to go.

His fingers brushed over sword hilts, invisibility cloaks, and storms in jam jars.

What a life they'd had together. And how quickly such a life could vanish—no matter how many wards, locks, or enchantments you wrapped it in. But that was what made life so special, wasn't it? That it ended. All good stories had a beginning, a middle, and an end. But the real stories—their stories—well, they lived on. And that was the magic of them. Though magic, he knew, had a habit of running out.

'Mr Luckyhand? Are you all right?'

'Yes, lad. I think I am. Now—it's time to get the old girl fired up. I believe we have some shit to sell!'

THE LAST STAND BEGINS

Poppy was digging a hole on the front lawn, and Granny Grack was sitting on a beach chair, watching her. It hadn't occurred to Poppy at the time that she would be the one doing the digging, but in hindsight, it should have been obvious.

'This is deep enough,' said Poppy. 'Surely?'

Granny looked over the top of her glasses from her spell book to Poppy, who was now up to her knees in a hole.

'Deeper. Much deeper.'

Poppy groaned. 'I don't even get paid for this shit, you know.'

'What was that, dear?' said Granny.

'*"What was that, dear?"*' She mimicked.

She dug away with fever and fury, jabbing at the earth, hard and fast. Poppy became so focused on the digging that she didn't see Huk and Janey appear at the edge of the woods and walk towards them.

'Why're you digging a hole, Poppy?' Janey asked. She and Huk were holding hands.

Poppy was, embarrassingly, entirely out of breath. 'Where the hell have you two been?'

'Exploring the woods,' said Huk.

'And guess what, Poppy?' Janey grinned—missing front tooth and all.

'What?'

'Huk said I could—' Huk nudged Janey, cutting her off. He made a face; he clearly didn't mean for Poppy to see it.

'Did you just mime chopping her head off?' said Poppy.

'No.'

'Yes, you did. I just saw you do it.'

'Then why ask me if you saw it?' said Huk, exasperated.

There was a loud noise behind them: like a great engine starting, followed by a high-pitched whine that grew deeper and deeper. It was so loud that Poppy couldn't hear her own voice. The earth she'd just shovelled trembled. The ground beneath her feet shook furiously.

'What is that?' she shouted.

But no one was listening. They all had their fingers jammed into their ears. There was a sudden loud bang—followed by complete and utter silence.

'Where's he off to in such a hurry, then?' said Huk.

'He's selling it all,' said Granny.

'What do you mean he's selling it all?'

It clicked for Poppy then. 'That was Kelzu?'

'I mean all of it. Everything. He said he wasn't coming back until every last thing was sold.'

'Why?' Huk looked shaken.

Granny went quiet.

Poppy wiped dirt from her cheek. 'Because we're broke, Huk. Because if we don't pay the bank what we owe them, they're going to take Sunnywood. Not in a couple of months, but next week.'

Shocked though Huk looked, he didn't miss a beat in replying. 'OH, FUCK OFF!'

Janey laughed.

Huk looked at her. 'Sorry, kid.' He looked at Poppy again. 'But seriously, they can FUCK OFFFFF! Who do they think they are, threatening to take our home? And how, might I ask, would they even do that exactly?'

'I don't think it matters how, just that they will,' said Poppy. And that "how" wouldn't be as simple as papers and signatures—it would be war, if this lot had anything to do with it.

Huk stormed inside, flinging the door open with such force that the glass panels shattered.

Bernard sprinted past him towards Janey, whimpering.

Granny sighed and went back to her spell book. 'He took that better than I expected, honestly. The old Huk would've strolled into the village and threatened the nearest bank he could find. Wouldn't matter if it was the right one. He'd do it just to prove a point.'

Poppy looked at Janey and Bernard, hugging each other on the grass. 'Are you all right, Janey?'

'Did Mr Luckyhand fly off in his magic wagon?'

Poppy nodded.

'All by himself?'

'I suppose so, yes.'

'And Mr Huk's upset because the bad men are coming to take away your home?'

Poppy exhaled—a long, exhausted breath. She nodded and looked at Granny. 'Surely this is deep enough now?'

Granny got out of her beach chair and looked down at the hole Poppy had dug.

'You know, if anything, love, it's too deep now.'

Poppy looked at Granny like she meant to thump her, then, without a word, climbed out of the hole and headed inside.

She met Huk at the door. He had his great-sword holstered at his back and a face that said anyone who looked at him funny was going to be thumped—and thumped hard.

Poppy sighed. She was far too tired for this. 'Huk, what are you doing?'

'What's it look like I'm doing? I'm going to—'

'What? Head into the village? Threaten a bank teller?'

'No, I'm going to—'

'Wave your sword around menacingly?'

'Well, yes, but—'

'Don't be ridiculous,' said Poppy, with a little more venom than she intended.

Huk's shoulders slumped.

He looked, suddenly, very old. And in that moment, Poppy realised it wasn't just the fight over Sunnywood weighing him down —it was the knowledge this might be one of the last battles he had in him.

'I don't know what else to do,' he said. 'But I have to do something.'

Poppy reached for his sword and took it from his back, leaning it against the wall.

Huk sighed. He slouched against the wall and slid down until he was sitting, head in his hands.

Poppy sat beside him and leaned her head against his shoulder.

They stayed like that for a long time, not saying a word—just looking around at their home. And Poppy couldn't shake the question pressing heavier each minute: would this still be their home when the following week came? Or would they, like Kelzu, be forced to leave with whatever they could carry?

HUNGER AND HAVOC

Clay pulled the clockwork wagon to a stop in front of the house. They all clambered in—Poppy, Huk, Granny, Janey. Bernard was left inside with only Alfred for company, and they could still hear him crying.

They were headed to the village, spirits uncharacteristically high thanks to the promise of a good meal. Hiro had left that morning to get work at the local inn, swearing it meant he could at the very least organise them a proper feed, free of charge—or so they hoped.

They spoke of the wonders Hiro might cook with a fully stocked kitchen at his disposal and found they could barely contain their excitement.

'A big old roast,' said Granny. 'Juicy meat, falling off the bone, with buttery whipped potato.'

'And gravy,' added Huk. 'Swimming in it. Like soup on a plate.'

'With crusty bread smothered in cold butter and flaky sea salt,' said Poppy.

Even Clay laughed. 'And for dessert—chocolate pudding so chocolatey it makes you feel sick. Physically sick.'

'It's like at that point we're not even eating pudding, just fudge,' said Poppy. 'But we don't care because—'

Clay revved the wagon, and it bounded forward in a cloud of steam.

They all laughed.

'If I don't get us there shortly,' Clay shouted above the rush of air, 'we'll start to eat each other.'

They tore towards the village, faster than was sensible, but all the better for it. Poppy's stomach growled. All they'd had all day were Hiro's breakfast scones and a few stolen apples. No wonder they were all irritable, emotional wrecks.

Janey curled into Clay's side, the fallen star clasped between her hands. Its silver light lit them against the darkening sky—so bright that Poppy didn't see the figure ahead until Clay swerved violently.

The wagon skidded to a stop, swaying so hard Poppy thought it might topple.

They sat breathing heavily in silence.

Janey began to laugh.

Poppy looked at Granny with wide eyes. 'What the hell was that?'

There was a voice then, distant and groaning.

'It was me, I'm afraid,' shouted Hiro.

Clay leapt down and half ran, half tripped towards Hiro, lying in the grass.

They crowded round as Clay checked him for injuries. Finding none, he hugged him tight, then grabbed his face and kissed him repeatedly on the forehead, cheek, and lips.

'I'm sorry. I'm so sorry,' Clay pulled his face away. 'What were you doing in the middle of the road in the middle of the bloody night anyway? You could have been killed! What if I'd killed you? How would that have made me feel?'

He resumed kissing. Hiro went beetroot red.

Janey made retching noises.

Huk chuckled. 'It's about time you two stopped sneaking around and made a proper go of it.'

'Only took nearly killing each other,' said Granny. 'But you got there in the end.'

Hiro pushed Clay off, groaning. 'You knew?'

'Of course. We're old, not stupid. It's the worst-kept secret in the history of secrets.'

'What are you doing out here?' Poppy asked, her relief fading to hunger. 'I thought you'd—'

'Got a job at the inn? I did. I also got fired from my job at the inn.'

'You move quick,' said Granny. 'I'd be impressed if I wasn't so devastated.'

'They get sick of your temper?' said Huk, helping him up.

'I threw a knife at someone's head,' said Hiro, nodding. 'They kept telling me my steak was undercooked. Though it was a perfect medium-rare. I wouldn't be told how to cook by some undereducated village idiot with the culinary palette of a five-year-old. No offence, Janey.'

Poppy sighed—louder than intended.

'What?' she said when they all looked at her. 'I was really looking forward to a roast.'

'Can we go back to the part where I nearly died?' said Hiro.

'I'd quite like to kill you anyway, now dinner's off,' Huk replied.

Granny laughed, then groaned. 'Gods, I'm hungry.'

They all started to laugh then, Janey included, though she didn't seem to understand why. Because if they didn't laugh, what would they do? Cry, probably. Almost definitely, they would cry, thought Poppy.

Clay tried to start the wagon so they could return to Sunnywood. It coughed steam into the night but wouldn't start.

'Please don't tell me we have to walk,' said Poppy.

'Fine,' said Clay. 'I won't.'

They watched him climb down, coat pulled tight against the cold/ He started walking home.

'What's he doing?' asked Poppy.

'Not telling you you have to walk,' said Granny. 'But walking all the same.'

'How far's the inn?' Huk asked.

'Half an hour on foot,' Hiro replied. 'Why?'

'We could rob them,' said Huk.

'I'm not robbing an inn.'

'Who said you? You can't even swing a sword.'

'We're not robbing an inn, Huklin,' said Granny. 'We're better than that.'

Janey yawned. 'I'll help you rob it, Mr Huk.'

Poppy glared. 'You can explain to her father why she thinks robbing an inn's a good idea.'

'That's if she doesn't starve first,' Hiro muttered.

Clay called back: 'Hurry up—I'm sure there's a tin of old biscuits in my bottom drawer.'

Meanwhile, Bernard was scratching at the door anxiously. He'd been scratching at it ever since they'd left him behind. First, Hiro had gone, left the kitchen and Sunnywood for the first time in... well, ever, that Bernard could remember. It unsettled the book-wyrm to be in Sunnywood and for Hiro not to be there with him. And not to mention the food situation had gotten rather sad of late. No big cream cakes that, with a subtle nudge, could be persuaded to fall to the floor and licked clean. Bernard had had to resort to a mouse that morning. A mouse! The shame of it. And now they'd all gone and left him. Left him with the ghost like some common house pet.

And there was something else. Bernard could sense it, sense it in the way all animals can sense things. A ripple in the ether, maybe. But something was coming, of that he was sure. And he wanted to be there for it when it did.

So, he had to get out of here.

He ran around the house in a frenzy, jumping on the tables in the dining room to look outside the windows, making sure whatever it was that was going to happen hadn't happened yet.

He howled, much like a dog.

He flapped his wings, useless though they were. He cried, and he cried, and he cried. Why would no one let him out? He scratched at the door. The ghost man yelled at him. Bernard pretended not to notice.

He pounded against the door. Leaping against it. It buckled in its frame. He could do this. If he really tried. And he would.

There was a loud rumbling thunder that rolled across the sky. Bernard felt its vibrations before he heard it.

He howled again, louder and more desperate.

He couldn't miss this.

Lightning cracked through the air. Thunder growled and thumped the sky.

The gods were playing drums, and they were awful at it.

There was a burst of light, as if someone had taken to the air with a great big knife and revealed another world behind it, leaving a gaping wound in the sky.

Out of it dropped a wagon.

It landed in a field of wild-flowers, not far from where the residents of Sunnywood were walking back towards the manor.

Steam rolled off of it in the cold night air.

The door flung open, and a gnome leaned out of it.

He looked up at Sunnywood House.

'Not bad aim,' said Kelzu cheerily. 'Not bad at all.'

They hadn't landed in the wall outside of his bedroom like last time. Kelzu considered this a win.

ONE LAST HOORAH

Poppy, meanwhile, had nearly shit herself for the second time that night. First, they'd almost run clean over Hiro, and now wagons were falling out of the sky with great big thunderous booms.

'What's he doing back so early?' said Granny.

'Did you forget something?' shouted Huk.

Kelzu spun around to look at them, smiling, hands on hips.

'You know, Huk, I believe I did.'

The gnome sat down on the small deck at the edge of his wagon, feet swinging happily. He looked, Poppy thought, like a child much too impressed with themselves.

'Why are you looking at us like that?' she asked.

Granny sighed. 'I know that look.' She turned to Poppy, Hiro, and Clay. 'He's about to say he had an idea,' she murmured, just for them.

'I had an idea, you see,' said Kelzu.

'He was somewhere exotic,' Granny whispered, leaning into Poppy. 'Eating the local cuisine when it hit him.'

'I was in Stibbles,' proclaimed Kelzu. 'About to eat some deliciously oily focaccia when it hit me.'

Granny raised her eyebrows twice, as if to say, are you impressed or what?

Poppy shook her head, grinning.

'...I couldn't eat it,' said Kelzu.

'Why not?' said Clay. 'I bloody would have.'

The rest of them chuckled and agreed. What they wouldn't give for some oily focaccia. Gods, what Poppy wouldn't do for even just a lick of the plate it was served on—it didn't bear thinking about.

'It felt wrong without you lot there,' said Kelzu. 'Like something was missing.'

Huk frowned. 'When's that ever stopped you?'

Kelzu groaned. 'Alright, fine. I ran off my mouth in a local tavern and got into more trouble than I could handle on my own. And I found myself wishing you lot were there to protect me. And then I thought—hang on. Why aren't you? Why aren't we off, travelling the world together?'

'Because we're too old for that shit, Kelzu,' said Granny, rather fiercely.

Huk looked from Kelzu to Granny. Poppy couldn't help but notice the hope in his eyes—the deep-seated yearning for adventure.

'No. We're retired. And we like it like that. Or we did, at least, when there was plenty of food.'

Kelzu turned to Huk. 'Well, what d'you say, old boy—one last hoorah?'

Huk smiled nervously.

Kelzu smiled back.

'We can't just go off on a whim,' said Granny.

'Why not? We used to go off on whims all the time. Our whole life was one big whim going off,' said Huk.

'We said goodbye to that life, though, Huk. We said goodbye to that a long time ago.'

'So? Goodbyes don't have to be forever.'

Kelzu looked at Granny, pleadingly. 'Come on, Grack. We filled this shop together, it only feels right we empty it together.'

Granny groaned and tilted her head back to look at the sky. 'Fine. But I want to be back before the end of the week. We've got to start work on alternative arrangements if we don't make the money and the bank turns up.'

'Alternative arrangements?' repeated Huk.

'She means prepare for war,' said Poppy.

'I thought we said goodbye to that life?' Huk was grinning.

'We did. But it turns out that life wasn't ready to say goodbye to us.'

Poppy shook her head, but she smiled despite herself. No matter what, they weren't going to give up Sunnywood. Not without one hell of a fight. She hugged Janey from behind and stood back with Clay and Hiro, watching as Kelzu helped Huk and Granny onto the wagon. They were laughing quietly and already arguing.

'It'll be a miracle if they don't kill each other,' said Hiro, dryly.

Clay hit him lightly in the stomach.

They watched as the door to Luckyhand's Lootland opened, revealing enough space inside to fill several warehouses.

Janey looked up at Poppy. 'I want to go with them.'

Poppy squeezed her shoulder. Of course she did. Poppy wanted to go, too. You'd have to be mad not to. To see the world from the comfort of a magical wagon—what could be better?

'I know... I know, kid,' said Poppy. 'Me too.'

Granny tottered inside the wagon, Kelzu following closely behind. But Huk stood there. He looked at Kelzu and Granny, then back at Poppy and the crew.

He stopped.

'Are you lot coming or what?' he said.

'Coming? With you?' said Poppy.

'Unless you've got something else you'd rather be doing?'

Poppy looked at Clay and Hiro.

'Don't look at me. You couldn't pay me to go travelling. And you're not even paying me now, so no, I don't think I will. It sounds bloody awful,' said Hiro.

'We'll stay here, keep an eye on the place,' said Clay. 'You go, though. Have fun. Keep them in line. And we'll work on fending anyone off if they turn up.'

Poppy's heart skipped a beat.

Here was her chance.

An adventure.

A real one.

Out in the world—a different place every day.

'Will it be dangerous?' she asked.

'I hope so,' said Huk.

Poppy sighed. She couldn't go. Not when she had Janey to look after. Not when the vegetable patch needed digging up and the seeds sowing. And then she had to evict Miss Trevor and her babies from the third floor and start cleaning that. There was too much to do. She couldn't just leave it all to go travelling.

Her smile fell. 'I can't.'

'And why not?'

'I promised Janey's dad I'd take care of her. I can't just... take her around the world.'

Huk frowned. 'Do you want to come, kid?'

Janey nodded, jumping up and down with pure excitement.

Huk shrugged. 'There, problem solved. Come on, kid.'

Janey sprinted towards the magic wagon.

Poppy folded her arms. 'You can be the one who explains to her father what happened if she gets hurt, then.'

'Yeah, sure. Whatever,' said Huk, waving his hand dismissively.

He helped lift Janey onto the wagon, and she sprinted down the aisles after Granny and Kelzu.

'No. Not whatever. I mean it. If anything happens to her, we'll never—'

Huk rolled his eyes and cut her off. 'Shut up and stop worrying. We're off to see the world, remember?'

Poppy's stomach lurched. Was it excitement or nerves?

No, come to think of it, did she even want to travel the world?

'Oh, fucking hell,' she whispered to herself.

Huk grabbed her hand and pulled her up onto the wagon with surprising strength for an elderly half-orc with arthritis. Poppy looked into the open door. The magic of Kelzu's wagon still took her breath away—more so now than ever. How could there be an entire shop contained within its tiny walls when all around it was nothing but a grass-covered paddock?

'Word to the wise,' said Huk. 'I'd find something big and solid to hold onto. Kelzu's driving ain't what it used to be.' And with that, he closed the door behind them. Hiro and Clay were waving goodbye, and then, in a blink, they were gone—and so too was Sunnywood.

'And it was never much good to begin with.'

Bernard had finally knocked the front door off its hinges. He'd landed atop it, skidding across the gravel with a bang, and then he was off—sprinting down the driveway towards town. He didn't know what it was exactly, but the distinct feeling he was missing out on something had grown so strong he felt suddenly like he might be able to roar fire.

Bernard ran faster than he had ever run—through the garden and across the field. He jumped the stacked stone fence with ease. It felt good to run like this. He felt wild and free. And although he'd normally prefer to feel lazy and full, this was a close second.

There—the wagon. Kelzu's wagon.

He watched as Poppy and Janey piled in. Watched as the door closed behind them. He still had time. He still had time—

The wagon folded in on itself, and where it had been moments before, it was gone.

Bernard cried—an almighty dragon cry to do book-wyrms the world over proud.

Hiro and Clay were still there, standing where the wagon had been. Bernard stopped and circled the spot frantically, sniffing the air. The scent of expelled magic was so strong it made his nostrils flare.

'They're gone, buddy,' said Hiro, kneeling to pat him. 'But don't worry—they'll be back soon enough.'

Bernard bent his head back and howled like a dire wolf at the full moon.

Clay knelt beside him and scratched his chest. 'How'd he know?'

Hiro shrugged. 'They just do. Don't they?

And with that, they started back towards Sunnywood. A big empty house for just the two of them—well, three, including Bernard. Or four, if you wanted to worry about Alfred. And then there was Miss Trevor. Look, it was mostly to themselves. And hungry though they might be, the prospect of being wildly in love and left mostly alone in a big old house—well, it was cause for excitement.

Hiro realised, after a while, that Bernard wasn't following. He whistled. But the dragon merely gave him the cold shoulder and sat precisely where the wagon had been.

No more than ten minutes later, there was a loud thunderous crack. The sky tore open with light, and the wagon appeared once more.

The door opened.

Huk whistled.

'Hurry up, Bernie, quick!' shouted Janey. 'Get in!'

The dragon leapt up the steps and disappeared inside.

The door to the wagon slammed shut.

If you'd been standing in the field that night, you might have heard a voice shout:

'NOW ARE WE SURE THAT'S IT? BECAUSE I SWEAR TO THE GODS I WILL NOT BE COMING BACK—'

And then there was the great big thundering clap of magic as the wagon disappeared once more.

But not before you could hear, 'Oh shut up, Luckyhand.'

And so ends the first part of Poppy's story. She has no idea what she's just set in motion, or how much she's about to lose—but that's the strange grace of beginnings. They never feel like beginnings until much, much later.

THE NEXT CHAPTER AWAITS
BOOK TWO COMING SOON.

HUK

Will the residents of Sunnywood be able to save their home from the dreaded Troll Bank?

KELZU

All we know is... the story isn't over yet. Not by a long shot.

[Kelzu's wagon creaks violently. Outro music swells—chaotic, magical, ominous—and then fades into static.]

ACKNOWLEDGMENTS

I wrote large swathes of this book in a good friend's house. Life happened, and we barely see each other anymore, but your beautiful kitchen—full of dappled light, an automatic coffee machine, and an assortment of coffee cups—saw a great deal of this book written. Thank you, Lesley, for the impact you've had on my life. Thank you for your friendship and for introducing me to pottery, which, in large part, allows me to spend all this time writing my silly little stories.

Alice, I think you might be getting an acknowledgement in every single book I write. Is that okay? Good. Stiff bloody shit if it's not. I genuinely think I might have given all this up if it weren't for you checking in every so often, asking how the writing's going—and for invariably listening to me moan that it's going awful, that I hate it and everyone and everything—and for reminding me that, like a child, I'm most likely just tired or hungry, and that I should take a break.

Caleb, have you thought about how you should shut up? (My way of saying thanks for everything.)

To my family, as always. You're a bunch of good eggs. Mum, Dad, Monique, Nan and Pop. The best eggs. Prize-winning eggs. Eggs with fancy spots and marvellous colours. This metaphor got away from me. I love you all.

To Mae, editor extraordinaire: I will forever be grateful to have crossed paths with you. Your time spent in Sunnywood with these idiots has been one of the greatest creative collaborations of my life.

Hearing your thoughts and excitement for this story has been a light amidst the ever-encroaching dread of *Am I cut out for this?*

And finally, to you—the person reading this book. I do hope you enjoyed your time here in Sunnywood. I hope it was a safe place for you to laugh. I hope it brought you even a fraction of the joy it brought me to write it. If it did, tell a friend. Then hopefully that friend will tell another friend, until, what do you know, there's an army of us. An army of book lovers, which, in my opinion, sounds like quite a lovely thing.

ABOUT THE AUTHOR

Blake Polden lives in Tasmania, Australia—a place of wild beauty and quiet magic. Once an avid traveller, he now happily explores imaginary worlds from the comfort of home, accompanied by his dog Kip, his favourite humans, and an alarmingly high stack of empty coffee cups. Sunnywood House is his second novel, with plenty more on the way.

 instagram.com/blakepolden